The
Railroad

Other fiction by Tony Holtzman

Axton Landing (Book One of Adirondack Trilogy)

Forever Wild (Book Three of Adirondack Trilogy)

Blame

The Bethune Murals

The Strange Malady of Alessandro's Uncle and other stories

The Railroad

A Novel by
Tony Holtzman

CLOUD
SPLITTER
PRESS

BOOK TWO OF ADIRONDACK TRILOGY

Cover design by Eva Cohen
Author photo by Robert Holtzman

For wholesale orders, visit North Country Books at
www.northcountrybooks.com

For information on Tony Holtzman's Adirondack Trilogy and
other works of fiction visit www.cloudsplitterpress.com

For individual orders contact your local bookstore or
www.amazon.com

ISBN 978-0-9984893-1-5

Cover design by Eva Cohen
Author photo by Robert Holtzman

For wholesale orders, visit North Country Books at
www.northcountrybooks.com

For information on Tony Holtzman's Adirondack Trilogy and
other works of fiction visit www.cloudsplitterpress.com

For individual orders contact your local bookstore or
www.amazon.com

ISBN 978-0-9984893-1-5

The Railroad

A Novel by
Tony Holtzman

CLOUD
SPLITTER
PRESS

BOOK TWO OF ADIRONDACK TRILOGY

To

Barbara Starfield, 1932-2011

Come again!
Sweet love doth now invite thy graces
that refrain to do me due delight.
To see, to hear, to touch, to kiss, to die
with thee again in sweetest sympathy.

—John Dowland, circa 1600

Acknowledgments

Many of the books I acknowledged in Book One were sources for *The Railroad*, and I will not repeat them here except to mention Michael Kudish's *Railroads in the Adirondacks: A History* (Purple Mountain) as particularly helpful. I have attempted to use mountain names that were in use in the 1870s. In that regard, RML Carson's *Peaks and People of the Adirondacks* (Adirondack Mountain Club) was invaluable. The Adirondack Museum, courtesy of Angela Snye, provided the photograph that served as the basis for the cover. Michele Tucker, archivist of the Adirondack Room of the Saranac Lake Library, provided an old map of the village of Saranac Lake from which I have adapted my own map. The students and teachers of a Stanford online course on writing fiction provided useful feedback on the first several chapters.

My daughter Deborah did a remarkable editing job, despite a full-time job and two small children. Not only did she pick up innumerable typos but she made substantive suggestions that greatly strengthened the novel. Thanks also to Maryhelen Snyder, Phoebe Leboy, Carol Bernstein for comments on the manuscript, and to Ron Donaghe for the final edit.

I would be incomplete if I did not acknowledge the enormous help that Google provided, leading me to calendars for specific years in the nineteenth century, to information about the construction of the State Capitol in Albany, and to other useful information. Google maps provided a first approximation of distances despite the development of roads and highways since the period about which I write.

Until her untimely death, my wife, Barbara Starfield, gave insightful comments on the early drafts and continued encouragement. Book Two is dedicated to her memory.

Preface

The first book in this trilogy, *Axton Landing,* became available on June 10, 2011, the day my wife, Barbara Starfield, died suddenly and unexpectedly while swimming. Her death removed my most cogent critic. Barbara read an early version of *The Railroad*, which I revised, based partly on her comments. She did not see the many deletions and few additions that I made between then and now, and the novel, as with its author, is the worse off for her absence.

The places in this novel are real, but the main characters are not. Corey's Inn stood between Saranac and Tupper Lakes, but any resemblance between William Corey and any of the real Coreys is coincidental. The Adirondack Railroad did not run along the Raquette River from Long Lake to Tupper Lake, and the Smead Lumber Company did not own land along the river's banks. Virgil and Caroline Bartlett operated The Sportsmen's Home between Round (Middle) and Upper Saranac Lake, but since Jared Mason is a fictitious character Virgil could not have sold him land. Several readers of *Axton Landing* who are familiar with the area, including the current owner of the property, asked whether Virgil and Caroline started a cemetery on their property overlooking the Saranac River, also mentioned in the current volume. To the best of my knowledge they did not.

William West Durant built a camp, Pine Knot, at Raquette Lake. However, the circumstances in which I place him are fictitious. The song, "We Shall Not Be Moved," based on a hymn, was probably not used as a labor song of protest until the twentieth century. I could not identify the author of this song; there were probably many.

I have made no attempt at local dialect, but vernacular words and phrases have, in most instances, been checked for usage by the 1880s in the *Oxford English Dictionary*. For example, the term "suffragette" was not used until the twentieth century according to the OED, but "suffragist" was used earlier. I use only the latter term, usually modified with "woman."

I have endeavored in *Adirondack Trilogy* to introduce the antecedents of many of the problems with which the people of the Adirondacks grapple today. I hope I have succeeded in presenting the concerns of the people who made—and make—their livelihood in the Adirondacks.

Maple Lodge
The Bartlett Carry Club
August 2011

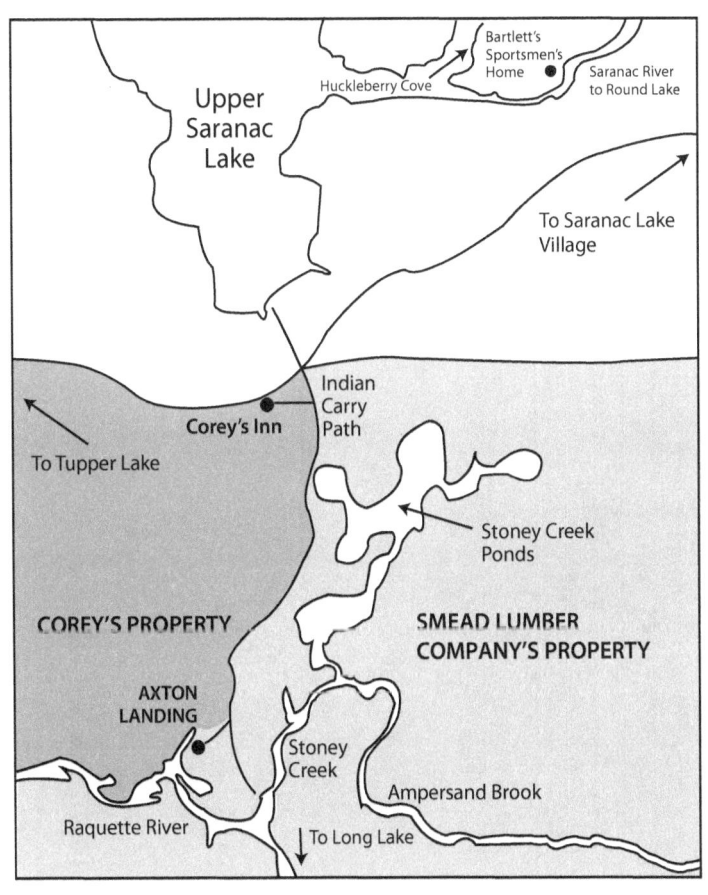

Corey's Inn and surrounding area, circa 1870

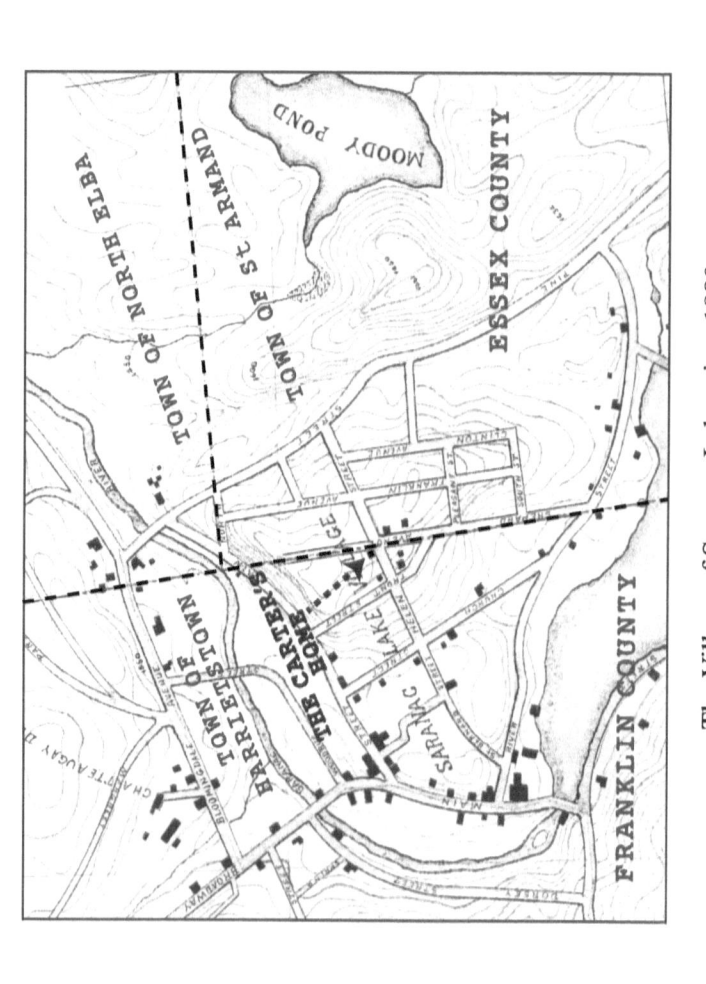

The Village of Saranac Lake, circa 1880

PART I

1

Job Hunting

ONE Sunday in July 1870, Mary Carter raised the possibility of teaching as she walked down the Indian Carry to Upper Saranac Lake with her husband, Cyrus, and their children. Cyrus had been waiting for the topic to arise ever since June when the Harrietstown School Board had announced its intention to hire teachers. "Are you asking whether I think you should apply?" Cyrus had reservations. They still lived at Corey's Inn, ten miles from the village where the school would be located. Of their three children only the older two, John and Tommy, were old enough for school; Mary had been teaching them at Corey's. Lisa was only five, just beginning to recognize the letters of the alphabet.

"Well, we haven't discussed it before," Mary replied. "Before I make up my mind, I wanted your views."

"Do you think they'll hire you?"

"Do you not think I'm qualified?" The children ran ahead, and Mary called out to them, "Don't go in the water until we get there." They were quickly out of sight as the trail turned around a fallen tree. Sloping downward toward the lake, the trail was barely wide enough for two, the summer foliage encroaching on it further. By the time Mary and Cyrus passed the fallen tree, the children had been engulfed by the dense forest.

"If you could teach me, you must be qualified, but the Council has elected Reverend Jones to head the School Board. He refused to marry us, remember?" The Reverend's words still echoed in Cyrus's head, *Do you, Sir, expect that a woman who has slept with another man, a woman who could not wait until her wedding bed, do you, Sir, expect that she will be faithful to you?*"

"How could I forget?" John's birth in January 1859 had halted Mary's formal teaching career. When John was one and a half, Mary and Cyrus married.

Mary took Cyrus's arm in hers. "The Reverend is not the only one on the Board. I think your tutor for the New York Bar would vote for me."

"Lawyer Venable is a fair man. It would depend on your competition."

"I doubt there are others near here with my qualifications."

They walked on quietly for a few minutes, only the songbirds interrupting the quiet, until Cyrus asked, "If you get the job, how are you going to get to the village?"

Mary dropped Cyrus's arm and turned to face him. "Surely you did not forget that I'm an expert horsewoman."

Now Cyrus took Mary's arm. "Of course not, Dear. But riding astride won't get you very far in the snow, and what if a storm brews while you're in school? You know how changeable the weather can be."

"There's always the sleigh or Uncle's trap."

"But if a blizzard comes in after you've ridden to the village, how will you get home?"

"I'd have to stay in the village overnight." She thought for a moment. "You know, Cyrus, some of my students will have to travel even farther. I'd be responsible for them and would need to spend the night even if I had transport."

"Leaving Uncle William and me to take care of the children," Cyrus said, throwing out what he knew to be a straw man.

"John and Tommy are already reading and doing arithmetic. Lisa's just about ready. I can take them to school with me. If not, Dear," she continued sarcastically, "you and Uncle can see how easy it is to take on a mother's role."

Cyrus would not be put on the defensive. "There's another solution."

"You mean moving to the village?" She stopped and bent down. "Oh my! Tommy dropped his towel. That boy is so active, he forgets his wits sometimes."

Cyrus laughed. "Who does he get that from?" They both laughed and stopped to kiss. They were about the same height and to Cyrus, Mary was more beautiful than the day they married. He wrapped his muscular arms around her and thought again how lucky he was. Mary picked up the towel, draping it around her neck as they continued toward the lake holding hands.

"We don't have the money to buy a house, Cyrus. Besides, I don't want to give up living in the country."

"Saranac Lake is not New York City. It's sparsely settled and there are lakes—Lower Saranac, Colby, Moody, Oseetah—and woods. We'd only be an hour's ride from here."

"If the weather's right," she teased. "What about the money?"

"I've saved some from jacking, and guiding is paying off. August should be an even better month. Your uncle has encouraged me to guide." He stopped to pluck a cluster of pine needles, on which he chewed. "We'd still have to borrow, even with the salary you'll bring in—if they give you the job."

"What about Uncle? He adores the children. He's getting old. Could he manage the cooking and cleaning without us? I would miss him."

"This has been Corey's best season, what with Adirondack Murray sending tourists up here. He'll be able to hire people to take our place—work wise, I mean—next summer. I can come out to lend a hand. I owe him for all he's done for us."

As they approached the beach, Tommy ran up, almost knocking them down. "What's the matter, Tommy?" his mother asked. He hardly stopped to look at them as he ran past, mumbling about losing something.

"Thomas," his father called sternly. "Your mother asked you a question."

Reluctantly, Tommy stopped. He gazed at his mother, broke into a grin, grabbed the towel from her neck, and without a thank you ran back to the beach. Cyrus and Mary were still holding hands when they reached the beach. The kids dashed into the water, requiring their parents' full attention.

———•———

A month later, Mary saddled one of her uncle's horses and headed to Saranac Lake, covering the eleven miles in a little over an hour. She slowed the horse to a trot as she descended to the sturdy bridge over Second Pond, admiring the peaks of the Seward Mountains to the south. She slowed again as the road passed near Lower Saranac Lake to the north, its tree-studded islands standing like jewels, the water around them sparkling in the summer sun. When she arrived in the village, the clock in the Town Hall tower was chiming three-quarters past the hour, the hands showing past ten. She hitched her horse in front of the combination Town Hall, Courthouse, and Jail. No one was in sight; she smoothed her loose skirt, let her dark hair down to capture the strands that had escaped during her ride, and tied them back in a neat bun. Fifteen minutes early for her appointment with the School Board, she walked to the rear of the building and gazed at the Saranac River coursing below. The village had been settled along its banks and at the foot of the hills rising above the river. With a population of three hundred, the village harbored a sawmill, lumberyard, and small furniture factory; grocery, hardware, dry goods, and furniture stores; a bar, hotel, and a bank. Most of the village's residents were the descendants of the original settlers. When the New York State legislature declared public education to be free in 1867, it left the building of schools and the payment of teachers to the cities and towns. Not until 1869 did the Harrietstown Council raise sufficient funds to procure an old house and convert it into a school, and not until June of 1870 did the town's School Board interview prospective teachers.

Mary walked back to the front of the Town Hall and entered through the swinging double doors. "Good morning, Mrs. Carter," the receptionist called, directing her to the antechamber of the room in which the School Board was meeting. Mary sat on one of the high-backed wooden benches. If she was nervous, her placid face gave no clue. Promptly at eleven the door opened and Reverend Jones ushered her in.

The five Board members had already reviewed her written application: thirty-three years old, graduate of the Teachers' College in Syracuse (she had submitted her diploma), two years' teaching experience. Of the two other applicants, both men who had been interviewed on the preceding days, one made no claim of college and the other had no teaching experience.

Mary told the Board how she had come from Syracuse to the Adirondacks to stay with her Uncle William Corey, help tend his inn, and teach in a one-room school he had built for her.

Reverend Jones interrupted. "That's when you had your two years of teaching. Is that right, Mrs. Carter?" Mary nodded. Her palms were moist.

"Why did you stop?"

"I had a baby," she said softly.

"Was your husband, Cyrus Carter, the father?"

You know he wasn't, she said to herself. "No he wasn't," she said clearly.

"Had you been married previously?"

Cyrus was right, Mary thought. *He's going to punish me again.*

Before she could answer, Lawrence Venable interrupted. "You and Cyrus Carter were married a year after your baby was born, weren't you?"

"A year and a half," Mary corrected him.

"Why didn't you return to teaching?"

"Because, Mr. Venable, I had to take care of John, my oldest, and then Cyrus and I had two children, Thomas and Lisa. Now they are old enough to go to the public school you are starting in the village."

"Don't you think a woman's place is in the home?" asked Tobias Brown, the owner of the dry goods store.

Mary felt her heart beating and pressed her lips together before speaking. Then she said evenly, "If you can find a man as well qualified to teach your children, Mr. Brown, then I could stay at home, but if you can't it will be your children who will be losing out. I love my children dearly and whether this Board appoints me or not, Cyrus and I will make sure they will be cared for."

Milo Miller, who sold real estate in and around the Village, asked, "Will you be able to make it from Corey's to school every day?"

"We may move to the village, Mr. Miller, but I've been riding horses since I arrived in Harrietstown thirteen years ago. In inclement weather, or when I take my children, my uncle will let me use his carriage, and his sleigh in the winter."

"Still, that's a long trip, Mary. Do you want the job that badly?" Miller asked.

"Mr. Miller," Mary replied. "I was fortunate enough in Syracuse to have parents who wanted their daughters educated and could afford to pay for it. I believe I have a responsibility to impart the knowledge I have obtained to others less fortunate than myself who can, for the first time, attend school free—"

"Except for the taxes their parents pay," Reverend Jones interjected.

"Yes, of course," Mary said impatiently, resenting the interruption, "and take the opportunity to better themselves and their community."

"Brava!" said Lawrence Venable.

None of the other board members echoed his enthusiasm, and silence reigned until Reverend Jones asked, "Does anyone have anything further for Mrs. Carter?" No one said anything. The Reverend stood. "Very well, Mary. Thank you for coming."

Mary stood, offering her hand to the Reverend. "I appreciate the opportunity." Jones regarded her hand for a moment before grasping it loosely. "Oh yes, one more thing, Mary." He dropped her hand. "We are likely to have enough children of school age to warrant two teachers, one for the younger and one for the older. If the Board decides to hire you, do you have a preference?"

Mary thought for a moment. *They're not going to hire me so why bother.* "I'll leave it up to the wisdom of the Board," she replied. Informing Mary that she would be notified, the Reverend showed her out, closed the heavy oak door, and returned to preside over the Board.

Leaving her horse at the hitching post, Mary walked the few blocks to the Venables' house where she visited with Mrs. Venable, awaiting the return of Mr. Venable.

The Board now sat in judgment. Returning to his seat at the head of the table, Reverend Jones began. "There's no doubt Mary Carter is the best qualified of our three candidates." He paused, looked at the impassive faces of the Board members. "But do we really want her teaching our children?"

Venable was the first to answer, asking in feigned innocence, "Do you mean because she's a woman, Reverend Jones?"

"That's only part of it, Mr. Venable. Mary had a bastard son by a Canuck lumberjack."

Virgil Bartlett, the fifth Board member who had been silent throughout Mary's interview, spoke up. "I've known Mary since she arrived in these parts in 1857." Virgil and his wife Caroline ran The Sportsmen's Club two miles northeast of Corey's. "We had Becky and Paul in her classroom and now they can read, write, and calculate better than me. Seems a pity to deprive the town's kids of such a smart woman because of one past indiscretion."

Milo Miller spoke. "She's been married to Cyrus Carter for ten years, a faithful wife and caring mother. Do you want her to wear a scarlet letter anyway?"

"No. I wouldn't go that far, Milo," Jones said in all seriousness, "but I wouldn't want my children tutored by a loose woman." Jones turned to Brown. "What are your thoughts, Tobias?"

"I hear Mrs. Carter favors women's suffrage. She might indoctrinate the children with wild ideas."

"It's always been a puzzle to me," Virgil replied, scratching his head. "If we're willing to educate our girls—and I haven't heard any objection to that—why shouldn't they vote once they're old enough?"

A brief debate ensued on women's suffrage in which Brown and the Reverend argued with Venable and Bartlett while Milo Miller remained quiet.

Reverend Jones pulled his watch from his vest pocket. "We're getting off the matter at hand," he said loudly. The room grew quiet. "Does anyone have anything to add about Mary Carter or the other candidates?"

Venable noted that one of them, Arthur Bumblecombe, had claimed to have been to college in Boston but had not presented any credentials. The third candidate had not claimed matriculating anywhere.

"I suggest," said the Reverend, "that we each vote for one candidate and select the two with the most votes." He passed out small rectangles of blank paper for ballots. The board members marked and folded their ballots and passed them to Mr. Venable who tallied the results and announced that Mary had received three votes and Bumblecombe two.

Mr. Venable suggested they send for Bumblecombe's credentials, to which the Reverend agreed but added that with school beginning in three weeks, they should hire Bumblecombe provisionally. "And," he added, "Mr. Bumblecombe will teach the children over thirteen and Mary the younger ones."

"We know Mary's graduated college," Mr. Venable said. "Why not let her teach the older ones?" Milo Miller and Virgil Bartlett agreed.

"Mary is an attractive woman," the Reverend replied. "I think the older boys might be distracted. With her past indiscretion, you never can tell what she would do." Venable guffawed but said nothing. Nor did the others. There being no further business, the Reverend adjourned the meeting.

Returning home immediately after the meeting, Lawrence Venable was pleased to convey the news to Mary. "You'll be teaching the younger children, Mary. Arthur Bumblecombe—I don't know that you've met him—will teach the older ones." He paused for a moment. "If I were you, Mary, I'd watch out for Reverend Jones. He doesn't think you're morally fit to teach the older boys."

—————•—————

While Mary was interviewing for the teaching job, Cyrus walked south on the Indian Carry to Axton Landing where he sought the Smead Lumber Company's jobber, Lewis Fairweather, who had taken over from Ben Anderson after the Miller trial. At the trial, Lawrence Venable had shown that Anderson had masterminded the plot that led to the murder of Sean O'Rourke; Frank Miller was only an accomplice. Venable's defense of Miller had impressed Cyrus with the majesty of the law and had started him studying for the New York bar with Venable's help. Fearing arrest, Anderson had not set foot in Harrietstown since the trial.

Fairweather had continued the arrangement that Cyrus had made with Anderson, letting Carter spend the night with his family at Corey's as long as he was on the job at daybreak. Cyrus never broke his word. Every spring after the logs had been floated down the Raquette, the loggers, including Cyrus, were laid off. Those that remained in the area had to apply again in the fall.

As he walked down the path, catching glimpses of the Stoney Creek Ponds on his left, flotillas of water lilies advancing out from the shore, Cyrus wondered, *how long can I continue jacking?* At forty-three, Cyrus was old for a lumberjack. For many years his back had ached, but swinging an axe limbered him—until the next morning at any rate. The fracture of his right leg in the logjam eleven years ago had left him with a limp, and the ache in his hip was no longer relieved by activity. Yet he needed the money. If he used the meager amount he had saved from jacking and guiding to put money down on a house in the village, assuming Mary got the teaching job, the couple would have little left, even with Mary's salary. In a year or two, he would know enough law to earn a little money helping Lawrence Venable with simple legal matters, but it would be years before he would be able to pass the New York Bar and become Venable's partner or have his own law practice.

He took the cutoff to Axton Landing and walked into the camp. "Hey, Pop," a young man sitting on a stump in front of the office, called to him. "What can we do for you?"

Cyrus had never been called "Pop" before and the appellation depressed him. Forgetting that his hair was heavily streaked with gray, Cyrus thought he must have conveyed his self-perception of being old to the youngster. "You're new here, aren't you?" Cyrus asked. The young man nodded. "I've been working in this camp since you were just a baby."

"No offense, Grandpa. Mr. Fairweather don't want no trespassers."

"Is he in?"

The young man pointed to the office door and said

nothing.

The uneven sound of Cyrus's footsteps as he clunked along the floor to Fairweather's desk emphasized his age. Fairweather looked up. "Hello, Cyrus. Not still thinking of jacking, are you?" Cyrus was reminded how he had first walked across that floor with Jean Entremont in 1859, almost begging Anderson for jobs for both of them.

"I've got a family to feed, Mr. Fairweather. You know I'm a good worker."

"I know you mean well, Cyrus, but I can't pay you an hourly wage when you didn't cut the number of trees last year that would have earned you that much if I had paid you piece rate." Several years earlier, Cyrus had negotiated an hourly wage for himself while the other jacks were still getting paid piece rate.

Fairweather's humiliating remark deepened Cyrus's depression. "I far exceeded that in early years, you know."

"I know," the jobber replied. Unlike his predecessor, Lewis Fairweather showed some sympathy for his workers. He picked up a pencil and twirled it, thinking what he could do for Cyrus. The proposition that he considered was one that might cause him and Cyrus trouble. Cyrus had always spoken up when he thought the men had legitimate griev-ances and he had, starting in Anderson's time, been a thorn in the company's side, extracting more from the jobbers by his ability to unite the men. *Still*, thought Fairweather, *my proposition will make it easier for the company, if he accepts it.* "It may seem strange, Cyrus, but while I can't profitably hire you as a jack, I can hire you as a foreman."

For many years, Cyrus had wondered what he would

do if he were ever offered a foreman's job. His loyalty had always been to his fellow loggers and the idea of lording it over them was repugnant. After Mary had taught him rudimentary reading, Jed Mason, a lumberjack with a college education, gave Cyrus his first adult reading, *The Communist Manifesto*. Still, Cyrus knew foremen who had been decent to the men and usually extracted more work from them as a result. "Are you making an offer?" he asked Fairweather.

"I'll have to clear it with Smead but, yes, I am."

"What will you pay?"

Again Fairweather twirled his pencil. "We've been paying you seven dollars for a sixty-hour week. Considering how long you've worked for the company, I'll up it to ten dollars, which is more than some of the foremen are making—"

"But less than others." Cyrus completed Fairweather's sentence.

"That's true, but you've never supervised before and I don't know how you'll work out. With time, you could earn more. We'll have to see."

Cyrus thought about asking whether he could still spend the nights at Corey's with his family, but when he considered they might be moving to the village, he decided to postpone this part of the negotiation. "I'll have to think about it, Mr. Fairweather. I'm not sure I'm good at giving orders."

Fairweather had now persuaded himself that Cyrus would make a fine foreman. "We're just beginning to hire now, so if you let me know by the beginning of November, I'll hold a position for you." He paused for a moment. "I'm sure you'd get the hang of bossing."

What should have been a happy occasion when Mary and Cyrus returned to the inn with their respective news was tinged with bitterness and uncertainty. Although Mary was pleased to be appointed teacher, the Reverend Jones's interrogation infuriated her, especially with Lawrence Venable's warning to be on guard. She was also annoyed to be teaching the younger students. She had only met Arthur Bumblecombe once, but his intellectual ability to teach the older children seemed dubious. Cyrus was anguished about accepting the foreman's job. "It's like going over to the other side," he told Mary.

"But it is more money and if we're thinking of moving to the village, money will be important."

"Moving to the village does create a problem, Mary. I won't be able to spend the nights with you and the children. Anderson and Fairweather let me do that when I could walk from Corey's to Axton Landing in fifteen minutes. I didn't even mention living in the village to Fairweather."

"You know it will suit me fine to stay here at the inn with Uncle William. Maybe we'll have a mild winter and we can postpone the decision."

2

Working

T HE school year started auspiciously for Mary. Little rain fell, and while the first frosts came in September, the air warmed as the sun traversed the southern sky on cloudless days. John and Tommy accompanied Mary to school in Corey's trap. Lisa balked, saying she'd rather stay home with her dolls, Uncle William, and Cyrus. John was the youngest student in Mr. Bumblecombe's class; Tommy was in his mother's. The children in Mary's class loved her and she was pleased with their progress. Despite her initial annoyance, she was glad to have the younger children; none of them were old enough to remember her past indiscretion, which Reverend Jones was reluctant to forget, and which the older children in Mr. Bumblecombe's class might also have heard from their parents. She worried they might tease John that Cyrus was not his father.

Cyrus delayed visiting Mr. Fairweather, staying around the inn, helping William and caring for Lisa. In his spare moments he opened his law books. Finally, on a blustery Halloween, Cyrus walked to Axton Landing and asked Fairweather if Smead had approved his becoming a foreman. He was a little disappointed when the jobber told him the company had. "In that case," said Cyrus, "I'll accept the job at ten dollars a week."

"Men are turning up every day looking to jack, Cyrus. I think we'll have a full crew by first snow. In the meantime, we have to extend the tote roads so we can cut farther into the forest. I want to have logs to skid when it does snow. Can you report on Monday?"

"Yessir," Cyrus replied.

———•———

In the middle of her history lesson one Friday in November, Mary posed a question to one of her brighter students who was looking out the window. The girl turned from the window, fiddled with her pencil in the groove on her wooden desk, and looked blankly at Mary, who repeated the question. The girl did not answer but blurted, "It's snowing, Mrs. Carter." Mary walked to the window. Large flakes floated in the air and settled slowly to the ground. The other children turned to look.

"Just a flurry, children. Let's get back to work," Mary scolded, returning to her desk. She was able to get the attention of most of the children over the next fifteen minutes, but the classroom grew darker and the flakes swirled with greater intensity. She knew she had lost the battle as most heads turned back to the window. "You'd think you'd never seen snow before," Mary said in exasperation. Walking to the window, she was surprised to find an inch of snow on the street and no sign of the storm abating. As the air darkened, she felt a chill and drew her shawl around her. *It's never too early for a blizzard in the Adirondacks*, she thought, and then took the requisite action. "Well, children, school will close early today. Get your coats and walk home quickly. No dawdling."

As the children gathered their books and retrieved their coats, Mr. Bumblecombe came in abruptly. "Mary," he said, stating what was now obvious, "it's snowing. I've got to get to my family. I'll leave the children who can't walk home in your charge." In contrast to Mary, who had eleven miles to travel, Bumblecombe lived in the village. He was gone before Mary could utter a word. Soon after, John and eighteen-year-old Alan Phillips came into Mary's classroom.

Mary stood at the door as the children who could walk home left, making sure their coats were buttoned and wishing them a pleasant weekend. Jane and Sally Parker remained, waiting for their father to come from their house in Bloomingdale, six miles to the north. Alan Phillips, who traveled the twelve miles to and from his house by horse, also stayed and, of course, John and Tommy. Alan had been Mary's youngest student in her school at Corey's in 1858 and was now the oldest in the school, coming only when his parents could spare him from farm work. Cyrus had teased Mary that Alan had a crush on her. Mary laughed, telling Cyrus that Alan was an excellent student. "Besides," she said, "he's not in my class."

As the blizzard gathered force and the temperature dropped, the classroom grew colder and gloomier. "Alan," Mary asked, "would you mind bringing in some wood from the pile in the shed?" She turned to John. "John, you can help Alan but put your jacket on and button it." Alan obliged, making several trips with John while Mary arranged kindling in the potbelly stove in the center of the room and lit a match to a piece of birch bark she had used in her science lessons. To the small fire she added a few of the logs the boys brought in. Then she lit the school's kerosene lantern, placing it on her desk. Soon the room was warmer and brighter.

Eight inches of snow had accumulated by the time school was usually dismissed without sign that the storm would abate. Mary resigned to spend the night in the village, glad that John and Tommy were with her but worrying about Lisa who would be in William's care, since Cyrus was working for Smead.

Alan dumped another armload of wood near the stove. "I think we've got enough to last until morning." He had not worn a jacket to school and his heavy woolen shirt was now soaked through. Mary urged him to take it off. "No ma'am, I don't think that's proper."

"You'll catch a death of a chill, if you don't." She pulled up a chair and set its back facing the stove. Reluctantly Alan removed his shirt and Mary hung it on the chair.

At that moment, the door burst open. The girls were disappointed it was not their father but Reverend Jones, whose church was just down the street. Shaking the snow off his great coat on to the schoolroom floor, he scolded, "Mrs. Carter, I thought you'd have enough sense to send the children home early." Mary flushed. The Reverend looked around and realized that most of the children were gone. "Oh, I see you've done that." Then he looked at Alan, bare-chested, standing next to Mary. Instead of addressing Alan, he faced Mary. "Is it proper for this young man to walk around half naked?" Alan blushed and wrapped his arms around his chest.

Mary pointed to the chair where Alan's shirt emitted a

thin veil of steam. "Alan was good enough to gather wood for our stove; his shirt got soaked." She walked to the coat hooks on the side of the room and removed a shawl that she used when the room was cold. "We don't want to offend the Reverend, Alan," she said acidly. "Please wrap the shawl around you." Alan complied meekly. The Parker girls giggled. "You look like a lady," said Sally, the older one, adding to his discomfort.

"Are you planning to spend the night here?" Reverend Jones asked, looking at Mary and then at Alan.

"We have enough wood to keep the room warm."

With the shawl wrapped around him, Alan piped up, "We could use some food, though."

"Are you sure you wouldn't like to come over to the rectory? We don't have enough beds, but we have plenty of blankets. We can put the lad in a separate room."

Reverend Jones's rectory held a very unpleasant memory for Mary. "What do you think?" she asked the children. Much to her delight, the girls, who had been looking through picture books, said together, "We'd rather stay here, Mrs. Carter." John and Tommy agreed.

"What about you, Alan?"

"If we could get some food, Mrs. Carter, that would be fine with me."

"Very well," replied the Reverend, "I'll see what I can do." He stamped out.

By the time it was dark, workers hired by the Village had shoveled paths along the main streets although the snow kept falling. The Reverend's wife walked over to the school around six o'clock, carrying a kettle of steaming vegetable soup. She asked Alan and John to walk back to the church with her to carry over bowls and utensils. They made three trips in all, carrying bowls and utensils, then sweet rolls, and finally blankets. The children slept well that night, but Mary only dozed, keeping the stove fired.

Lewis Fairweather was delighted with the heavy snow. It meant the men could finish chopping the trees they had notched, load them on the sledges, and get them to skidways on the bank of the Raquette. He called his foremen to the office to tell them the plan. "Do you mean we start when the blizzard stops?" Cyrus asked.

"Just then," Fairweather replied. "This early in the year we might see a rapid thaw and we may not get our quota of logs to the river if we wait."

Another foreman spoke up. "But tomorrow's Saturday and half the men will be off until Monday."

Fairweather had not expected objections from any of his foreman. He looked at Cyrus suspiciously although he had only asked for clarification. "The men have only been working for a couple of weeks. I am going to cancel their days off and make it up later in the year."

Cyrus was in a bind. He knew Mary and the boys were trapped in the village and that William would be pulling his hair out caring for young Lisa. Yet he did not want self-interest to influence his argument with Fairweather and he decided to keep quiet.

When the full force of the blizzard struck, the foremen had told their men to go to the tool shed to sharpen their axes. After their meeting with Fairweather, the foremen went to the shed, gathered their teams around them, and conveyed the jobber's order. The teams that were scheduled to have half Saturday and all of Sunday off grumbled. Cyrus apologized and urged his team to finish sharpening their axes. Quietly, he appointed Carl Johannson, with whom he'd worked in previous years, to take charge of his fellow jacks the next morning and told Carl what the team should do in case he was not there.

The storm raged as darkness fell, and after their evening meal, the men retired to the bunkhouse. Cyrus slept fitfully, finally drifting off despite the heavy wind and the cracking of branches under heavy loads of wet snow. It was still dark when he awoke and was immediately aware of the silence and a blue glow of moonlight coming through the small windows, half covered with snow. *Foreman job be damned,* he said to himself as he quietly put on his outer garments and tramped through the snow to the stable. In the darkness, Cyrus groped his way past the large sledges and wagons to the back of the stable where he found the small sleigh with one bench seat. The half dozen horses neighed nervously. He dragged the sleigh toward the entrance and hitched one of Smead's horses to it. Outside, the animal awkwardly ploughed through a foot of snow while the sled's runners floated near the surface.

By the time Cyrus reached the village, the sun was long up and he was sure his presence at Axton would be missed. Mary was surprised to see him and they hugged indecorously in the doorway, John and Tommy coming up quickly behind their mother. "I guess you could say I've stolen Smead's sleigh and Fairweather may well fire me, but I couldn't leave you stranded in the village. The trap's not going to get you and the boys anywhere for quite a while." By this time, the Parker girls' father had picked them up and Alan Phillips said he would stay with friends just outside the village until he could get home. "Let's get back to Corey's, and I'll return the horse and sleigh to Axton, come what may."

Cyrus held the reins with Mary sitting to the right of him, John to Mary's right, and Tommy to Cyrus's left. He had thought to bring a horse blanket from Smead's stable and, before starting out, he spread it over their laps. A few sleds had already traveled to and from the village so the road to Tupper was partially packed and the going was easier than before.

Mary let loose against Reverend Jones. She related what had happened when the minister came to her classroom. "How do such arrogant men gain prominence?"

"Their arrogance has something to do with it," conjectured Cyrus.

They rode on in silence, admiring the snow-covered trees and mountains under the sapphire sky. Finally, Cyrus said, "Don't you think it's time to look into buying a house in the village?"

"If you lose your job you can transport us in Uncle William's sled," Mary teased. She cuddled closer to Cyrus and whispered, "I miss you at night, you know." Cyrus transferred the reins to his left hand and put his arm around Mary, gently squeezing her shoulder.

"I've only earned twenty dollars so far. If I'm fired that

won't get us very far."

"But it will help. So will my meager salary—unless Reverend Jones dismisses me." She paused for a moment to admire Lower Saranac Lake on their right, with plates of ice extending from the shore, but the lake was not yet frozen solid. "Uncle William has been expecting our move. Still, he'll be disappointed. If we move before next summer, he'll have to hire people to take our place."

"If Fairweather fires me, I can always help out. Your uncle has been very generous to us."

With the clop of the horses and swoosh of the runners, the boys heard only part of the conversation, but enough to know what their parents were contemplating. "Are you thinking of moving to the village?" John asked.

Mary replied, "Unless you want to be trapped there, or at Uncle William's over the winter—"

"And miss school?" Tommy interrupted. "What fun!"

"Tommy," Cyrus rebuked, "You're fortunate to be able to go to school. And to have the best teacher in the world." Tommy became quiet.

"It will be sad to leave the inn and the lake and the trails—and Uncle William," John said thoughtfully.

They were all silent for the rest of the ride. When they arrived, Mary rushed in to see her daughter, who was equally happy to be reunited with her mother. The boys marked a spot on the side of the shed as a target and took turns throwing snowballs at it. Mary came out holding Lisa's hand as Cyrus was feeding Smead's horse. He turned to Mary. "I don't know when I'll be home. Fairweather's going to work us pretty hard as long as there's snow on the ground. He canceled leave for this weekend."

Mary let go of Lisa and hugged and kissed Cyrus. "I'll miss you." She whispered, "Don't get hurt."

"There's less of chance of that now that I'm a foreman."

———•———

When Cyrus arrived back at Axton Landing, the camp appeared deserted, but he could hear the thumps of axes from the surrounding forest. He walked to the office, and then stopped. Why announce his presence? He turned, picked up his axe from the shed, and walked upriver, along the Raquette where his crew was chopping.

They gave him a friendly greeting. So far, he had managed to stay on their good side by not making excessive demands and listening when they had complaints or suggestions. His men told the members of other teams how he performed and as a result they were less willing to take unjust orders or treatment from their foremen. Cyrus's team was chopping and bucking more trees than the other teams. Carl Johansson had no idea whether Fairweather knew that Cyrus had gone missing. This puzzled Cyrus because the foremen met every morning with the jobber before they went out with their crews. "I gathered our team right after breakfast and started them out fast," Carl explained. "Mr. Fairweather must have thought you were eager to get the trees down and skidded as fast as possible."

Cyrus chuckled. "I am lucky this once, but I don't think I can make a habit of it." If the men were curious about where Cyrus went, they did not show it. No longer attempting to swing his axe at the giant white pines, Cyrus went to work lopping off the branches that had to be removed before the trunks could be levered on to the sledges. He also seemed to be setting an example for the other foremen who had seldom lifted a finger to help their men.

The winter proved a rough one. The ground was not bare of snow until April and the temperature seldom rose above freezing, permitting a record number of softwood trees to be chopped and skidded to the river. Stumps were the only sign of where these giants had stood, leaving the forest sparsely inhabited by the relatively slender hardwoods—maple, birch, beech—that did not float. Sunlight penetrated to the forest floor far more than it had for a millennium.

The blizzards often kept Mary at home with her children. Only when the tracks of sleighs coalesced after the storms abated, making the road a ribbon of packed snow, was travel possible. After the storms had trapped Mary and the boys in the village on a few occasions, she insisted that Lisa begin school, allowing her daughter to bring one doll with her. The School Board, under Reverend Jones, had arranged with families living nearby to shelter the children who could not get home when storms struck. The Venables took in Mary and her brood. The Board also debated whether to dock the teachers' pay for the days they missed because of weather. Mr. Venable pointed out that the teachers they hired would not be able to support their families if their pay was cut. Tobias Brown, knowing that Cyrus was now a foreman with Smead, commented that Mrs. Carter's husband was earning enough to support his family and he wondered whether they should cut Mary's pay while they maintained Mr. Bumblecombe's. The other Board members, even Reverend Jones, thought this would be unfair, and the proposal was dropped.

In December, one of Cyrus's crew lost his footing in the snow and gashed the calf of his left leg with his axe. Cyrus reacted with anger, blaming the jack. "Haven't I told you to make sure your footing was secure before raising your axe?"

The man was writhing as blood soaked through his trousers. "My wife's expecting, Sir. I've got to chop as many trees as possible to make sure we can pay for the doctor."

Cyrus's anger shifted. "Damn this piece rate. If that wound festers, you'll lose the leg and earn nothing." Carl Johansson helped Cyrus carry the man back to the bunkhouse where they pulled off the man's trousers. The gash was a deep one, revealing muscle for a length of three inches. He asked Carl to go to the cook shed and get a pot of boiling water. From jacking with Jed Mason, who was now a doctor in New York City, he remembered that boiled water helped cleanse wounds. When Carl arrived with the pot, Cyrus first poured water over the wound. To Cyrus's dismay, this increased the bleeding. He tore apart the less bloody trouser leg and dropped it in the hot water. After a minute he pulled it out and used it to bind the man's wound. Leaving Carl with the injured man, Cyrus walked to the office and described the situation to Mr. Fairweather. "Unless we get him to a doctor who can sew up his leg, the man could bleed to death."

"Why don't we wait to see if the bleeding stops?" Fairweather replied.

Cyrus shook his head. "I'm afraid the wound will fester. Pouring boiled water over it may prevent that but it has made the bleeding worse. We should take him to see Doctor Weinberg in Tupper Lake. He's the doctor who set my fractured leg. I wouldn't be here now if it weren't for him."

"Very well. Take the small sled and do it as fast as you can. Send Johansson back to work. Missing two men is quite enough."

Cyrus and Carl loaded the man on to the sled. Cyrus did not stop at Corey's but turned left from the Indian Carry on to the road, heading to the tiny village of Tupper Lake ten miles to the west.

Cyrus had kept in touch with Henry Weinberg over the years and was pleased that this time he was not the patient. "This man's pale from blood loss," Henry said as he tore off the crude bandage. "His pulse is rapid, as I'd suspect, and he's barely conscious. Still, I'll need your help Cyrus when I suture his leg." Henry went to a small table and lifted the lid off a metal container. He removed a bottle from a shelf above the table, went to the sink and poured liquid over his hands. The liquid emitted a powerful smell. "Carbolic acid," Henry told Cyrus. "This English physician, Joseph Lister, maintains that it is antiseptic and cuts down wound infection when he bathes his instruments and hands in it." Weinberg pulled a curved needle and some thread from the metal container, which was filled with the liquid. He poured some carbolic acid over the gash and the man winced in agony. "We'd better tie his arms down, Cyrus. Otherwise he might disrupt me sewing." The doctor proceeded to sew the wound and pour more carbolic acid over it when he had finished. "Jared Mason writes me from New York that most of the surgeons there think it's a lot of hokum and refuse to adopt it. They don't like the smell, he says."

Cyrus remembered the lecture Dr. Weinberg had given him and Jed eleven years earlier. "They still don't believe in Semmelweiss either, I guess."

"I'm afraid not," Henry replied. "Jared is infuriated at the surgeons, but as an inspector for the Health Department there's little he can do."

The man was awake and Henry offered him a swig of brandy to ease his pain. The doctor gave Cyrus some clean bandages to dress the wound and told him to bring the patient back if the wound swelled, turned red, or exuded pus. In the days that followed, with the man confined to his bunk (and denied pay), Cyrus watched the wound carefully, doing as Weinberg had said. It healed without further complication, Weinberg removed the sutures, and the man resumed jacking just after the New Year.

In March, Cyrus came across two men fighting near a large white pine that had been notched. The men had thrown their axes down and were slogging with bare fists. One's eye was swollen shut and the other had blood pouring from his nose. Crimson drops stained the packed snow. Cyrus separated them and demanded to know what had happened. The one with the bloody nose put his hand on the pine above the notch, pointing to the other. "He stole my tree."

"I did not," the other replied.

With further inquiry, Cyrus learned that the man who claimed theft had started to notch the tree the previous day but was cut short by the mess call. The next morning, when he returned to finish the job, he found the thief cutting a counter notch. "He's looking to get credit for work

I started."

Cyrus again cursed piece rate, but silently. Out loud, he chided the thief. "I know you're not making a living wage, but you can't steal another man's tree to get another dime." He paused, wondering whether he should say more. By now several other men had gathered around the tree. "You men should demand a daily wage that you get regardless of how many trees you cut. Getting paid by each tree you cut is dangerous. It also makes you competitors with one another rather than comrades."

"That makes sense, Carter," one of the men said. "Maybe after our next pay period we should demand a daily wage from Fairweather." Cyrus knew that Fairweather would discover he was an instigator and might fire him. At this point, however, he didn't care. He missed being away from his family, and he had managed to save one hundred dollars of his salary. He picked up the men's axes and handed them back. To the man who had started notching the tree he said, "Finish cutting your tree." He ordered the others back to work.

Cyrus's friend Carl Johansson soon became the leader of the group demanding a daily wage of seventy-five cents a day. Not all the men were in favor of it; most of those that cut more than seven large trees a day at a dime a tree were content to leave the pay as it was.

At noon on Saturday, April 2, the men lined up in front of Fairweather's office to get their pay. Johansson was at the front of the line. When he walked into the office he received his pay from Fairweather. Two of the foremen—neither of them Cyrus—stood in back of Fairweather. Johansson counted it and instead of turning to go spoke politely to Mr. Fairweather. "With all respect, Sir, from now on I would like to get six bits a day, or four dollars and twenty cents for six days' work." He paused, holding the cash that he had just received in one hand. "That's a dime less than you paid me for this past week."

Fairweather was incredulous. "You mean you're willing to work for less if I pay you a weekly wage instead of piece rate?"

"Not only me, Sir, but all of the men."

Fairweather looked at his ledger and found that Johansson usually cut more than seven trees in a ten-hour day. "I'll tell you what, Carl. I'll grant your request, but it stays between you and me."

"The men won't like that, Mr. Fairweather."

"We'll see. Get out." The two foremen moved menacingly toward Johansson, but he turned and left.

The next man accepted his piece rate wage without complaint, but the third, fourth, and fifth men followed Johansson's lead. Fairweather looked at the number of trees each had cut in the previous weeks. If they had cut more than seven, he granted their request. If they had cut less, he refused. He told these men to cut more trees and come back and he'd consider it. The next payday, Fairweather paid out less than the previous one. Dealt with one by one, the demand for a weekly wage had saved the Smead Company money.

Cyrus learned what had happened. On his next weekend off, he mentioned it at Sunday dinner in front of the whole family. "The men made a terrible mistake," Cyrus concluded. "If Jed Mason were here, he'd have gotten all the men to agree. He wouldn't have let Fairweather split them. Those cutting fewer trees are now going to try harder and are more likely to injure themselves."

"What about the men who got the weekly wage?" William asked. "Might they not slacken off?"

"I suppose some of them would. Fairweather is no dope. For those that do, he'll go back to paying them piece rate."

As the snows receded in the spring the men prepared for floating the logs down the Raquette to the mill at Tupper Lake. The pay each received was now in the hands of the foremen, who used the number of logs each man levered off the skidways into the river to decide on his wage. Often the foremen modified the piece rate depending on how friendly a man was to him. It was not unheard of for a jack to give his foreman a fraction of his wages. Cyrus told his team that he was going to pay them each the same amount. The harder they worked together the more logs they would get into the water, and every man's pay would be higher, but they would share equally.

Word spread quickly to the other crews and the foremen who had gained from the old system complained to Fairweather. "I'm on to you, Carter," Fairweather said to him in front of the other foremen. "Anderson warned me about you. You're trying to get the men to stand together." He glowered at Cyrus.

"It's the only fair way, Mr. Fairweather. I've seen Smead do a lot of cheating in my years as a jack, and I'm not going to be a part of it. You've succeeded in splitting the men by paying the stronger men a weekly wage but not the others. They'll catch on to you fast."

Fairweather smiled. "We'll see. Jobs up here are not easy to come by. They'll take what they can get." He paused, deciding what to do with Carter. "That goes for you too, Carter."

Cyrus returned to Corey's that evening angrier than ever. "I'm tired of playing the stooge for Smead. I won't be part of exploiting the jacks for another year."

"Are you going to quit?" Mary asked with some alarm.

"I'll work until Fairwather lays me off. Then we'll see."

That evening, Cyrus and Mary emptied the satchels in which they kept their money and counted up one hundred and fifty dollars, a sum that surprised them both. "We can be grateful to your uncle that we've been able to save so much. He's been generous with food and board."

Cyrus was laid off at the end of April, along with most of the jacks. The next week, he accompanied Mary and the children to the village in Corey's wagon. While they were in school, he visited Milo Miller who had inherited a large amount of real estate throughout the village and had bought some more. Together, they looked at houses the Carters might be able to afford. The one Cyrus liked best was on Helen Street as it climbed above the banks of the river, close to Mt. Baker with Moody Pond beyond.

After school, he drove Mary and the children to the site. The children explored the surrounding area, discovering the pond close by. Mary fell in love with the land instantly. "It's in the village, we can all walk to school, but it's like the country—a mountain looming over us and a pond we can swim in."

She was less taken with the house. Cyrus saw the look of alarm as she walked gingerly through the rooms, trying not to trip on the broken floor. "I can have this place livable in a few months," he assured her. "When school ends, the boys can help; it will do them good to learn carpentry and do some painting."

Milo Miller agreed to the one hundred and fifty dollars the Carters were willing to put down, holding the mortgage for the balance plus interest. When school let out in June, John and Tommy accompanied Cyrus to work on the house. Their work was interrupted only when tourists staying at Corey's offered Cyrus a guiding job. Mary saw less of her husband and her sons than during previous summers. By August, work on the house was far enough along that Cyrus and the boys could sleep on the floor, although the boys preferred sleeping outside. When the renovation was complete, they would share a room, and Lisa would have her own.

Tourists filled Corey's to capacity that summer. With Cyrus seldom available to help, William hired a young couple to take the Carters' place. Mary spent her time showing them how the place was run.

In September, Mary and Cyrus borrowed Corey's wagon to move their possessions and their children to the village. After school started, Cyrus resumed his study of the law, spending a lot of time with Lawrence Venable who, with increasing frequency, paid Cyrus for researching deeds, drawing contracts, and other such legal matters.

3
An Offer

COREY'S Inn stood midway between the villages of Saranac Lake and Tupper Lake, just off the road that connected them. The summer of 1871 had been warm and dry and the road was hard packed, with occasional ruts, the remnants of gashes made by wagons in the spring when the melting snows and rains made it a river of mud.

The land on which the inn stood was purchased by William Corey, a veteran of the War of 1812, and passed, on his death in 1850, to his son, William Jr. Before his father died, the son promised not to sell the property to the lumber companies that were gobbling adjacent plots. Father and son loved the cloistered serenity of their land.

Built by them in 1830, the inn stood near the northeast edge of the property, which was bounded by the road between Saranac and Tupper Lake villages on the north, the Indian Carry on the east, the Raquette River on the south, and a line parallel to the Indian Carry one mile to the west of it. Except for the clearing around the inn, Corey's six hundred acres was virgin forest, dominated by white pines six feet across and smaller spruce, fir, and hemlock.

Thanks to William H.H. Murray's book, *Adventures in the Wilderness*, tourists flocked to the Adirondacks during the summers of 1870 and 1871. Arriving by stagecoaches from

Saratoga or Utica they came to hunt and fish, paddle and swim, occasionally climb the mountains, and rest. For the first time, Corey's Inn turned a profit, enabling William Jr. to hire a couple to take Mary and Cyrus's place.

By fall, the last of the tourists had departed and William had discharged the couple, not expecting any guests. He had cleaned the cabins in back of the inn and was sitting on the front porch sipping a sarsaparilla, admiring the birches that flashed yellow and the fiery red maples amidst the dense green of the softwoods. The Carters had only been gone a month but he missed them, especially the boisterousness of his nephews and niece, which he did not appreciate until they were gone. He had treated them as might a grandfather, and they reciprocated. He chuckled at their occasional lack of respect, hiding his pipe, for instance. The first time, he offered to pay them a penny each if they would make it reappear. This got to be an expensive game, with John rapidly increasing the price for retrieval.

Reminiscing this way, he did not see the cloud of dust rising from the east until he heard the clatter of hoofs on the hard-packed surface. Then two horsemen appeared as the road emerged from a copse, slowing their pace as they approached the inn. They pulled up, dismounted, and tied their horses to the post in front of the inn. William put his hands on the porch rail and pushed himself up slowly, his joints no longer limber. The men, well dressed, with black hats, long coats, and string ties, walked up the steps to the porch.

"Are you gentlemen wanting accommodation?" William asked.

"No, Mr. Corey, but we would like lunch."

"How is it you know my name?"

"You're well known in these parts. Besides, we've come not only for lunch but for business."

"Well, I don't like to do business with hungry people, so let me feed you first. Then I'll hear what you have to say."

It was an Indian summer day, with the barest of breezes riffling the trees. William set a table on the front porch and retreated to the kitchen from which he emerged a few minutes later with chicken and venison salads. His guests refused wine.

The men were not drawn to talk while they ate and William retreated into the inn. When they had finished, he cleared the table, returning with cups and a pot of coffee. One drew a cigar from his coat and a cutter from his vest pocket. After clipping the cigar, he lit it and sat back in his chair, puffing contentedly. William placed an ashtray on the table and pulled a chair up. "If you're comfortable, gentlemen, we can conduct our business here." They nodded agreement. "What can I do for you?"

"Mr. Corey, have you heard of Dr. Thomas Durant?" the one without the cigar asked.

"Railroad magnate, isn't he? Financed the railroad that runs across the United States, the uhh—"

"Union Pacific. That's right. Well Dr. Durant and a few others are financing the Adirondack Railroad Company to run a line from Saratoga to Malone. We're Dr. Durant's personal representatives."

"Gentlemen, I'm sorry. Although I've had a very good season, I'm not in a position to invest in this venture. If I could give you anything it would be a pittance."

The other tapped his cigar into the ashtray. "We're not looking for your money, Mr. Corey. Quite the opposite."

William was puzzled. "Really?"

"Construction has already started on the southern end and we'll have the track laid to North Creek by the end of next year. We've made several land purchases along the route."

"The plan is to run the line from North Creek northwest to Long Lake," the other added, "then along the Raquette River into Tupper Lake."

William got the picture quickly. "Seems like my property might be in your path."

The smoker picked up his cigar. "It could be. If you sell us a strip of land, we can put a station near your inn. Think what that would do for business."

"I reckon it'd help, but you'd be messing up the woods. Folks come up here for the beauty of the place, for peace and quiet."

"I doubt there'll be more than one passenger train a day, if that many, so far as peace and quiet goes. We won't cut a path any wider than we need for the track, less than one hundred feet, so your guests will hardly notice it."

"And I'll bet you double or triple the number of guests in the first year of the railroad's operation," the other interjected.

William scratched his head. "Surely Dr. Durant's not going to make a whole lot of money out of this venture. If the fares he charged were high enough for the railroad to make a profit, he wouldn't get many customers."

"Well, Mr. Corey, I'll be frank with you, Dr. Durant and

his son William have made land purchases in the Adirondacks and they want to see more folks come up here to share the beauty."

"And make a pretty penny from those folks' enjoyment."

"You could share in that wealth," the cigar smoker continued.

"Might be," replied William. The original cabins and those that he and Cyrus had added had all been rented for half of the past summer. If they could be rented for the entire summer, he would make enough to build more cabins if the demand warranted. "What sort of price are you offering?" he asked.

"If you're interested, we'd have our surveyors get up-to-date measurements, but from the deeds filed in Malone we'd estimate a purchase of about thirty acres, which would include a station. We're offering ten dollars an acre; three hundred dollars is a tidy sum," said the cigar smoker. "That's probably more than you clear in an entire season."

Doing his own calculation, William reached a similar conclusion. His guest offered him a cigar. William refused but took his pipe and a pouch of tobacco from his pants pocket, stoked, lit up, stood, and walked to the porch rail. He could see Stoney Creek Mountain and the long ridge of Ampersand beyond. In a few weeks, when the leaves were off the trees he would catch a glimpse of Upper Saranac Lake. He had lived his entire life here and, except for the gradually widening road and the inn, nothing had changed.

He returned to the table. "You know, gentlemen, before he died, I promised my father I wouldn't sell this land to the lumber companies."

"We're not a lumber company, Mr. Corey," the man without the cigar responded briskly.

"I know that, Sir. But you'll be cutting trees to clear the railbed, and when your engines come puffing through, they'll make a darn sight more noise than axes and saws. God knows what other havoc they'll wreak."

Durant's representative relit his cigar. "You know, Mr. Corey, from the deed I've examined, the amount we offer to purchase is less than five percent of your property. I think you're exaggerating the harmful effects."

"What if I don't sell?" William asked.

"We've been talking to the Smead Lumber Company, your neighbor to the east and south. They're very interested in selling us a strip on their side of the Raquette."

William stood. "I see," he said. "Gentlemen, I need to think about it."

The two men rose as he did. "You understand, Mr. Corey, we're eager to move ahead on this." The man with the cigar took a card from his vest pocket. "Write me at this address. But you'd better decide soon or you'll miss this opportunity." He reached for his wallet, asking William, "How much was lunch? It was delicious."

William looked up at the sky where white clouds were coalescing. "I'd say the equivalent of a half acre."

"You mean five dollars?"

"If that's your land price."

Both men laughed. "That's the current price, Mr. Corey," one said. "It could go up or it could go down." The men paid their bill, mounted, and headed back toward Saranac Lake village.

William cleaned up and returned to the porch, sitting this time in a high-backed rocker. His vision was failing; he could see the outline of the mountains, but the vivid fall colors were just a blur. He didn't know how much longer he could manage the inn. A few years ago he thought that when he was no longer able, Cyrus and Mary could take it over. But now they had moved to the village so Mary could teach in the new public school. She had helped him for fourteen years; he couldn't ask for more. Cyrus, who had continued to jack in the winters, worked for him in the warmer months, adding on cabins, keeping them and the inn in good shape, and guiding tourists who wanted to hunt, fish, and climb, in his spare time studying for the bar, convinced he could do more that way for his fellow laborers than continuing to be one. If he succeeded, Cyrus wouldn't be interested in tying himself to the inn. Could he pass it on to the Carter children? In ten years he'd be sixty-six and John would be twenty-two. He might be interested, but who could tell? *Besides I might not last that long*, he thought. If John would want it, wouldn't it be best to have the inn on a sound financial footing—the railroad delivering tourists right to its doorstep? And if he had to sell it out of the family, he'd get a better price with the railroad close by. But then he thought, *I'm already an old man. What do I need the money for?*

He must have dozed off, for when he awoke, a chill had pervaded the air as dark clouds obscured the sun. He smiled to himself: *Adirondack weather sure is changeable. Maybe I'll take the trap and visit the Carters. I suppose they're settled in by now. It's awfully lonely out here without the children, and I'd rather eat Mary's cooking than my own.*

William arrived at the Carter house in a steady rain. He hitched the horse to a tree at the side of the house and walked as quickly as he could up the steps to the front door. Tommy responded to the knock. "Uncle. It's so good to see you." The two hugged. John and Lisa came into the entry way and also hugged the old man.

"Are your folks here?" William asked.

"In the kitchen," John replied. "We were just teaching Lisa how to play jacks in the parlor. Do you want to join us?"

"I'll give it a try." William got down on the floor but quickly gave up competing in dexterity with John and Tommy. As he stood, Mary walked in, surprised to see her uncle.

They hugged. Mary said to Lisa, "Let's give Uncle William a tour of the house, starting here." Waving her hand around, she said, "The parlor was enormous when we bought the place."

"Couldn't have been as big as at the inn," he commented dryly.

"That's true, Uncle, but it's big enough for us. And with the fireplace it will be cozy warm in the winter. Cyrus subdivided the parlor, building a study for himself— he's earnest about the law, Uncle." She pointed to a door at the far end. "And there he added a bedroom for Lisa."

Mother and daughter led William back to the entrance hall where Lisa proudly opened one of the doors off the hall. "This is my room!" she proclaimed. A few dolls were propped on her bed. Mary opened the second door, to a bigger bedroom. "The boys share this one." Then they led

William down a short hall that led to the kitchen, where Cyrus was peeling potatoes. "Look who's here, Dear," Mary announced as William entered.

"Hello William." Cyrus noticed William eyeing the potato in his hand. "I'm embarrassed, William, to say that these potatoes come from your garden."

"Well, if you allow me to partake, I'll excuse the theft."

"Of course, you're invited to dinner, and from the looks of the weather, overnight as well." Mary added, "We'll fix up the sofa in the parlor if that's all right, Uncle?"

"I prefer my own bed but I also prefer to keep dry, so with this rain, I'll accept your invitation with pleasure." Mary ended the tour by showing him the master bedroom just beyond the kitchen.

They had a plain but ample dinner with a blueberry pie that Mary had baked for dessert. "Did you steal these berries too?" William asked.

"No, Sir," Tommy piped up. "Mama sent us out with pots and pans to pick them near Moody Pond. After we got through, they were just about gone."

After dinner, William took out his pipe and tobacco and filled it. He caught Tommy eyeing the pipe as he put it down to fetch a match from his pocket. "Don't try any of your tricks, young man," he said to Tommy and quickly picked up his pipe and lit it.

After his pipe was well stoked and Mary had returned from putting Lisa to bed and cleaning up the dishes, William mentioned that he'd had visitors from the Adirondack Railroad Company the previous day. "They want to buy a parcel of my property for a railroad that will run from North

Creek to Malone."

John and Tommy were playing near the table. "A railroad. Wow! That'll be fun," said Tommy.

"Maybe, Son," Cyrus said. "Building it won't be easy."

"I bet we could travel all the way to New York City in a day," John exclaimed.

"What did you tell them, Uncle?" Mary asked.

Taking his pipe from his mouth William replied, "I told them I'd have to think about it. They tried to read me the rush act. I wanted to talk to the two—or maybe I should say the four—of you first." He resumed puffing.

Cyrus began pondering. "Building the railroad would mean jobs. And after it was finished, more people coming here for vacation would mean more jobs."

"Cyrus dear," Mary interrupted, "you're always thinking about jobs."

"You know why that is. A father's got to feed his family."

"A mother does, too," Mary replied. "Right now most people up here have work."

"You're right, Dear," Cyrus replied. "But I don't know how long that will last. Smead's cut just about all the large softwoods in the forest, at least at the distance that makes it profitable to get them to the Raquette. I hear the Company's going to close some camps. The railroad will bring jobs. It will extend the reach of the lumber companies; if they can get the logs to the rails they won't have to depend on the rivers. They might be able to harvest timber all year round."

"And having the railroad will let them cut the hardwoods that don't float," Mary interrupted. "The hills will be naked. Just stumps, and they'll rot, along with us."

"And if that happens," William observed, "the tourists will stop coming." He relit his pipe. "Of course, that's not the way the gentlemen from the railroad company put it. They emphasized the tourist aspect. Even wanted to build a station on the strip they'd buy from me so tourists would flock to the inn."

William's remark made Cyrus realize for the first time that continued cutting could interfere with the tourist trade, a source of jobs not only for guides but for people employed to build more inns and other resorts to feed and house the visitors and then for people hired to work in them.

"I don't understand," William commented, "why this Dr. Durant, who owns the railroad, bought a lot of land up here."

"I'd guess either he wants to keep it for his private use or sell tracts profitably, after the railroad's built, to other wealthy men, hotel builders." Cyrus paused. "Or maybe to lumber companies. His railroads would make a pretty penny hauling logs to the mills."

"Do you think if I helped build the railroad, the boss'd give me a free pass to ride on it?" Tommy asked his father.

Cyrus and William laughed. "First of all, Son," Cyrus replied, "you're too young. From what Uncle William says, they'll have it built by the time you're out of school."

"And if you think Dr. Durant's gonna give free passes to his workers," William added, "you've got another guess coming. He'll want to keep the riff raff out—the likes of people like us—especially if he's gonna use the land for his own domain."

Mary couldn't bear to think that Tommy might work for the railroads when he grew up, but all she said was, "They'll never build the railroad. They won't get enough people to pay to ride on it. Coming up here is just a novelty for city folk. Once they learn the discomforts they won't keep coming."

"What do you mean by 'discomforts,' Mama?" John asked. He and Tommy loved camping in the woods and when Cyrus had a job guiding he'd often take them along.

They would gather firewood, fetch water from the nearest stream, help Cyrus prepare the fire, cook the evening meal, and build lean-tos, none of which their clients deigned or knew how to do, and the boys loved every minute. Often the boys and Cyrus would have to slow down to keep up with their guests. John and Tommy got good at telling which guests would give up on an ascent, whispering their predictions to Cyrus. "They're not used to the woods, boys. They're more to be pitied than scorned," he'd reply.

Cyrus answered John's question. "Back at the inn I've heard them complain of blisters and mosquitoes, of getting wet and being hungry. They realize camping is not as glamorous as 'Adirondack' Murray claimed. That's why guides ask for payment in advance."

Nobody spoke for a few minutes. Tommy asked, "Dad, can we have a fire? It's getting cold in here."

"Sure, Son. You and John bring in some wood. Try to keep dry." He turned to John, "You can build it and I'll even let you light it." The boys went out.

William took the opportunity of their absence. "I know it's too early to ask, but do you think either of your boys would take over the inn? I can probably hold on for another ten years but after that I'd have to sell or hand it down to one or both of them. The question then is would it be more valuable with the railroad or without it?"

Mary stood. "With all due respect, Uncle. I'd rather see my boys go on to college and maybe a profession. I haven't imagined them as inn keepers."

Mary's words stung William, but he replied politely. "Yes, of course. I see your point. You've given them a better education so far than I've ever had."

"Better than I've had, too," Cyrus added.

"Don't sell yourselves short, either of you," Mary replied. "You're plenty smart without formal education. And if Cyrus eventually gets admitted to the bar, that will prove it for him."

The boys brought in some kindling and short logs. John built and lit the fire on one match.

William asked, "What would the fall be like up here without the maples and birches?"

"The leaves are the least of it," Mary said.

———•———

William didn't write to the railroad representatives; they came by a few weeks later. He told them flat out he wasn't going to sell. They didn't stay for lunch. "Oh, by the way," one of them said as he mounted his horse, "we've made a deal with Smead. They're going to lease us land south of yours. Except for their loading platforms across the river from Axton Landing, there won't be any stations between Long Lake and Tupper."

"Suits me," William replied, knowing he had missed a chance to increase his clientele. He was aware that a move was afoot to improve the road between Saranac and Tupper lakes. That would be a less intrusive way to improve business than the railroad.

Trains began to run between Saratoga and North Creek in 1872, the same year that construction of track started between North Creek and Long Lake by way of Minerva and Newcomb.

4

Panic and Politics

THE Carters adapted to life in the village. By the time Lisa had reached her sixth birthday in May 1872 she was enjoying school. Her brothers also thrived; all three children had friends living close by, something they did not have at Corey's. The Carters missed fewer school days than when they had to travel from the inn.

With Cyrus essentially apprenticed to Lawrence Venable, Mary was the principal breadwinner. Cyrus worked as a guide over the summer, which supplemented Mary's nine-month salary. They were able to keep up with mortgage payments and in June they bought a horse along with a wagon big enough to hold them all. The purchase enabled them to visit Uncle William and swim in Upper Saranac Lake, their favorite site. The next year went well for them as well, Cyrus earning more money as his skill as a law clerk increased.

In September 1873, panic struck the nation after financier Jay Cooke declared bankruptcy. Construction of the Adirondack Railroad halted just beyond North Creek. Unable to borrow money, people who were building houses and stores had to stop construction. As demand for houses fell, the lumber companies curtailed their operations; more men were laid off. Unemployment reached fourteen percent.

Initially, Lawrence Venable had a flurry of clients who wanted to make sure their deeds protected their property and a few others who declared bankruptcy—matters that kept Cyrus afloat—but soon Venable's law practice petered out and with it Cyrus's source of income.

By the end of 1873, the Harrietstown Council recognized that its revenues for the following year were going to fall. The Council informed Reverend Jones that the School Board would have to trim its budget. Venable and Miller argued for reducing both teachers' salaries, but Jones, Bartlett, and Brown pointed out that Bumblecombe's family would be devastated if he had to work for less. Venable noted they had never received Bumblecombe's credentials from Boston, but no one else seemed to care. The majority, on the other hand, said Mary could rely on her husband to bring in an income. Tobias Brown said he still believed that "a woman's place is in the home" just as he had commented when they had interviewed Mary. Only Venable knew how little Cyrus was making.

Reverend Jones delivered the bad news to Mary on the last school day before the Christmas holiday. "The town no longer has enough to pay you and Mr. Bumblecombe. We will have to let you go. I suspect that some of our families, perhaps including yours, will no longer be able to send their children to school. The Board thinks Mr. Bumblecombe will ably handle the students who return after holiday."

"Regardless of what happens to me," Mary responded simply, "my children will be to school in January. Goodbye, Reverend."

As they walked home together, her children were buoyant with the holiday in front of them. They were surprised that their mother was glum.

Fortunately, the summer of '73 had been a good one for guiding in the Adirondacks, but even with what Mary earned until the Board fired her, the Carters were hard pressed to get through the winter. They were determined to keep up their mortgage payments to Milo Miller, but other purchases were cut back. There would be no new clothes for the children, although the boys were growing rapidly. Without a job, Mary had plenty of time for mending. The family was able to get winter vegetables from Uncle William's garden, and Cyrus went ice fishing and did some hunting. But the family was in more difficult straits than it had been before.

Others were worse off. Without a reliable source of food, hunger increased, followed by illness. While the Carter children continued school under Mr. Bumblecombe, others did not. Illness, pride, having to help at home, or worn or inadequate clothing kept them away.

A pall hung over the Village.

In the spring of '74, the unemployed began to congregate in small knots. They were bewildered. What had happened? The year before everything was going well, and now, nothing. Fearing insurrection, the Harrietstown Council ordered the sheriff and his deputies to disperse any gathering of three or more men.

The idea of running for the Harrietstown Council gnawed at Cyrus. No workingman sat on the Council, and its members were more concerned about protecting the town's privileged residents than keeping its poorer ones from slipping into poverty. After many discussions with Mary, Cyrus decided to file his candidacy for the 1874 election. He had little doubt he would garner the votes of the unemployed and others who had earned their living by physical labor—if they voted. With the ban on congregating, Cyrus would have to travel from farm to farm, from hovel to hovel, introducing himself and letting people know that he was running.

Mary kept pestering him. "Why do you want to run?" She wasn't questioning whether he *should* run but was helping hone his platform. Sometimes she phrased the question, "Why should I vote for you?" or "What do you stand for?"

"We need someone to represent the plain folks of Saranac Lake." No one, Cyrus knew, wanted to admit poverty; "plain folks" was less obtrusive than "poor folks."

"But what are you going to do for them?" Mary pressed.

Cyrus chuckled. "I'll sponsor a resolution to let women vote in the local elections."

"Thank you, Cyrus. If women could vote, you'd surely win on that platform," Mary replied, "but they don't, so forget it." She stopped to reflect. "Well, I don't mean forget it, but it won't elect you."

Still smiling, Cyrus continued, "I'd make a big thing about education, how we can't afford to hire enough teachers—"

"You'd better not, Cyrus. They'll accuse you of favoritism."

"I'll tell them that the Town should set aside a fund from tax revenues to assist families in time of need."

"That's good."

"I'd tell them the Town should hire local workers instead of contracting out to private firms for work on Town land.

Cut out the middle man." Mary nodded agreement.

"I'd propose to change our local taxes so large landholders paid a higher percentage on the number of acres they
owned than small landholders. I'd put a tax on earnings,
with the rich paying a higher percentage."

"Those policies will get you in trouble with the wealthy
folks," she interrupted.   Cyrus nodded agreement. "And as
I visit around the village, I'll ask people what they think and
maybe adopt what they say."

The Town Council was not elected along party lines,
although the affiliations of most of the candidates were
known. Cyrus wasn't sure to which party he gravitated and
decided not to assume a party label. Nationally, the Republican Party—the party of Lincoln—was becoming the party
of the rich. Cyrus was not happy about that. The Democrats
were considered the more corrupt party.

By the time Cyrus, accompanied by his wife and children, walked to the Courthouse on a lovely June day in 1874,
three other candidates had filed for the two vacancies on the
Council. One was Tobias Brown, School Board member and
owner of the dry goods store. After Cyrus filed the necessary
papers, he and Mary looked up and copied the names of all
of the registered voters in Harrietstown. Few of the men he
knew from jacking or guiding were on the list. In the areas
outside the village no one had yet registered, although they
were still inside the town boundaries. By visiting families on
the Bloomingdale Road and out toward Ampersand, Cyrus
learned that many of them didn't even know there was an
election or that men over twenty-one, whether they owned
property or not, had the right to vote; he encouraged these

men to register, telling them that he was a candidate and that he thought the Town Council had a responsibility to help those in need. By October he had doubled the number of registered men and was promoting his candidacy among all registered voters. With little over one hundred votes needed to win, Cyrus was able to convince many of those he visited that their vote really counted.

———◆———

One day in early October, as he was walking past Brown's dry goods store, Cyrus heard his name called: "Mr. Carter, Mr. Carter." He turned and saw a lovely young woman approaching. "You probably don't remember me. Eleanor Weinberg, Henry's daughter."

Cyrus's face brightened. "Of course. You've changed since I last saw you." She had blossomed into an attractive woman, standing straight, her dark hair spilling down her back, her figure slender but full. "Your father said you were going off to college. That must have been five years ago. How are your parents?"

"They are both well, thank you. Yes, I graduated from Cornell University last year. I'm trying to decide what to do next. I do have something important to tell you—not about me. Your old friend Jared Mason has just returned to the Adirondacks. I'm afraid he's not well; he's staying with us."

Jared and Cyrus had jacked together for two years in the late 1850s. Then Jed, as his friends called him, went to medical school in New York City and became an inspector for the City's Board of Health after he graduated.

"I haven't heard from Jed for some time. He wrote me

once about ten years ago that he had to take time off because of illness. Is this the same problem?"

"I don't know what he had then. But now, Papa and Jared think he's got consumption. He was deathly ill when he came off the train at North Creek last week. He's getting better though. Mama said that if I ran into you I should invite you and Mary and her uncle to dinner." Eleanor removed a small diary from her purse and leafed through it. "How about Friday, October twenty-third? We want to surprise Jared with your visit."

"We'll look forward to it. We're living here in the village but we have a wagon and can collect Mary's uncle on the way to Tupper Lake. Our children are old enough to stay home by themselves."

"Excellent," Eleanor said. "The children are welcome to come, you know."

"I'm afraid they'd be bored. Besides, once they taste your mother's cooking, I'm not sure they'll want to return home."

Eleanor laughed. "As you like. But come as early as you can so you can return before dark. I'm sure there'll be a lot to talk about."

5

The Return of Jared Mason

AS an inspector for the New York City Board of Health, Jared Mason worked hard, visiting the teeming tenements where disease ran rampant. His coughing bouts went back to his early days as an inspector. Despite remissions when he took time off and rented a room near Central Park in the northern part of the city, Jared's health deteriorated. He coughed up blood; his night sweats became more persistent. Finally, he admitted what he had known subconsciously for ten years: he had tuberculosis. He had fought back before, but now everything conspired against him. For a while after the end of the war he thought the world would be a better place. If the nation could see the evil of chattel slavery, surely it would see the evils of low wages that resulted in starvation worse than many slaves had faced. He saw this every day on his visits to the tenements.

He did not count on the greed of the steel, railroad, and banking magnates who had little regard for the workers as they took advantage of new technology and the seemingly limitless markets that the west provided, until the financiers overextended and panic ensued. He did not foresee that the wealthy planters would regain control of the south and put "free" Negroes to work under hideous conditions. Physically and mentally, Jared was beaten.

One last time, he wrote to his old friend, Henry Wein-berg, at Tupper Lake.

New York City
September 15, 1874

Dear Henry,

The sad state of affairs of this nation and my own meager efforts to improve health in the City has exacted a price. I have to admit what you probably have long suspected from the clinical details in my previous letters: I have consumption. Fortunately, no one depends on my earnings and, fortunately, I have not been intimate with other people. (I do believe it is an infectious disease.) I am barely strong enough to walk and I have quit my job.

I am grateful to you for encouraging me to stick with my medical studies and become a doctor. I am proud that I went to work for the City and believe that I have accomplished something. Perhaps civilization spirals up-ward and what I have done will have some lasting effect, but at the moment it is difficult to believe.

This may be my last letter. My best to your wife and daughter.

I will try to write Cyrus Carter, but now I must rest.

With gratitude,
Jared Mason, M.D.

———◆———

Within days after writing to Henry, Jed received a money order for his train fare from New York City to North Creek, along with the following telegram:

COME AT ONCE STOP BUY RAILROAD
TICKET TO NORTH CREEK STOP WILL
MEET YOU THERE ON MONDAY OCTOBER
5 STOP WIRE ACCEPTANCE STOP HENRY

Jed read the message, lay back on his pillow, and examined his prospects. Was he prepared to die alone in his rooms? Would he survive the trip to Tupper Lake? Would he infect Weinberg or his family? Would the Adirondacks help him? He had acquaintances in the City; if he asked, they would help, but the clean air of the mountains and his old friends, Henry and Cyrus, had appeal.

Jed dressed, put Henry's money order in his pocket as well as some of his own earnings, and dragged himself to the nearest Western Union office. Should he return the money or tell Henry he would come? At the office, a young Jewish woman was on line ahead of him. Through sobs and tears, she could not get the telegrapher to understand that she wanted to notify her parents in Austria that her brother had died. With his limited German, Jed patiently helped her write out the message. She dabbed at her eyes with a handkerchief and stopped crying to listen as he read the brief message back to her. She nodded that the wording was correct. Jed handed the message to the telegrapher. As he finished, the woman grasped Jed's arm and smiled. "*Danke*," she said, and then falteringly, "Thank you."

Jed wired Henry:

**WILL COME MONDAY OCTOBER 5 STOP
DON'T NEED YOUR MONEY**

The agent said he could add more words for the same price. Jed told him he had nothing more to say.

Jed walked sluggishly to the Board of Health office and showed one of the other inspectors Henry's telegram. "Are you going?" the other doctor asked.

"Yes, but—"

Before Jed could go further, the doctor said, "I think you're making the right decision." Handing several dollars to his friend, Jed asked if he would purchase the ticket for him. "Certainly," he replied, "and we'll get you to Grand Central Depot in time to catch your train." With tears in his sunken eyes, Jed grasped his arm and thanked him.

The train carrying Jed Mason arrived in North Creek at 4:30 P.M., two hours late. Henry Weinberg had borrowed a wagon from his neighbor and fitted it with a mattress, pillows, and blankets so Jed could lie back on the arduous trip. Henry and his daughter Eleanor waited expectantly. They first saw the white cloud of steam against the deep blue Adirondack sky and then heard the whistle and the rumble of the engine as it came into view. The train disgorged its passengers, but Jed did not appear. Finally, a conductor walked down the steps of one car, extending his arm back into the train. A gaunt man emerged, holding the conductor's arm with one hand and a cane in the other. Once the man was planted on the ground, leaning heavily against his cane, the conductor went back into the train and brought out a carpetbag, which he set next to the man. They shook hands and the conductor climbed aboard the train.

Henry was astonished. The man looked twice Jed's age and half his former weight. "Wait here," Henry bade Eleanor, as he walked from the wagon to the side of the train. As he approached, he recognized a caricature of Jed's features. "It's so good to see you, Jed." Henry picked up Jed's bag and slipped his free arm around Jed's waist, practically carrying him to the wagon. Eleanor stepped forward to take Jed's bag from her father. "Let me see," Henry said, "Eleanor was ten years old the last you saw her. She's grown a bit, wouldn't you say?"

Jed smiled weakly but said nothing. He reached in his pocket and pulled out Henry's money order. "Here," he said in a barely audible voice as he handed it to Henry. "I didn't need your money to make the trip."

Henry knew better than to argue with a man in Jed's condition. He took the money order and led Jed to the wagon. With Eleanor's help he settled Jed into the makeshift bed on the wagon floor. "If the train had been on time, we might have made the sixty miles home today, but now we'll have to stay overnight in Newcomb or Long Lake. Freda packed a picnic basket that may be our supper." Henry climbed on to the driver's bench and Eleanor sat beside him. She peered back at Jed from time to time. Sometimes his eyes were closed. Other times he stared at the sky. At Mary

and Cyrus's wedding, Jed had towered over her. He had
been smooth shaven with a finely chiseled nose and mouth
and blue eyes that flashed when he spoke a few words to
her after the ceremony. She remembered his hair as long
and straight, neatly tied in the back. That he'd been formally
dressed for the occasion enhanced his handsomeness in her
memory. She had harbored a crush on him ever since. Now,
with lusterless, graying hair, gray stubble on his face, and dull
sunken eyes, he had changed almost as much as she had.

Darkness overtook them at Newcomb where they
sought lodging at a small inn. Jed had his own room and
Henry and Eleanor shared another. They saved the food
Freda had packed for the next morning and had a light supper at the inn. Jed ate very little. His eyes had a glaze that
suggested to Henry that any significant conversation was
fruitless. The next morning he seemed somewhat better. He
smiled and nodded when Henry asked if he had slept well.

They arrived at Tupper Lake in mid-afternoon. Freda
greeted them at the door. She too was astonished at Jed's
appearance.

Eleanor had volunteered to give her room to Jed and
sleep on the sofa in the living room. The Weinbergs did not
tell Jed that he was sleeping in Eleanor's room, knowing he
would object. They had no place else to put him.

Jed slept that first afternoon. He awoke to savory aromas. For the first time in weeks, the idea of eating appealed
to him. Relishing Freda's cooking, he swung his feet over
the side of the bed and reached for his cane, hanging on
the doorknob. The tap of the cane alerted Eleanor, sitting
in the living room below, that he was awake. Henry was

seeing patients in his adjoining office. Eleanor stopped in the kitchen where her mother was busy cooking to ladle water that was simmering on the stove into a large porcelain pitcher. Carrying the pitcher, Eleanor went up the stairs and knocked on Jed's door.

"Come in, please."

"I brought some water for you to wash with." She set the pitcher on the washstand. Jed looked directly at Eleanor for the first time. "You have grown, haven't you? I've probably lost about as much as you've gained," he said, echoing Eleanor's observation of the previous day.

Ignoring his attempt at humor, she said primly, "Dr. Mason, you are already looking better than yesterday. With Mama's cooking, you'll soon be back to the way I remember you at the Carters' wedding."

"That was a long time ago."

"Yes, I was only ten." Jed saw her blush. "I thought you were the handsomest man there."

A warm glow settled over him. He laughed, "And there was some pretty stiff competition, too. I remember, though, that Cyrus didn't look as good in his coat as he did in a lumberjack's shirt. Your father was handsome too, and still is. Reverend Loguen was elegant."

"I'll bet you don't remember me."

Jed hesitated. "Well you had pretty stiff competition from the ladies, including your mother. Mary was gorgeous in her wedding dress, and her sister Rachel..."

Eleanor changed the subject. "Mama's cooking one of her special dinners. I hope you're up to it."

"I think it was the aromas that awakened me. I've more

of an appetite than I've had for weeks."

"Good. Perhaps you'd like to wash first." She poured water into a large basin cradled in the washstand and showed him soap and towel. He started to roll up his sleeves before she left; he was accustomed to washing in the presence of women. "If you like, I'll come back in fifteen minutes to help you downstairs."

"That's very kind of you, Miss Weinberg."

"It's Eleanor."

Recalling how she had addressed him a few minutes earlier he replied, "I'm Jed." But Eleanor preferred calling him Jared.

After breakfast on October 23rd, Freda Weinberg announced to Jed that she was having a surprise dinner in his honor that evening. Not quite two weeks since his return, Jed was able to walk up and down the stairs without his cane, although he did hold the banister. A few hours after Freda's announcement, he strolled through the dining room and noticed the table set for seven. From the kitchen, the smells were tantalizing. Jed was not sure he could hold out.

His theory about the guests was accurate. Cyrus, Mary, and William sat on one side; Jed and Eleanor on the other, while Henry and Freda sat at the ends. They began the meal with Freda lighting the Shabbat candles, even though it was before sundown.

"Do you do this before every dinner?" Mary asked.

"No, only on the meal before the Sabbath."

"It's about the only religious thing we do on a regular

basis," Henry added. "When Eleanor was little we celebrated some Jewish holidays so she would know something about her heritage."

"It's more a matter of culture than religion," Eleanor commented. "I still like to celebrate Chanukah and Passover. They are reminders that freedom and justice are not the natural state."

Cyrus turned to Mary. "Was Eleanor ever a student of yours? She sounds like you."

"Women can come to their judgments independently," Mary chided Cyrus then turned to Eleanor. "You should join our women's suffrage group. Women have neither freedom nor justice."

"Or not as much as you'd like," Cyrus added jokingly. "I wanted to put women's suffrage on my platform, but Mary wouldn't let me."

"What platform?" Jed spoke for the first time.

"The Weinbergs haven't told you?" Mary asked. Glancing at Henry's puzzled face, she continued, "Oh! I guess they don't know. I've been so absorbed in Cyrus's campaign I've forgotten there's a world beyond Saranac Lake."

"What campaign?" Jed persisted.

"I'm running for the Harrietstown Council," Cyrus explained.

Jed dropped his fork with a clatter. Everyone looked at him. "What ever possessed you?" he asked incredulously.

"I think I can get something done," Cyrus replied calmly. Gently he set his fork and knife on his plate. "This panic, depression, or whatever you want to call it, has hit hard. Some families didn't get through this past winter. One man up near

Mackenzie Pond shot his wife, two children, and then took his own life. They were starving to death. All the Town Councils have done is lower taxes, which only helps the rich; most people don't own enough property to pay taxes."

Jed had continued to eat while Cyrus talked. Now he laid down his fork and sat upright. His face was flushed. To Henry Weinberg sitting diagonally across from him, it seemed that the Jed Mason he knew was coming back to life.

"How many members on your Council, Cyrus?" Jed asked blandly.

"Six." Cyrus picked up his fork and resumed eating.

"Do you stand a chance of getting elected?" Jed was not eating.

"He'd better for all the work we've put into it," William answered. "Cyrus and Mary have even put their children to work making posters and handing out leaflets."

"I'm one of four candidates for two vacancies," Cyrus said.

"So you'll be one out of six if you're elected. Any other laborers on the Council?" Jed wiped his lips with his napkin and coughed.

"No. Right now, two are big property owners, one is an official of Smead, one owns the village's only hotel, one is a minister, and one owns the furniture factory."

"What makes you think you'll get a majority behind proposals to help the working man?" Jed picked up his fork, adding, "If you are elected."

"You're being unfair, Jed." Mary chimed in. "Cyrus knows it's unlikely. But he'll be raising issues the Council's never considered before. If he gets the people behind him, we might get somewhere. He'll encourage other lumber-jacks, small farmers, the few mechanics around to run in the next election."

"If I could get elected," Cyrus interjected, "why couldn't they?"

"You can bet," Jed replied to both of them, "that those wealthy property owners and the others are not going to sit idly by and let workers get elected. These aristocrats want to hold office not to help others but to help themselves." He barely got the words out when he started to cough parox-ysmally, covering his mouth with a handkerchief he pulled from his pocket. Eleanor offered him a glass of water, but he waved it away. Finally, the attack subsided, he returned his handkerchief to his pocket without looking at it, and accepted the water. "Maybe it happens more in the City than up here, but the greatest value to holding office is the privilege it brings, privilege to help oneself and preserve the privileges the elected officials have already garnered for themselves or their class. The amount of graft and corrup-tion is astounding. On the remote chance you get elected, Cyrus, I only hope you don't fall prey." He started to cough again. These were the first bouts he'd had since arriving in the Adirondacks.

Jed's tirade made Cyrus blanch. Mary put her hand over Cyrus's on his lap. She held it tighter as Jed continued to cough. Both of them had expected Jed to be pleased to learn of Cyrus's candidacy.

"Jed," Cyrus said when the coughing ended. "I'm sorry to have upset you. Maybe we should change the subject."

Jed brushed Cyrus's suggestion aside. "I've had my say.

Now it's your turn." Freda got up to clear the plates away. Eleanor knew she should help but sat glued to her seat. Returning to Tupper Lake after graduating from Cornell, she was usually her father's adversary at the dinner table, but the arguments were never as charged as this. She wondered what Cyrus would say.

"Jed, remember when I first met you, jacking at Fourth Lake, and I walked out complaining about the food? I reached the edge of the camp and when I turned around there you were with nine others, fighting the foremen. I'd never seen that before."

"I remember," Jed resumed eating as Cyrus talked. He added, "I also remember that you turned your back on us."

"I should have known better," Cyrus admitted. "The next year you and I went to work at Axton." He turned from Jed to Henry and then back. "I'm sure you both remember that winter. Bad food again, two deaths from cholera, and two more due to poor management." Mary clutched his hand under the table. "Knowing Ben Anderson, the jobber, had an illegal operation going, we protested—together— threatening to reveal it to Smead unless Ben improved our situation." He paused to take a drink of water. "Yeah, we won a few concessions but they didn't stick." He looked at Jed earnestly. "We can change the laws to make it harder for these tycoons—that's a word I've learned recently—to beat us down. The battle can't be fought one lumber camp at a time. These tycoons can be held accountable under the law."

Eleanor realized she was holding her breath while Cyrus spoke. Now she let it out slowly and as surreptitiously as possible. She turned sideways to look at Jed. He had shaved before dinner and his smooth cheeks were glistening as he responded. "The tycoons, as you call them, *are* the law. Workingmen will have to fight tooth and nail to gain concessions from the tycoons. They will need unions that can negotiate on behalf of all workers. That means strikes and scabs. That means cops. That means violence."

Cyrus remained calm. "When you were in medical school, Jed, you wrote me about the shoemakers' strike in Lynn. As I recall, you said they won their demand for higher wages, but the shoe companies rejected their demand for a union that could bargain for them."

"The strike is a potent weapon," Jed replied, "but unions are the ultimate demand. Wealth buys power, Cyrus, and only direct action by working men will gain them anything lasting."

"You have a point, Jed. Last year, when those of us without jobs tried to meet in the village, the sheriff ordered us to disband. We couldn't talk to more than one person at a time. I figured as a Council member I could get an ordinance allowing people to assemble peaceably. That's in the Bill of Rights, you know?"

"There it is, Cyrus," Jed could not resist one last dart. "It's in the Constitution and still the Council got away with it."

Cyrus brushed the crumbs around his place into a neat small pile. "That's why I'm studying to be a lawyer. We won't let the sheriffs, the police, the lawmakers themselves get away with breaking the law."

For the second time, Jed was incredulous. "What? Can you become a lawyer without going to law school?" Cyrus's revelation abruptly ended Jed's tirade, starting him in a new direction. "I wish I could have become a doctor without going to medical school," he said. "I would have apprenticed myself to Dr. Weinberg here and learned a lot more a lot faster." Everyone around the table except Henry clapped. From the kitchen, Freda brought out two apple pies she had baked. The table grew silent as she cut them. "I hope you are not quiet on my account," she said.

"Of course, they are, Dear." Henry replied. "Your creations stop the show every time." As soon as they finished dessert, Mary got up. "Freda, Henry, we really must be going. The sun's set and it will be dark soon."

———•———

A few days before the election, Lawrence Venable knocked on the Carters' door. Cyrus was home alone. "Cyrus, I've just learned that your opponent Tobias Brown is going to claim that you're neither eligible to vote nor to hold office on the Harrietstown Council."

Cyrus was stunned. "On what basis?"

"He says your house is in Essex County, in the town of St. Armand, not Harrietstown."

Cyrus got out the deed. It defined the boundaries of his property as distances from Helen Street and Shepard Avenue, but said nothing about the property in relation to county or town boundaries.

Using his meager savings, Cyrus hired surveyors from Keene Valley to establish the boundaries in relation to the county and town lines. They found that the line between Franklin and Essex Counties ran close to the Carters' property.

Shortly before the election, the Council relaxed its ban

on gatherings to allow the four candidates to debate in the town hall. Tobias Brown was the first speaker. He stood and pointed at Cyrus. "This gentleman, my friends, is a fraud. He doesn't live in Harrietstown or even in Franklin County. He is ineligible to run in this election." All heads turned to Cyrus who sat implacable at the front of the room with the other candidates.

When it was his turn, Cyrus rose slowly. He wore the same coat as at his wedding fourteen years earlier. His neatly trimmed beard and hair were now more white than gray or brown, and lines were etched across his forehead. Although not tall he stood erect, with a confident and distinguished bearing. "My friends and fellow candidates," he began, turning his head to smile graciously at his opponents. "The first families that settled in what we now call the village of Saranac Lake—the Moodys, the Millers, and the Bakers—must have picked their spots for beauty and convenience, not because they were in one county or another. Little did Jacob Moody, one of this village's founders, worry that his farm was mostly in Essex, not in Franklin County." The audience did not seem impressed. Cyrus paused for a drink of water.

"I was very surprised when I learned of Tobias Brown's concern that I was not a bona fide citizen of Franklin County, so I did a little research." He reached into his coat pocket and pulled out a folded paper. Spreading the paper before him on the lectern, he held it up, first for his opponents on the stage and then for the audience, to see. "I've gone to the expense, which I could ill afford, of having my property surveyed in relation to the county and town lines." Holding the top of the map with the fingers of his left hand, he drew his right index finger down a vertical line, commenting as he did so. "This here's the line that separates Franklin from Essex County, and Harrietstown from the town of St. Armand." He walked down the aisle so everyone could see what he was talking about. Returning to the front of the room, he said, "Now, I call your attention to the fact that Helen Street is not entirely within Franklin County." He traced the street on the map as it proceeded in a northeasterly direction, making sure everyone saw it. A few in the crowd chuckled.

"Next, I call your attention to the location of my property." With his right index finger he pointed to his house, which abutted the boundary along Shepard Avenue but was entirely in Franklin County and Harrietstown. He didn't say a word. A few people sitting in the front row began to laugh as they realized that Tobias Brown had not made his case. Map in hand, once again Cyrus walked down the aisle. The laughter spread as he walked to the back. On the stage, Brown looked glum.

When the laughing subsided, Cyrus returned to the lectern and continued. "The honorable Mr. Brown was almost right. If and when my wife should throw me out of the house for unruly behavior and I have to sleep under the chestnut tree on the other side of Shepard Avenue, I would be in Essex County and the town of St. Armand." Mary, sitting close to the front, suppressed a smile. "I'm pleased to say, however, that has never happened and, as you can see, my home, including the bedroom, is entirely within Franklin County and Harrietstown." The audience broke into applause.

"Now for some more serious business."

6

Huckleberry Cove

IN November, days after Cyrus won a seat on the Harrietstown Council, Eleanor came down with a cold. Freda expressed her worry to Henry that maybe it wasn't such a good idea to have Jed stay with them. The thought lingered with Henry although Eleanor quickly regained her health. A few days later, on a brisk fall afternoon, Henry and Jed went for a walk, Jed no longer needing a cane. He had put on weight and, despite the lines on his face and his gray-tinged hair, he was starting to resemble his younger self.

As light breezes gently shook the trees, a few of the remaining leaves floated slowly to the ground.

"I owe you my life, Henry."

"Not me. Maybe I was *der Katalysator*," Henry said in a rare reversion to German, "but it's more likely Freda's cooking, the fresh air, lots of sleep, lack of—in German we might say '*die psychische Belastung*'—I don't know how to say it in English."

Jed thought for a moment. "The first word is easy, *psychological*. The second word, uhh—*pressure*. No, *stress*; *stress* is a better word. You might be right."

"'Stress,' thank you. I've learned a new English word." Weinberg paused. "It would be nice to know whether you really have this tuberculosis and what it is. I hear many scientists are working on it."

"It must be a germ, probably spread through coughing." Jed hesitated. "I'm afraid I am putting your family in harm's way."

"The thought has occurred to Freda and me. Eleanor is so happy to have you around. I doubt she's thought about it."

"I've taken her room, haven't I?" Henry nodded. "She's a lovely young woman, smart, beautiful. What will she do?"

"Up here, her prospects for marriage are not great. There are no Jewish boys who interest her. No gentile would marry her. Really, though, I don't think she's thinking about marriage. She wants to go to medical school, but for a Jewish woman, that's out of the question."

"There are women doctors, you know."

"But a Jewish woman? I doubt it. She's also interested in women's suffrage. I'm glad Mary Carter invited her to join her group."

"Henry, maybe I should move out," Jed blurted out suddenly.

"Go back to the City?"

"No, I'm not ready for that. Maybe build a place of my own or buy a house."

"William Corey would probably rent you a cabin. He doesn't have much business over the winter. Maybe you should ride over there, or take our carriage, before the snow flies."

Henry noticed that Jed had become short of breath and steered him back toward the house.

"I'll have to admit, Henry, that I'll miss seeing you, Freda, and Eleanor."

"You'll still be a lot closer than New York City."

Corey was agreeable to the idea. Jed would be a paying guest and stay in one of the older cabins over the winter. He moved just after he celebrated Thanksgiving at the Carters' along with the Weinbergs and Corey. They gave thanks that they were surviving the Depression and for Cyrus's victory at the polls. Even Jed congratulated him. "Maybe you'll prove me wrong, Cyrus, and accomplish something."

⎯⎯•⎯⎯

In the spring, Jed purchased a small plot of land from Virgil Bartlett. It was adjacent to an out-pocketing in the large bay that came off Upper Saranac Lake, which had acquired Bartlett's name and ended at his beach. Jared named the out-pocketing Huckleberry Cove; its shores were covered with shrubs that would bear fruit in late summer.

Cyrus had kept his boat at Corey's, maintaining it for fishing. One Saturday after the ice had melted, he, William, and Jed, with the help of John and Tommy, hauled it down Indian Carry, storing it on the beach on the southern shore of the lake. In the ensuing weeks, Jed used it to travel to and from his plot of land. He outfitted himself with axe, saw, hammer, and nails and gradually transported his tools and materials in the boat to a little beach on his property. At first he rowed the half-mile slowly, resting frequently, too tired to do much work once he arrived. He would rest on a large sloping boulder and look out across the cove to the bay, eating the lunch William had packed for him and doze in the afternoon sun. Awaking refreshed, he would row out to the bay, then west, against the prevailing wind, to the main lake and south to Indian Carry. The pull of the oars on his shoulders and stomach felt good as he worked muscles that he had not used for years. He would rest a few moments after he pulled the boat out of the water at the foot of the Carry and then trudge back up to Corey's.

Each day his strength grew. In five days in June, by chopping seven saplings, as well as three pines and a hemlock, each about a foot in diameter, he cleared a rectangular plot about ten feet by twelve feet, enough for a small cabin. His plan was to cut enough trees of about a foot in diameter to form the walls of a log cabin. He would purchase planks from the mill in Tupper Lake for the floor and the frame, using cedar shingles for the roof.

To help Jed, Cyrus brought John and Tommy out on weekends. They stopped at Bartlett's and got permission to drive their wagon across Virgil's property on the path used to carry canoes from Round Lake to Upper Saranac Lake. If Mrs. Bartlett was at home, the boys were likely to get a gift of cookies from her. The end of the Carry at Upper Saranac was about one hundred yards south of Jed's clearing. Cyrus and his boys blazed a footpath along the shore from the Carry to the clearing.

John was now sixteen and Tommy fourteen. John towered over Cyrus and was slightly taller than Jed. Tommy was about an inch shorter than Cyrus and hoped to at least equal his father's height. He doubted he would be as tall as John. John was also darker than Cyrus and Tommy, and his mother for that matter. His hair was black.

One Saturday in early June, Cyrus and his boys hitched their wagon to a rail they had built at the foot of the Carry and walked to Jed's clearing. Jed had not yet arrived. Having discussed the layout with Jed, Cyrus decided to start without him. He sent John back to the wagon to get the bucking saws. When he got back, Cyrus was marking off twelve-foot lengths from the trees that Jed had felled, making notches with his axe. "John, and you, Son, use the saws to buck the tree down to size for the cabin walls. Let's see if you can each get one done before Jed gets here."

Tommy walked a short distance to his tree. As he did so, John asked, "Dad, how come you call me 'John' and Tommy 'Son?'"

Cyrus, who had started measuring off another twelve-foot length, stopped his tandem walking, planted his feet about a foot apart, and stood silently facing John. "I didn't realize I did." He wiped the back of his hand across his brow. "Do I always do that?" Looking at his father and brother from his tree, Tommy noticed their mood had changed.

"Most of the time," John replied.

"Hey, Tommy! How about a hand?" Tommy turned to the lake, where Jed was about ten feet off shore. Tommy ran to pull the bow up on the shallow beach and gave Jed a hand getting out of the boat. Cyrus continued speaking to John. "There's a reason, but now's not the time to discuss it. Can you wait until tomorrow?"

"I've wondered for a long time. Another day won't matter." He grabbed his saw. The two boys bucked the tree into logs in a short time. No small banter interrupted the rhythm of the saws as they cut through the trunks.

Jed noticed the somber mood. He knew better than to ask what was wrong and tried to lighten the atmosphere. "Well, Councilman Carter, have you legislated this excellent weather for us?" Cyrus replied with a wan smile, but no words. Jed tried again. "If I paid these boys a living wage do you think they'd work for me over the summer?" The boys heard the question.

"Jed, don't ask Dad," Tommy replied. "We're old enough to decide for ourselves." Cyrus nodded, again with a wan smile. He resumed pacing off twelve-foot lengths.

"Do you two belong to a union?" Jed asked.

"Yeah," Tommy said. "The Brotherhood of Brothers."

"Fair enough. Which of you is the Brotherhood's bargaining agent?"

"John is, of course. He can stand up to you better."

"All right. When should we have our first bargaining session?"

"Right now," Tommy replied.

"No, right now you're on the job."

"Wait a minute," Cyrus interrupted. "You're not paying them anything yet." He smiled more broadly, finally caught up in the negotiations.

"Well, I thought you boys came here to work not to palaver, but how about we negotiate over lunch?" Jed countered.

"No," John answered. "That's our time to recuperate from being exploited."

They decided to postpone the negotiations until school recessed for the year.

———————

Cyrus and the boys returned home late in the afternoon. Mary, wearing her new reading glasses, was preparing her lessons for the following week while Lisa was doing her homework. The boys went to their room. Cyrus came up behind Mary and rubbed her shoulders. She purred contentment. "How about a walk, Mary? I have to discuss something with you."

She got up, took her glasses off, laid them on the table, and smiled. "It will be a relief to take a break." She took her shawl off a hook near the door and they went out, heading farther up the hillside on a path just wide enough for them to walk side by side.

"We can't be gone too long. I've got to get dinner ready."

"John asked me today why I call him 'John' while I call Tommy 'Son.'"

"I've noticed your doing that lately. I thought maybe you were using that as a way to get John to ask you the question we've been waiting for."

"I wish I was that foresighted. I've been doing it unconsciously. At any rate, now it means we have to answer the question. I told him we'd talk about it tomorrow. I think you should be there, too."

"Yes, of course. What will we say to him?"

"We will tell him the truth. I don't think either of us ever doubted that the time would come."

⸻

The next day, Tommy and Lisa went to visit friends. John could have gone, too, but he realized with his siblings out of the house it would be easier for Cyrus to answer his question. Mary and Cyrus were cleaning up the kitchen when John entered.

"About the question you asked yesterday," Cyrus began, "your mother and I thought it best if the three of us discussed it." They took seats around the kitchen table but no one spoke for a minute. Then Cyrus asked, "Do you think you know what the answer might be?"

John looked straight at Cyrus. "Yes." He paused, took a deep breath. "You know, over the last few years as I've grown to be the tallest in the family and to look different from you and Tommy, I've wondered whether you were my father."

"You were right to wonder," Cyrus replied.

Mary spoke up. "John, do you remember when Tommy was born, you asked me whether a couple had a wedding every time they planted a seed for a new baby. I wondered whether you were remembering being at my wedding to Cyrus."

John remained silent. "I don't remember what you told me when Tommy was born, or being at your wedding. But if I was at your wedding—and I guess you're telling me I was—then that must have been after my seed was planted."

"That's right," Mary and Cyrus answered together.

John looked at them, expectantly.

"Very well. I'll begin," Cyrus said. "Your father's name was Jean Entremont. You are named after him. In the fall of 1857, he came down from Quebec after his father had died, looking for work, and I was rowing north from Fourth Lake, in the boat that Jed uses now, also looking for work. He hailed me from the shore of Long Lake, and I offered to take him up the lake and then down the Raquette to find jobs." Cyrus paused, reflecting back on that day.

"How did you get the boat over the falls on the river?"

"I have to admit, one of the reasons I gave Jean a ride was so that he could help me carry the boat around the falls. I would have had a hard time by myself. Your father was strong, as strong as you are."

"What happened to him—to my father?"

"We got jobs as jacks at Smead's Axton Landing camp. In April 1858, we were ordered to break a logjam on the Raquette to get the logs to the mill at Tupper Lake. Jean and I and two other men were in my boat, in front of the jam. I asked Jean to row as I worked with the pike pole from the stern to break the jam. A thunderstorm blew up. All of a sudden, the jam broke. Jean pulled hard on the oars to stay ahead of the jam, and I fell overboard. I was able to keep on top of the logs for a while. As they moved faster, I lost my grip and fell. Jean jumped out of the boat to rescue me. The logs had gathered speed and were churning the water." Cyrus paused again. He hadn't thought that retelling the story would affect him, but now he felt he was reliving it. He swallowed hard, and tears came to his eyes.

Mary continued for him. "A log hit your father in the head, knocking him unconscious." Her voice wavered.

Cyrus regained his composure. "Sean and Peter O'Rourke, who also worked in the camp, found Jean's body down river two days later. You can visit his grave at the Bartlett's Cemetery above Round Lake."

Nobody spoke.

After a few moments, Mary broke the silence. "The night before he died, your father—Jean—and I agreed to marry. We got close that night, the first and only time. That's when your seed was planted." She wiped away a tear. "Cyrus was hit by a log as he tried to get back in the boat. It broke his leg. Dr. Weinberg in Tupper Lake set it and Uncle William agreed to let him recover at the inn. When he was better, Cyrus stayed on to work at Corey's. You were born at Corey's. Cyrus played with you a lot and loved you. When you were about a year old, he asked me to marry him for your sake as well as mine."

"And mine," Cyrus interrupted. "I couldn't love anybody more than I love Mary and you."

Mary continued. "He was right. Neither of us would have done as well if I hadn't married him."

The three of them sat silently around the table. Then John grasped his mother's hand with his right and Cyrus's with his left. Mary took Cyrus's free hand in hers. They sat silently, hands clasped in a circle on the table.

———◆———

Jed's health improved steadily. He put on weight and was able to clear land for his cabin and row both ways without getting short of breath. He had not had a coughing bout for several months. Periodically, he borrowed Corey's horse and cutter and paid visits to the Weinbergs. On one of the visits in June, Henry took Jed into his office, percussed his chest, and listened with his stethoscope. "You have good breath sounds and no rales. Much different from what I heard when you arrived." Jed put his shirt back on. "Freda and Eleanor, and, of course, I, are expecting you to stay for dinner."

"It will be my pleasure."

Eleanor's conversation at the table and in the parlor afterwards reminded Jed of Mary's. She was well informed and was not intimidated by him or her father. She was particularly interested in his medical school experiences and what it was like taking care of patients.

"Most of the really sick ones are poor. If they come to see a doctor at all it is in the late stages."

"If they came earlier could you have helped them?"

"Not really. We have few effective treatments."

"But small pox can be prevented by vaccination."

"I see you're up to date. Yes, before I left, the Board of Health was organizing a vaccination campaign. But we don't have vaccines against diphtheria, measles, and tetanus, which can kill within days. And no vaccines against slower killers like rheumatic fever and tuberculosis."

"They don't always kill. Look at you."

"That's an interesting observation," Dr. Weinberg interjected. "Maybe he doesn't have tuberculosis."

"I daresay if I had stayed in the City I would be dead by now. Only an autopsy would prove whether I died of tuberculosis." His statement evoked a new thought and he paused to formulate it. "An interesting question is what would happen if I returned to the City?"

Eleanor sat up straight and looked at Jed with alarm. "Surely you're not thinking of doing that?"

"Not right away. After all, I'm a property owner here. I want to get my cabin finished. After that, who knows?"

Eleanor tried to conceal that Jed's rhetorical question unsettled her. "How is the cabin coming?" she asked blithely.

"Excellent. With school out next week, I'm expecting the Carter boys to work every day. They've demanded I negotiate an agreement with them—they have their own union," he said and smiled at Henry, "the Brotherhood of Brothers. If they're like Cyrus, they'll drive a hard bargain, but I made enough money in New York to afford it." He smiled at Eleanor. "You should come out sometime and have a look at it."

Eleanor felt her heart flutter. "I'd like that. Maybe I can bring you and the boys some nourishment." She turned to her father. "Do you think I could do that?"

"I don't see why not? You handle the horses expertly, and

driving the carriage—if you want to bring them a picnic basket—is not difficult."

"We do work up quite an appetite," Jed said, which Eleanor interpreted as further encouragement.

"Yes," Henry said. "I've noticed that yours has improved. I'd say you're back to the weight I remember."

On the last day of school, John brought an envelope for Mary. Opening it, she was surprised to see a note from Reverend Jones asking if she could visit him in his rectory the next Monday. She asked John if he knew why the head of the School Board might want to see her. Then she asked Tommy, the more obstreperous of the two boys whether he was in any trouble. "No more than usual," he replied jokingly.

Not quite satisfied, she persisted. "You're not getting on Mr. Bumblecombe's bad side?"

"Mama, the man's too stupid to know when he's being teased. Besides, he ignores the boys, gives all his attention to the girls."

Mary looked up. "What do you mean, 'stupid?'"

Both boys laughed. "His knowledge is limited," John replied. "He had us memorize the multiplication table up to twelve times twelve, but when a student asked him how to multiply fifteen times fifteen he got the answer wrong."

"I taught you to do that. Did you show the student?"

"Behind Mr. Bumblecombe's back; I didn't want to embarrass him." John paused. "Two hundred and twenty-five, right?"

When Mary entered the rectory and the Reverend seated her, he got right to the point. "Mr. Bumblecombe will not be returning to teach in September. Mary, uh, Mrs. Carter, I'd like to offer your job back until we can find another teacher."

"Excuse me for asking, but was it due to his lack of competence?"

"I have no reason to believe he was incompetent, although we never received his credentials." The Reverend looked down at some notes on his desk. Mary waited quietly. "The father of one of the students insisted he leave."

"A girl's?"

"Yes. How did you know?"

"I had a fifty percent chance of guessing right, didn't I?" She smiled. "I've heard rumors that my colleague favored our fair sex. I imagine he went too far." She stopped, debating whether to continue. "I'm surprised you didn't expel the girl rather than Mr. Bumblecombe, Reverend." Remembering what Lawrence Venable had told her about why Jones did not want her to teach the older children, she added, "I'm sure you see the irony in the matter." She quickly added, "No need to answer, Reverend." She reflected for a moment. "As for taking my job back, I will do it on one condition: that you pay me as much as you paid Mr. Bumblecombe."

The Reverend hesitated. "But Mr. Bumblecombe is a—" Mary rose to go. "Very well, Mrs. Carter. The job is yours on your terms."

And so in the new school year, Mary returned to teaching. In doing so, she became the family's major breadwinner; Cyrus was earning only a pittance as a town councilor, guide, and apprentice to Mr. Venable. Her tenure as a teacher turned out to be longer than Reverend Jones' tenure on the school board.

———•———

John and Tommy also contributed to the family income over the summer. As soon as school was out, they negotiated a contract with Jed. Cyrus had coached the boys not to accept a piece rate, although he doubted Jed would try to get away with that. Jed offered them a flat fifty cents a day. They countered with seventy-five cents, six bits. They agreed on sixty cents.

The boys became adept at chopping down and then bucking trees. Following Jed's plan, they dug a shallow pit and sank cedar posts at the four corners and the midpoints of each side of his cabin to be. They nailed joists to the posts around the perimeter and then nailed the floorboards to the joists. Working alongside Jed, they notched the logs for the walls, alternating the logs front and back with those on the sides in traditional log cabin fashion. The three of them built a fireplace with a chimney at the back of the cabin, cementing together local rocks, which also served as the hearth. As the logs went up, they cut out spaces for windows, two in the front and one on each side.

Early in July, Eleanor and Freda packed a large picnic basket. Eleanor placed it in the Weinbergs' carriage and then climbed on to the front seat. With a gentle flick, her whip started the horse moving east. With Virgil Bartlett's permission, she drove along the Carry to the Upper Lake where she tied the horse and carriage to the rail. Carrying the basket, she picked her way along the narrow path that Cyrus and the boys had blazed along the lake. She often had to step gingerly from rock to rock, which was difficult with the heavy basket in hand. She was glad she had worn bloomers instead of skirts.

John was the first to spot her. "Jed, you've got a visitor." Jed put down his saw and looked down the path. He was stripped to the waist, as were the boys. They grabbed their shirts as Eleanor approached. "You should have given us some warning."

Eleanor smiled and looked at the half completed walls. She walked over and peered into the cabin. "Did you want me to telegraph you? I didn't know you could receive messages here."

"No," Tommy quipped. "But you could have sent smoke signals."

"Don't treat our guest rudely, boys. In that basket I suspect she has something we want. Unless we're hospitable, she might turn around and go home."

"I might just do that," she teased, returning to the path.

Jed fell to his knees and the boys followed. "No, no, Miss Weinberg, don't do that, we implore you." They all clasped their hands in front of them.

"That's better," Eleanor scolded. "Why don't you men finish what you're doing, while I spread out the lunch?" She walked over to the large sloping boulder facing the cove, where Jed liked to sit. It was large enough to hold the basket and the four of them. The cove was unusually calm. The reflection of the trees in the water was as sharp as the trees themselves. John and Tommy clambered up the rock, while Jed helped Eleanor get a footing. As Eleanor prepared and then served their lunch, they talked about the work for the afternoon. When they finished eating, John said, "We're only allowed a half hour for lunch. Excuse us Miss Weinberg." John got up. Tommy seemed content to sit and admire the scene, including Eleanor. Her limpid dark eyes and single braid of black hair, which came down to her waist, appealed to him. John grabbed Tommy's wrist. "Come on, Tommy," he said and pulled him up. They jumped down and walked the few yards to the cabin. As Eleanor placed the plates and utensils back in the basket, Jed spread himself out on the boulder. He had trouble keeping his eyes open. "Do you think you could arrange this every day?"

"You're not serious are you, Jared?" Eleanor said, calling him by his full name while she finished her chores. When she looked at him again he was asleep.

By the end of July, the walls were completed and construction of the roof beams began. By mid-August the cabin was finished.

On a sizzling hot day in late August, Eleanor decided to ride out once again to Jed's cabin. She had just received a pair of jodhpurs by mail order and wanted to try them. They fit snugly. She told her mother where she was headed and set out in late morning, arriving within the hour at Bartlett's. Dutifully, she stopped to obtain permission to cross the Carry from Caroline Bartlett. "Jed and the Carter boys have finished the cabin, you know," Caroline told her.

"I can't wait to see it," Eleanor replied.

"Pretty sparsely furnished, so far as I can tell. In fact,

there isn't any furniture. Needs a woman's touch."

"I'll see what I can do," Eleanor said, as she swung into the saddle, riding astride. She hitched her horse to the rail at the end of the Carry.

All was quiet as she walked gingerly along the lakeshore path. Huckleberries were in full bloom and she plucked them off the bushes as she walked. The cabin was complete. It looked solidly built, but nothing distinguished it from other cabins she had looked at casually. She knocked. No answer. The breeze had kept her cool while she was riding, but now she was sweltering in the stillness, especially in her tight-fitting pants. She walked past the large boulder to the lakeshore. In the middle of the cove, something was splashing. After a few seconds, the splashing stopped and she recognized Jed. She waved and he started to swim into shore. When he was about forty yards away, he shouted. "Do you make a habit of sneaking up on people?"

"Don't be silly. If I wrote you first, it might be snowing by the time you replied. The heat in Tupper was unbearable. I thought it would be cooler out here."

"It is, especially where I am. Why don't you come in?"

"I didn't bring any bathing clothes."

"I don't have any either. Why don't you take off what you've got on, unless you want to get them wet?"

"Jared, surely you're not serious in either case?" She raised her hands to the top button of her blouse.

"I've seen plenty of naked women. It's part of being a doctor. If you're modest I'll turn around until you're in the water. The water is hard to see through, you know."

"You're sure there's no one else around."

"I've yet to see a beaver here. They must be trapped out. At this time of day, the river otters aren't likely to appear. Plenty in the early morning though. A couple of loons frequent the end of the cove. There are other birds, too: a blue heron flies over hourly and bald eagles can make a sudden appearance, especially when ducklings are in sight."

"I meant people."

"Haven't seen any of them since John and Tommy finished last week. Mrs. Bartlett had a peek in my cabin once."

"Turn around." She wriggled out of her jodhpurs and blouse and removed her undergarments, piling her clothes neatly near the door of the cabin. Quickly, she stepped into the water, which was colder than she expected.

"I can't tread here much longer," Jed shouted over his shoulder. "How many layers do you have on?"

She didn't answer but walked out until the water covered her thighs. The bottom was unpleasantly muddy. Then she took the plunge and started to swim toward him. He heard her splashing and turned to face her when she was about ten feet away.

She stopped swimming. "I told you not to turn around."

"I swear! I haven't seen a thing except your lovely face. When I heard you splashing I knew you were submerged. I have to admit, though, once, a long time ago—thirteen years to be exact—I was suspected of being a peeping Tom." They began sidestroking around the circumference of an imaginary ten-foot-diameter circle, looking at each other.

"Were you arrested?"

"No," he laughed. "I was accompanying a young lady who was trying on dresses. She asked me to stay near the fitting room so I could give my opinion on her outfits, but the salesman told me if I wasn't her husband I had to move."

Eleanor envisioned the "young lady" and had pangs of jealousy. "What happened?"

"I moved." Jed noticed Eleanor frown. "I saw the young lady the next day—and then never again. Our interests differed."

Imperceptibly, the diameter of the circle around which they swam began to narrow, as if by mutual consent, until they were four feet apart. Eleanor could see droplets of water clinging to Jed's eyebrows. Her heart was racing. They were no longer swimming but quietly treading. They looked intently at each other.

Eleanor said the first thing that popped into her mind. "When we're in deep water like this, it looks like we're of equal height."

"Yes, at least from the neck up." After a moment's pause he said, "Race you to that rock over there." Jed pointed to a rock protruding above the surface about twenty yards away.

"You're probably a better swimmer than I am. It won't be fair," she said defensively.

"No! You probably have more stamina. Go ahead, start."

Reluctantly, Eleanor began. She loved to swim and her stroke was rhythmic and graceful. Jed took off after her and was able to keep abreast of her until about five yards from the rock. Getting short of breath, he lagged behind.

Eleanor reached the rock first and put her hand on it. Jed came up a few seconds later.

"Not only do you have more stamina," he stopped, trying to catch his breath, "you're the better swimmer."

They were facing each other; Eleanor, her right hand on the rock, was standing on an underwater ledge. Jed moved closer, stood on the ledge, and bent to kiss Eleanor lightly on the lips.

"Is that my reward for winning?"

"Maybe. I don't know what it was for. I haven't kissed a woman for a very long time." As Jed moved closer to Eleanor, their bodies touching, she leaned back against the rock. Jed's legs encircled hers. Eleanor put her arms around Jed's neck and they kissed passionately. Jed felt Eleanor's heart pounding as he pressed his chest against her breasts.

The kiss stopped but they remained close. "I love you, Jed."

"Since when?"

"Since I was ten years old."

"And you waited all this time?" They kissed again.

"I wasn't going to tell you at Mary's wedding. Besides, you seemed interested in her sister."

"Very perceptive for a ten-year old. You were right. That 'young lady' I told you about was Mary's sister, Rachel."

"Oh! I should have figured that out. Thirteen years ago would have been 1862, two years after the wedding. Did you see her much before then?"

"Not the way I'm seeing you now," he teased. "Actually, I didn't see her at all except that one time in the City. We just exchanged letters." He kissed her again. "The letters weren't passionate, I can tell you."

Jed stepped slightly away from Eleanor and placed one hand on her neck. Slowly he moved it down, over her breasts to her belly. Her breath came quickly. She pulled him to her again. "Oh! Jared."

From the end of the cove a loon wailed. The answer came back a short distance away from where they stood.

"I told you we weren't alone."

"Maybe we should swim back to the cabin. We're likely to get cold."

"Being so close, I doubt it. But you're right. Do you want another race?"

"Sure."

"Okay. This time you have to give me a three-stroke head start," Jed demanded. Before she could answer he was off.

Jed was not a great swimmer. Eleanor started swimming when he was about five yards ahead. Without rushing she gained on him slowly, timing her stroke so they were swimming side by side when the shore was only a few feet away. Jed stopped just where the water was shallow enough for both of them to stand. Jed crouched so only his head was above water. Eleanor had to stand straight for her head to be above water.

"Do you still want me to turn around while you get out?" Jed asked.

She stood in front of him, her breasts just below the surface, and put her arms around him. "That won't be necessary, doctor." They kissed again. Then Jed picked her up, and carried her to shore. Being careful not to let their dripping bodies wet the clothes she had piled neatly near the door, he kicked the door open and went in. As Mrs. Bartlett had warned Eleanor, there were no furnishings. There was a thin mat and a blanket roll near the fireplace. Jed set Eleanor down on the mat.

"I thought only newly married women get carried

across the threshold."

Jed did not answer. He squatted on the mat. Eleanor was lying languidly on it, leaning on one elbow, her dark eyes fixed on Jed. Jed took in the sweep of her body, her narrow waist above hips that tapered into smooth, shapely legs. He lay on his back alongside of her. "I think I may have misled you, Eleanor."

She leaned over him, her breasts resting gently on his chest. "What do you mean?"

"I don't know what I mean." He paused. Both of their faces became serious. "I'm not proposing to you, at least not now."

She brightened. "You mean there's hope. I'll say 'yes' before you ask."

Jed was overcome and pulled her on top of him. They kissed again. Gently he let her slide off.

"There are problems." She peered at him, waiting. "First of all, I'm eighteen years older if I calculate correctly. Second of all, I have tuberculosis."

"Yes, and you may have infected me already. I took that risk when we kissed."

"Third of all, I'm not sure what I'm going to do. I may go back to the City. Life is too easy up here."

"Not if you're going to hole up in this cabin and live like a hermit over the winter. You might freeze to death. If by any chance you do survive," she teased, "it will be a strengthening experience." She laughed. "I may of course intrude on your privacy."

Jed got up, opened the door, and brought in Eleanor's clothes. "You'd better get dressed, Eleanor, before I lose any restraint I've got left. Your body and mind are irresistible."

Reluctantly, Eleanor started to dress. So did Jed.

As she dressed, she said, "You realize, Jared, I've thought of those reasons. You haven't thought of what I might want. If you go to the City, I could come. I want to go to medical school anyway. That's the only way I could become a doctor."

"What about children?"

"Look, Jared, I'd like to have kids but I want to go to medical school first. If it's too late after that, I'll forego children."

Sitting on the floor, Jed laced up his boots. "You probably could manage it. Thirty is old for a first child but if you started by 1877 you'd beat that deadline."

———◆———

The sun was casting long shadows by the time Eleanor rode back to Tupper Lake. It was still hot.

The next week, Jed bought a horse and cutter. He got standing permission from Virgil Bartlett to cross his property during daylight hours and told everyone he was tired of rowing to his cabin. In September, he used his new acquisitions to drive over to Tupper Lake and did so twice a week as long as the weather permitted. Eleanor had alerted her parents to the turn in her circumstances. They were overjoyed.

PART II

7
Tommy Goes to Work

ALTHOUGH Freda would have liked a rabbi to offi-
ciate at her daughter's wedding (neither Eleanor nor
Jed would have objected), there were none in the vicinity.
The Justice of the Peace in Saranac Lake married the couple
with Cyrus and Mary as witnesses. The wedding party
adjourned to Bartlett's Sportsmen's Home for a sumptuous
(non-kosher) meal for which Freda supplied pies to accompany Caroline's towering wedding cake.

Eleanor started Bellevue Medical School in September
1876, appropriating "Mason" as her surname in her application even though she and Jed were not married when she
applied. The newlyweds took a small apartment near Bellevue and Jed returned to his old job as an Inspector for the
New York Board of Health. Eleanor's medical education, like
Jed's before, consisted of attending lectures, making it easy to
regulate her hours—and Jed's as well. He remained healthy.
On weekends, they delighted in visiting Central Park, taking
walks and an occasional row when the weather permitted.

John Carter came to stay with them when Eleanor was
in her third year. The year before, when he was 19, he
left the village to go to Quebec in search of his paternal
grandmother, uncles, or cousins. All he had was the address
to which his father, Jean, had mailed his pay. Without suc-

cess he came home, took a job as a mill hand, and told his parents he was going to go west as soon as he had enough money. He could not name a final destination, but would travel first to New York City from where he would board a train going west.

When it was clear she could not dissuade him, Mary wrote to Jed imploring him to persuade John to stay in the City, where he would be closer, especially with the progress on the Adirondack Railroad, and where Jed and Eleanor could keep an eye on him. John stayed with the Masons while he worked as a copy boy for *The New York Sun*. With a little more money in his pocket he hopped a freight train and stopped in Chicago. Jed wrote to Mary, saying he and Eleanor had tried to keep John in the City, but to no avail. "He doesn't want help from anyone but wants to strike out on his own," Jed explained. "He feels you and Cyrus have protected him from the adversity that fate dealt him. He's got to prove himself a man. That doesn't mean he doesn't love you and Cyrus. He does, and I'm sure he'll keep you posted."

———◆———

Construction of the Adirondack Railroad resumed in 1876 and inched inexorably northward from North Creek. Word of its coming advanced much more quickly than new track. Tommy learned of it while still in school and was determined to work on it when he graduated in 1879, despite his mother's worries and her uncle's opposition to the railroad. Seven miles of track from North Creek to the town of Minerva had been completed by September 1877. By the summer of 1878 the track extended another eighteen miles to Newcomb. The fourteen-mile segment to the village of Long Lake was completed in late spring of 1879. In accord with their agreement with the Smead Lumber Company, Thomas Durant and his company planned to cut north-northeast, along the northwestern shore of Long Lake and then along the west bank of the Raquette, a distance of twenty miles to Axton Landing. There, the track would follow the river west to Tupper Lake, another nine miles.

Surveyors laid out the path for the rail bed, then like an advancing army of termites, lumberjacks cut a swath through the woods. Unlike the lumber companies, the railroad supplied the axes. The logs were bucked, brought to the current train terminus, and carried by train to the nearest mill where they were trimmed into cross ties and returned to the terminus by the train. Then trains brought workers recruited from the City and along the way to the current terminus. They laid the ties and spiked the rails brought from Midwest steel mills. As track was added, the terminus advanced, bringing the railroad farther north. New workers were recruited locally.

Mary hoped Tommy would go to college, although few of his friends did. She had instilled good learning habits in him; he read avidly, wrote well, and could hold his own in debate, but he preferred the outdoors and working. Like his brother, he wanted to be on his own. His mother pleaded with him not to delay college to work on the railroad, but he would not be dissuaded. Cyrus had mixed feelings. Tommy promised to return home for Thanksgiving when he and his parents would reevaluate college for the following year.

When Tommy told his parents he was going to leave right after the Fourth of July, Cyrus offered to row him up to Raquette Falls to shorten his journey to join the railroad at Long Lake, and Mary insisted on accompanying them. Never before had she been in the boat, which held frightful memories. When they got to the falls and Tommy picked up his few belongings, Mary asked if they couldn't carry the boat around the falls and continue up to Long Lake. Tommy was eager to set out on his own but was too polite to balk at the idea. Cyrus knew he could carry the boat up the Carry with Tommy's help, but he doubted he could carry it back down, even with Mary's help. Mary would have to accept the departure of her son sooner or later.

Tommy promised he would get letters to them, repeating that he would be home in the fall. Mary and Cyrus hugged Tommy and returned, silently, downstream. Tommy walked up the carry and then picked his way along the bank of the river. He camped where the Cold River joined the Raquette, sleeping in the open on the warm night. He awoke with more mosquito bites than he had ever had at one time. Stripping, he plunged into the river to relieve the itching, and then dressed quickly, taking off immediately to escape the bugs. As he walked, thinking of how he would ask for work, the itching abated. Tommy reached the narrow part of Long Lake before noon and crossed the bridge over the Lake. Swaying as Tommy crossed, the bridge consisted of planks laid on a float of logs held together in a boom. He reached the newly laid railroad tracks and followed them to the terminus two miles away. A small locomotive, a boxcar, and a flatcar stood on a siding close to the terminus. A path had been cleared two hundred yards farther. About ten men, most stripped to the waist, were laying ties. A smaller team lifted sections of rails off the flat car, carried them to the

newly laid ties, and laid them end-to-end. Two men aligned
the gleaming rails and another two, one for each track, alter-
nated swinging heavy mallets to drive the spikes in to set
the rails. In the dense forest farther ahead, Tommy heard the
thump of axes and an occasional shout of "timber." He esti-
mated about fifty men were doing the various jobs.

A stairway of stacked railroad ties led up to the open
door of the boxcar. Tommy climbed them and then stepped
into the car, his eyes taking a few seconds to adjust to the
darkness. He stopped in front of a large table while out of
the gloom two men walked to the back of the table. They
had a good look at Tommy, but he could barely see them.
"What can we do for you, young man?"

Tommy made his work preference known. "Can you use
another jack for the summer?"

Fully grown, Tommy was five feet eight inches, about
the same height as his father, with the same stocky build.
The previous summer he had tried to grow a beard but it
came out so wispy that his mother laughed at him, saying
he still wasn't all man. He shaved it off, and now had just a
day's growth of brown stubble that matched his hair. "Have
you jacked before?"

"Yes, Sir."

"Where?"

"On Upper Saranac Lake."

"For Smead?"

"No, clearing land for cabins," he exaggerated slightly. "I
chopped and bucked."

"We'll give you a try." The man pulled a ledger over to
him.

Tommy hesitated. "What are the wages?"

The men laughed. "You'll get paid ten cents for every tree one-foot or more thick you cut."

Tommy nodded. "Who keeps track?"

"Why the foreman, of course," one of them replied. "We also give you food and board."

Tommy knew he would be welcomed home with open arms. He had nothing to lose. "I want a daily wage: seventy-five cents for ten hours' honest labor a day. You can take off ten cents for every tree less than eight I cut in a day. If I cut more, you still pay me seventy-five cents a day."

The men laughed. "We don't pay the foremen much more than that."

Tommy thought to himself, *they don't work as hard as jacks do, probably don't know as much either.* He turned to go. "Sorry, you've lost a good jack."

"You young squirt. Still haven't shaved, I bet." The man speaking was no taller than Tommy and was slenderly built. Tommy was sure he could beat him in a fight. The other man was slightly taller but fat, not much of an opponent either. What would his father do in this case? Cyrus had told him how he had walked away from fights where winning gained nothing. Tommy shrugged and continued out.

As he reached the opening in the boxcar, the thin man called out, "How about sixty cents a day?"

Tommy grinned. He hadn't expected a deal so easily. "I guess that'll keep the doctor away," he answered, thinking of a rhyme his mother had taught him. He walked over to the table. The thin man had opened the ledger to the last page with entries. Tommy leaned forward to look at it.

The thin man looked up and covered the page with his hand. "Don't press your luck, Son."

"Just want you to make the right entry." The man grabbed a quill pen and dabbed it into the inkwell. He looked up, waiting for more information. "Thomas Carter, Saranac Lake." Next to his name, the man wrote. "Sixty cents a day for ten hours' work." He looked up. "Is that all right, Sir?" he asked mockingly.

"You'd better put in about ten cents off for every tree less than eight."

When he had finished the entry, which took two lines—more than for any other man—the thin man blotted the ledger and rose. Tommy offered his hand. Reluctantly, the thin man shook it.

"Go check in with Danny Miller. He's your foreman. He'll supply you with an axe."

Tommy jumped down from the boxcar and walked farther up the rail bed to a hastily constructed bunkhouse. A big tent nearby served as the mess hall. Tommy wondered whether the food and board were any better than in his father's time. He had no difficulty finding Danny Miller, a redheaded foreman who looked to be in his early thirties. "Mr. Miller, the man in the office told me to report to you. My name's Tommy Carter. I'm ready to chop."

Miller looked him over. "Glad to meet you, Mr. Carter. He walked to a makeshift rack where axes were propped up. "Pick an axe and follow me." The axe heads varied in weight, the axe handles in length. Tommy picked up one of the biggest axes. "That's a little big for you, don't you think?"

"I can handle it." The rail bed had petered out, replaced by string stretched between large wooden stakes in the ground that indicated the direction in which the bed was to be extended. Men were chopping trees on either side of the string, notching them so they fell away from the rail bed.

"You've done this before?" Tommy nodded. With a piece of chalk, Miller marked nine trees, varying in diameter between eight inches and two feet. See if you can get these down today." He walked away. Tommy cut them all plus one more. His hands had sufficient calluses that he avoided blisters, but his shoulders ached by evening.

Living close to twenty-five other men was harder to get used to than he imagined. The snoring, the smells, the bad mattresses, the stifling heat, and as he learned the next morning, the bedbugs, were all new experiences. At home, after John had gone, Tommy had had a room to himself.

The summer of 1879 was hot and dry. The Raquette River, about a quarter of a mile from the new railhead, was low. Some men in the bunkhouse said logging in the Adirondacks had caused the drought; with fewer trees, water ran off rather than penetrating the ground where the roots held it. Rain diminished. Others argued against them. "Trees don't make water," they said.

Working stripped to the waist, the men sweated profusely. The local bosses had made no provision for extra water despite the heat. On one particularly torrid day, an older man told his foreman he couldn't spike another rail unless he had some water. His foreman said, "You lose money if you don't spike. Just don't think about water." In the subdued bunkhouse that night, a lad from Newcomb, about Tommy's age, related what had happened. Laying crossties into the rail bed just ahead of the older man, he noticed that each stroke of the man's mallet on the spike got shorter. Instead of the loud clang after a full stroke, the note became softer and softer, the spike barely sinking. The older man took one last stroke. The head of the mallet slipped off the spike; the man dropped the mallet and collapsed. The lad ran back to him as the foreman came up and stared down at the man. "The man's eyes had rolled back in his head. He was burning up, but he wasn't sweating. I told the foreman that he needed water. The foreman told me to mind my own business and get back to work. He ordered a couple of the other crew members to carry the man into the shade and told another to run back to get water. By the time he returned, the man was dead."

The men took bets on whether the company would increase the ration of water the next day, working out a contingency plan if it didn't. When no change was announced, one of them stole a pail and ladle from the mess tent after breakfast and brought it to the railhead. By mid-morning the temperature was in the nineties. The loggers, who were under less supervision than the tracklayers, took turns carrying the pail to the Raquette. The man whose turn it was had to wade into the river to fill the pail with clear water. Some of the water inevitably sloshed out as the water-carrier ran back. When he returned, the other loggers lined up for a ladle full until the water ran out. On the next run, the bucket was passed to the men laying rails. Late in the afternoon, Tommy was caught carrying the pail. The foreman who had stood over the dying man the day before demanded that Tommy hand over the pail. "I'll do that after the men have their drink." The foreman stepped forward, but the workers formed a human wall around the pail so the men could drink their ladle-full. When the pail was empty, Tommy handed it over with the ladle.

"I could have you arrested for stealing company property."

Tommy could not contain himself. "And I could have you arrested for killing a man yesterday." The foreman glared at Tommy and raised his arm. The men crowded around Tommy to protect him.

His authority threatened, the foreman retreated but sneered, "Yeah? Who's gonna arrest me around here?" Pail and ladle in hand, he walked away.

In their bunkhouse that night, the men commended Tommy for talking back. Tommy was not pleased. "I should never have been caught." The men were sure that after the episode, the foremen would tighten their guard to prevent the relay to the river. They needed another plan. One of the older men, Aaron Howard, who had been working on railroad construction since the Civil War, finished rolling a cigarette, tamped it down, and said in a low voice heard only by those nearest him, "We should strike."

One of the younger workers asked incredulously, "You mean we should beat up the bosses?"

"No, strikers only fight in self-defense. A 'strike' means we refuse to work until we get what we deserve—more water in this case." Aaron struck a match against one of the posts. The flame cast eerie evanescent shadows on the men's faces as he lit his cigarette and then extinguished the match. Aaron inhaled deeply and spoke as he let the smoke out. He told the boys he was in Baltimore in 1877 when Maryland's Governor called out the National Guard to break a strike against the Baltimore & Ohio Railroad. "We surrounded the armory, hoping the protest would stop the Guardsmen from coming out. Seeing their friends out there, some of the Guardsmen quit. But others came out shooting. Ten protesters were killed. One soldier was wounded." Aaron took another puff. Attracted by the smoke and the knot of men gathered around him, other men in the bunkhouse came over.

"What were the men striking for?" Tommy asked.

"B&O cut wages by 10 percent. Down the line in Martinsburg the brakemen uncoupled the engines, ran them into the roundhouse, and said no trains would run until their wages were restored."

"Aaron, do you mean all the brakemen were getting the same wages?"

"Yep. They won a standard wage awhile back."

"We don't have that yet."

"That's because the bosses want to get the most work out of you," Aaron replied. "The more you cut, or the more track you lay, the more you get paid. It's not healthy; sometimes the men work so fast they hurt themselves, or others."

"'You lose money if you don't spike,'" the lad from Newcomb said. "'That's what the foreman told the man who asked for water. I've heard him say it many times." He paused, eying the ember at the tip of Aaron's cigarette. "Maybe we should strike for more water."

By now, Aaron had only a stub that he held between his thumb and forefinger. "That's a sorry state when we have to strike for something that should be as free as the air. But I guess we have to." He stubbed out his butt.

Most of the men in the bunkhouse had been drawn into the discussion. The idea of striking was new to them. They drifted back to their bunks mulling over the implications of this strategy. They knew intuitively that an unsuccessful strike could cause great hardship with loss of jobs and maybe violence.

The men were surprised at breakfast when the fat boss walked into the mess tent to announce an extra ration of water in the morning and again in the afternoon. It made a few of the men wonder if there was a spy in their midst.

Spy or not, the men felt their discussion had influenced the bosses to supply more water. The next evening the heat inside the bunkhouse was stifling. Sitting on his bunk, Aaron pulled out his pouch of precious tobacco, rolled another cigarette, walked outside, and sat on a stump near the steps to the bunkhouse, where he lit up. Tommy and a few others followed him, sitting on the ground or the steps of the bunkhouse. "You know," Aaron said, his face invisible, "we've got an advantage over workers in the cities: We're not easily replaceable. The company would have to import scabs."

Out of the dark, someone asked, "What's a scab?"

"Scabs are strikebreakers. There aren't many men up here to take our place."

"So we have an advantage," Tommy said. "Why don't we demand we all get paid a flat rate? That's what I'm getting." The door to the bunkhouse opened, illuminating Tommy's face, as another man stepped out. The men looked at Tommy in astonishment. "When I was thirteen, my brother and I negotiated our first contract for logging. It was with a friend of my father's who was building a cabin. We got sixty cents a day. When I got to the railhead and walked into that box car, I asked Mr. Fat and Mr. Thin for seventy-five cents."

The men gave several low whistles. "Did you get it?" asked the man who had just come out, closing the door as he spoke. Tommy could be heard but not seen.

"They offered sixty cents and I took it." He didn't mention having to lose ten cents for every tree less than eight he chopped. It never had happened.

Another of the older workers, not as muscular as the others, grumbled, "That's more than I get and I've been doing this a lot longer."

Aaron sensed some hostility to Tommy, the young whippersnapper. "What would you have done if they refused?"

"Gone home," Tommy answered. The men laughed. That was a luxury few of them could afford.

———•———

Tommy and Aaron had planted a seed that began to sprout as summer turned to fall. On two counts, however, the men objected to getting a flat rate, although they agreed it was better than working piece rate. First, the skill and experience needed for some jobs was greater than for others. Second, the men who thought they would make more from piecework objected to taking a cut in salary. For the first time, the men told each other what they were earning. They discovered that some of them never got more working piece rate than sixty cents a day, and several were averaging less than fifty. They decided to demand sixty cents a day for everyone.

"One more thing," Aaron pointed out, "if we get paid a flat rate, the bosses could make us work longer hours to earn it. We have to demand a limit on the number of work hours in each day." The men agreed on ten; with the days getting shorter that was about all the daylight there would soon be.

Tommy, the lad from Newcomb, Aaron, and a few others took it on themselves to persuade those who had not spoken in the discussions. Not all the men were eager to cooperate, but as more of the workers learned what was going on, a majority became interested and excited enough to pull most of the others along. It took until October before the organizers were confident the men backed their demands. Tommy and Aaron were elected to speak to the bosses.

Danny Miller and the other foremen noticed that the men were speaking more to each other before, during, and after work. They mentioned it to the two bosses in the boxcar on the evening of October 1, a Wednesday. The bosses replied, "Yeah. We know. They're up to no good. Try to break it up."

It was too late. The next morning the men's elected representatives did not report for work but went to the boxcar.

"Looks like a delegation," said the thin man.

"Yessir," answered Aaron, "an elected delegation."

"What can we do for you boys?"

"The men have been talking," Aaron began. "We refuse to get paid piece rate any longer." The bosses both laughed, the fat one's double chin quivering.

"We also know that the best-paid workers are making sixty cents a day," Tommy added.

"You should know, kid," the fat boss said to Tommy.

"What do you want?" the thin boss asked.

"Every man in this camp gets sixty cents a day for ten

hours' labor," Aaron replied.

The thin boss smiled graciously. "Boys, I can't do that. I don't have enough cash on hand."

"We thought of that. The supply train leaves here tomorrow and comes back on Monday. We're willing to start the new wages next week."

"And what if we don't agree?"

Flushed with excitement but keeping his voice calm, Tommy replied, "We'll strike."

"Lemme talk it over with my friend here." He pointed to the fat boss. "Come back tomorrow morning."

On the way back up the rail bed, Aaron and Tommy slapped each other on the back, congratulating themselves that they were not turned down outright—or fired.

Friday morning they reappeared at the office. The thin boss said, "We don't have the authority to bargain with you. We'll wire the main office and see what they say. Maybe we'll have an answer by Tuesday morning."

The men were disappointed but not surprised. Aaron said, "If we don't have an answer then, we'll strike."

"Unless we fire you first," the fat boss smiled maliciously.

"Fat chance," the representatives replied.

———— • ————

Later that morning, after the supply train left, the bosses boarded the train on the siding—used for short hauls to North Creek—and had it switched back to the main track. When they arrived at North Creek, they went to the Western Union office and telegraphed Durant and his associates at the main office in New York City.

WORKERS DEMANDING SIXTY CENTS A
DAY FOR ALL STOP THREATEN STRIKE
STOP NOT ENOUGH MONEY HERE TO
COMPLY STOP WHAT TO DO

They waited at the Western Union office for a reply. The office was about to close when the reply came over the wire.

HELP WILL ARRIVE MONDAY STOP DO
NOTHING

They looked at each other, puzzled. On the train back to Long Lake, they speculated what it meant. Was the Company capitulating? Were they sending a higher up to take over the negotiations? They had to wait.

The supply train left New York City on Sunday evening and arrived at Long Lake late Monday afternoon with the engine pushing the cars from the rear. In addition to the usual flat and boxcars, the train carried an elegant private sleeping and parlor car coupled to an ordinary passenger car. The two bosses were standing near them when the train stopped. They noticed that the passenger car had the shades drawn over all its windows. A man in a bowler hat, topcoat, and neatly pressed trousers walked down the steps of the parlor car and waited for the bosses to come to him, then offered his hand.

"William W. Durant, gentlemen, Dr. Thomas Durant's son. We can talk comfortably in the parlor." He turned and walked up the steps, opened the door for the bosses to follow him, and extended his arm indicating they should go inside while he held the door. The parlor took up half the car and was lined with sofas and a few dark leather swivel chairs facing the sofas at various angles. Durant removed his hat and invited the men to take seats on the sofa while he sat facing them in one of the leather chairs. He reached for a humidor from the drum table near his chair, removed the top, and offered them cigars. They refused, but Durant clipped his cigar and lit up.

The thin man asked if he'd had a pleasant journey.

"Yes, I always enjoy coming to the Adirondacks, even when the business is unpleasant. This little matter you brought to our attention gave me an excuse to see how work is progressing on my new camp at Raquette Lake."

"Pine Knot," the fat man said.

"It will be the most elegant structure in the Adirondacks," Durant said after his first puff. He puffed again. "Why didn't you just fire the trouble makers?"

"If it was only the two who came to see us we would have done that," the thin man replied. "But they claim to represent a majority of the laborers. We've checked that out and it's true. Our informers tell us most of the men would strike if we didn't give them what they wanted."

"Giving in to them would be a dangerous precedent, don't you think?" The bosses nodded. Durant continued, "We've gone to considerable expense to nip this in the bud. Indeed, it may cost us more than giving in to their demand." The bosses were puzzled. "Gentlemen," Durant continued, "in the adjacent car sit fifty men. Fifteen of them are armed. They are part of our private police force. The others are laborers who will take over the jobs of the men who refuse to work under the existing arrangements. I want you to tell the representatives that they will be fired if they persist in their demand, and that is the fate that awaits any other man who goes on strike."

"I hope we don't have another Baltimore," said the thin one.

"If we do," smiled Durant, "the world won't know about it. That's one nice thing about the woods." As he got up from his chair, the bosses quickly stood. "When do you expect the so-called representatives to return?"

"Tomorrow morning," both answered.

"Gentlemen, I will be watching from this window," Durant said, pointing to the heavily curtained window in back of the bosses. "If necessary, I will order my men out of the next car. The police will escort the leaders off our right-of-way. Then, the foremen will assign jobs to the new men, and our police will protect them. I won't make an appearance." He pulled his watch out of his vest pocket, glanced at it, and added, "My carriage will be waiting at North Creek to take me to Pine Knot tomorrow morning. I don't intend to be delayed."

On Tuesday morning, Aaron and Tommy led the workers toward the train. Durant and the bosses had not anticipated that the other men would follow them. With some trepidation, the bosses walked out to greet them in front of the private car.

"Do you have an answer?" Aaron asked.

"The company will not give in to your demand," the fat one said.

"Very well," Tommy replied. He turned, shouting to the men, "They've rejected our request. You know what that means."

The men grumbled. Aaron and Tommy led the workers

past the private car and the bosses, who were too stunned to move. The men did not stop until they were abreast of the engine. Then they turned sharply and marched on to the tracks: Five rows of eight men each.

Peering through the window, Durant watched the workers march by. He motioned for the bosses to join him. When they came in he said, "These men are pretty smart. How many men are left?"

"No more than ten," the fat one said.

One of the trainmen ran up to the car and then up the steps. He wrapped on the door. Durant let him in. "Sir, the men are blocking the track. We're due to pull out in fifteen minutes."

"Did you tell them?"

"Yes Sir. They said they're not moving until the company agrees to their demand."

"Tell the crew to fire up the engine. Blow the whistle one minute before departure. If the men don't leave the track, the engineer is to start the train."

The trainman hesitated. He squeezed his cap vary hard in his hands. He looked hard at Durant but said nothing before he turned and left the car.

"This is annoying," cursed Durant after the man left. "I wanted to be at Pine Knot for lunch." The three of them sat speechless. After five minutes, the engineer and brakeman came up to the car and knocked. "We will not start the train while the men are in front of it," they declared.

"Very well." Durant walked through the door to the next car. He came back with the chief of his private police. "The men have gone on strike before we could fire them.

They are blocking the tracks. I want your men to remove them from the tracks."

"At any cost, Sir?"

"At any cost."

"Even if we have to open fire?"

"At any cost," Durant repeated.

A few moments later, fifteen uniformed and armed men descended from the passenger car and marched to the engine. When they reached it, the engineer and brakeman were standing in front of the strikers.

"Out of the way," yelled the police chief to the trainmen. No one budged. In the back row of strikers, a man began singing:

> *We shall not*
> *We shall not be moved*
> *We shall not*
> *We shall not be moved*
> *Just like a tree that's standing by the water*
> *We shall not be moved.*

By the third line, five other men joined and when the voice started the stanza again almost all the men were singing.

Above the voices, the head of the police shouted, "Who's in charge here?"

Without hesitation, and before Aaron or Tommy could say anything, the engineer stepped forward, "I am."

"Tell the men to disperse or I will remove all of you forcibly."

"Remove me forcibly, and this train will never move," the engineer replied.

The men repeated the song for the third time.

Back in the parlor car, Durant pulled his watch out of his vest pocket. The two bosses squirmed restlessly in their seats. Through the slightly opened window they could hear the singing. Suddenly, they heard a fusillade of shots. All was silent for a few moments. Then the singing started up again. A moment later the head of the police came up to the car.

"What happened?" Durant asked.

"I ordered my men to fire. They know the first round goes over their heads. The strikers didn't budge. The engineer and brakemen are standing with them. My men are not being threatened. I don't think I can get them to fire into the men as long as they are just standing there."

Durant looked at his watch again. "Damn! Give the men their sixty cents and let's get this train out of here. My carriage is waiting at North Creek." Durant ushered everyone out of his car.

With the police chief, the two bosses walked to the engine. The singing died down.

The chief ordered his men back to the passenger car.

"Howard, Carter, come over here," the bosses called. Aaron and Tommy stepped toward the bosses.

"All right you boys," the thin man started quietly but with vindictiveness in his voice. "We'll pay you all sixty cents a day, but we're gonna build this railroad faster."

Aaron laughed, "And if we can't?" He didn't wait for an answer. "There was another part to our request."

"Yes, I heard it," the thin boss replied. "Ten hour days— that too."

The bosses walked to their office. Aaron turned and told the men what had happened. Cheers went up. They ran down the tracks to the jobs they had been assigned.

When Tommy learned that William Durant, one of the owners of the Adirondack Railroad, had been present and was in a hurry to get to his camp on Raquette Lake, he asked Aaron and the others why he didn't build the railroad closer to his camp.

"That's easy," Aaron replied. "Wait 'til you see what this place looks like after the railroad is in operation. I don't think Durant wants that to happen to his hunting preserve; there'll be nothing left to hunt." Tommy remembered listening to his great uncle tell how the Railroad had offered to buy some of his land adjacent to the inn and how disappointed he was when his uncle refused to sell. Maybe Uncle William was right. He also remembered his father talking about the jobs the railroad would bring. Maybe he was right too.

———•———

Mary and Cyrus invited the Weinbergs, Corey, and Susie O'Rourke and her son to Thanksgiving dinner that fall. Susie's husband, Peter, had died of small pox after enlisting in the Union Army. Before that he had worked at Corey's. Their son, Peter Jr., born in July 1862, went to school with the Carter children, and he and Tommy became best friends. As a young widow, raising a child alone, Susie did not have an easy time; Mary befriended her.

Early Thanksgiving morning, while Mary was in the midst of preparing dinner, Tommy arrived. It took a fleeting moment for his mother to recognize him. He now had a full brown beard, and his body was less fleshed out than when he had left five months earlier. She stopped what she was doing and ran to embrace him. "Oh, Tommy! You surprised me."

He threw his arms around her and glanced around the kitchen. "I promised I'd be home for Thanksgiving. You mean this banquet you're preparing isn't for me?" He turned around and pretended that he was going to leave. His mother grabbed him by the sleeve.

"Of course it is! We've invited a few friends and Uncle William in your honor."

What's on the menu?"

"Haven't I taught you that it's not polite to ask?" She smiled coyly. "That depends on your father."

A short while later Cyrus came in and dropped two geese inside the door.

"Cyrus, why did you do that?" Mary chided. "You'll get blood all over the floor." He was already walking toward Tommy.

"The blood's drained already. There'll just be a few feathers to clean up." He hugged Tommy. "You did make it after all."

"Did you have any doubts? When a son gives his parents his word, he's got to keep it."

"I knew you'd try," Cyrus replied, "but I wasn't sure the Adirondack Railroad would let you go."

"Oh! They're glad to be rid of me."

"Then you're not going back?" Mary asked hopefully.

"I didn't say that, Mom."

Cyrus changed the topic. "You must be hungry, Son. We can scramble up some eggs if you can't wait for the feast."

Over his breakfast, Tommy told them the track was now halfway to Axton Landing. He had followed the surveyor's string the previous afternoon, slept in the woods that night, awoke at dawn, got wet crossing the Raquette at a narrow point, bushwhacked to the road to Saranac Lake near

Corey's, and hiked to the village. He ate hungrily. "Where's Lisa?" he asked.

"She's gone over to pick up Susie and Peter Junior."

"You mean she's old enough to drive the wagon?"

"She's fourteen and a half. Wait 'til you see how your sister has grown," Cyrus told him. "She's as beautiful as her mother. She and Peter Junior seem to have something going."

Mary had put a large kettle on the stove to warm water. After breakfast Tommy took his first private warm-water bath since he'd left home.

The trees were mostly bare by now, leaving the woods around their house open. Through them one could see a few other houses that had been recently built. The day was overcast and chilly. It might even snow, Mary thought, hoping not.

The guests arrived in the early afternoon, within a half hour of each other. Everyone was happy to see Tommy, even his sister, who Tommy teased about her womanly appearance.

Uncle William had aged since Tommy had seen him last. His hair was completely white and he walked with a cane; he said his hip bothered him. The past summer he had hired more hands to help run the inn as business picked up. His voice was a little raspy but he was alert as ever.

Cyrus had slow roasted the trussed birds over an open-pit fire and brought them to the table where they were greeted by oohs and aahs. He carved and served them while Mary added her winter pudding, green beans, and candied wild cranberries to the plates as they were passed down the table.

When everyone had been served, Cyrus asked Henry Weinberg, "What do you hear from Eleanor and Jed?"

"Eleanor's finishing medical school at Bellevue."

"And of course she's close to the top of her class," Freda said proudly.

"How is Jed doing?"

"He's working as hard as ever for the Health Department. Eleanor writes that he has occasional bouts of coughing and has lost some weight. I've invited them to come to Tupper and take over my practice."

"Guess it would take two of them to do that," William interjected. "Especially if Jed is not well."

"We're hoping he'll recover up here as well as he did last time, but they are reluctant to leave the City." Henry looked across the table at Tommy who was the last to finish the main course. "What have you been up to, young man?"

Tommy gave them a detailed description of his experiences as he ate. He credited his father with his success in getting an hourly wage, first for himself and then for all the men. "We got almost all of the workers to agree to demand sixty cents a day before we negotiated."

"Thomas," his mother commanded, "either put your fork down or wait until you've finished."

"Yes, Mama," he replied dutifully, swallowing his food and putting his fork down. Everyone looked at him expectantly. "We made our demand on a Thursday. The bosses said they'd have to wire the main office in New York City and told us to come back the next Tuesday. Monday, the supply train came up from the City as usual, but it also carried a fancy parlor car and next to it a passenger car with the shades completely drawn. We speculated that William Durant himself had come up, but the passenger car puzzled us. My friend Aaron thought it might be full of scabs." He paused to explain, "Strike breakers, you know. Others thought it might contain the Company's private police force. Let me tell you, we were scared."

Mary, who had stopped eating when Tommy began, clutched her hand to her throat and turned pale. Tommy regarded his plate and took a mouthful of stuffing. All but Mary resumed eating. Tommy laid down his fork again and the others stopped.

"Monday night, we discussed what we should do if the Railroad turned down our demand. Aaron said above all we must remain calm, don't throw rocks or shout. He and I would do the talking. One of the workers had overheard the bosses talking about Durant's building a camp in the Adirondacks. We speculated that maybe Durant would want to take the train back to North Creek and then visit his camp after he settled with us. That's when we hit on the idea of marching to the front of the train and refusing to let it move. If the engineer and the train crew supported us, we might have a chance. Of course if there were cops in the car, they might start trouble."

Mary got up, agitated. "Even though I see you sitting at my table, Tommy, all in one piece, I've lost my appetite. Excuse me." She left the room. Cyrus went to fetch her from the parlor.

"I'm not going to let him go back to that job!" she sobbed.

Cyrus put his arm around her and kissed her hair. She hugged him and gradually settled down. "We may not have any choice, Mary," he whispered.

In a few minutes they returned to the dining table, finding everyone just as they had left them. "Why don't you continue, Son," Cyrus suggested to Tommy.

He looked at his mother. She nodded. "Well, there were cops in that car and they fired one round over our heads." Mary gasped. "But the engineer refused to start the train and risk mowing us down. The cops refused to shoot into us. It was Durant in the car, and he did want to go to his camp. We got our sixty cents an hour and a ten-hour day." He smiled at Mary. "And no one was hurt."

Cyrus got up and hugged Tommy. "You accomplished a lot. And without violence."

"It is remarkable," Henry commented. "There may yet be violence."

Mary regained her composure and finished her meal. After she had served dessert, she said, "We are thankful to have you home, Tommy." She paused, shifting her gaze to Cyrus. "We do have something else to celebrate. Cyrus went to Albany to sit for the bar exam in September. We just learned that he passed. Now he can practice law in New York." They all applauded.

"That's terrific, Papa," Tommy said. "I remember you once told me about an argument you had with Jed Mason. When John and I were working with him on his cabin, we asked him about it. To make life better for working men he argued for unions and you argued for legislation. Do I have it right?"

"You've got it right, Son. Now we have a union man in the family—I guess you don't have a name for your union yet—and maybe soon we'll have a legislator."

"What do you mean, 'soon'? You are on the Harrietstown Council, aren't you?"

"Yes, coming on six years, but the Council hasn't done anything to improve the lot of the plain folk in town." He turned to Freda and Henry. "I'm afraid Jed was right about that. The big landowners and shopkeepers are usually in the majority and I seldom am. Jed predicted that's what would happen."

Henry said, "He might have been right about that, Cyrus, but he was wrong if he thought you'd sell out."

"So what did you mean, Dad?"

"I'm going to run for the state legislature next year. Now that I can practice law, I'll be looking for cases around Franklin County. I am going into practice with Lawrence Venable: 'Venable and Carter, Attorneys at Law!' Since the Miller trial, Lawrence has earned a good reputation and has clients around the County. He wants to cut back on his traveling and would like to retire soon. The traveling will let me get acquainted with people in Malone, Franklin Falls, Dickinson Center, and Tupper Lake."

"And them with you," Mary joined in. "It's called 'campaigning.'"

"Papa, you mentioned the Miller trial. I'd forgotten about that. Was Miller the foreman at Axton who killed Sean O'Rourke?" He glanced at Susie, but she didn't seem upset to hear her late husband's brother mentioned.

"He was the one. The trial started me thinking about becoming a lawyer."

Tommy said, "Maybe it's just coincidence—Miller's a common name—but one of the lumber foremen for the Adirondack Railroad Company is Danny Miller."

"Does he have red hair?" Cyrus asked. Tommy nodded.

"Probably they're related. I don't know if it's a good idea to ask him though. I witnessed Frank's killing Sean and I testified at the trial."

Lisa and Peter Jr. sat next to each other and surreptitiously held hands below the table. Peter had listened intently as Tommy described what had happened at the railhead. Letting go of Lisa's hand and bringing his hands above the table, he asked Tommy, "Do you think they have work down there?" Susie, Lisa, and Mary looked at him anxiously.

Oblivious to the tension that Peter's question had raised, Tommy replied, "I expect that some of the men are not going to come back next week. I'll bet you can get a job."

"I don't think Peter was thinking of starting so soon," Susie quickly replied.

"As a matter of fact, Ma, I haven't been successful in getting jobs around here. I think it would be good for us if I could get a job building the railroad. Just imagine, sixty cents a day. We could come up in the world with wages like that."

Tommy now realized that he had stirred up a hornet's nest and stayed quiet. Mary turned to Tommy. "Your father made a real change in his life from laboring to legislating," she said, ending the silence. "Don't you think it's time for you to think ahead?"

"I don't know, Mama. It took Papa until he was about forty before he made a change. I'm not half his age."

"But your father didn't have the education you've had. Now that you've proven what you can accomplish by organizing a small band of workers, think what you'll be able to do with the skills you'll get in college."

"You'd be surprised how much you learn working—not only about the job, but about what bothers workers, what they want. You can't get that at college." He paused. Everyone was looking at him. No one spoke. "Mama, I've decided to go back to the railroad. I'd like to see the railroad get to Tupper Lake. Maybe then I'll think about college. I'm not even eighteen."

"I told those railroad men who wanted me to sell them land," William interjected, "that I wanted no part of it, but I have to admit a railroad to Axton might be good for business."

"The trouble, Uncle William, is that the railroad's coming this way because they leased the land from Smead. Smead has acquired property south of its holdings and is already logging along the new tracks north of Long Lake, hard woods as well as soft. When I first started, just the small right-of-way for the railroad was cleared, but as we extended the bed north, you could see for a half-mile through the thinned woods. That's Smead's doing. At least you've got your woods to serve as a barrier. There won't be many trees left standing around Axton, I can tell you." While Tommy was talking he was also thinking about Peter's interest. "You know, Peter, if you don't get a job with the railroad, there's always Smead and lumbering."

Susie's anguish was plainly visible. "Your father didn't do well with logging," she told Peter, not for the first time. "You're bigger than he was, but I'm not sure it would suit you." Lisa grabbed Peter's hand under the table as if to hold him at Saranac Lake.

8

The Trestle

TOMMY returned to the terminus of the railroad the Sunday after Thanksgiving, accompanied by Peter O'Rourke Jr. Before they left, Mary pulled Tommy aside to tell him how Peter's father came to work at Corey's: while jacking at Axton, he had developed blisters on his hands that had become badly infected and Uncle William had agreed to take him in to recuperate. Tommy promised he would look after Peter Jr. and make sure nothing like that happened.

Shortly after Tommy and Peter left, Cyrus traveled to Malone for the first time, ostensibly to meet clients who had been referred to him by Lawrence Venable. While there, he established a relationship with the Franklin County Democratic Party. By then it was clear that the Republicans had become the party of big business and no less corrupt than the Democrats, having "bought" the 1876 presidential election for their candidate, Rutherford Hayes, after he lost the popular vote to Samuel Tilden. Some Democrats, including Grover Cleveland from Buffalo, New York, criticized the "robber barons," including railroad builders like Thomas Durant, Leland Stanford, and Cornelius Vanderbilt. Cyrus thought the Democrats were closer to the interests of the workingman and in June of 1880, fed up with the Harrietstown Council, he filed as the Democratic candidate from Franklin County for the New York State Assembly.

Peter Jr. got a job bucking chopped trees into shorter lengths, using the saw rather than the axe. His hands thickened quickly and he was soon chopping as well as bucking. Neither Peter nor Tommy returned home for Christmas or New Year's. They spent most of their time off around the bunkhouse while the other men walked back along the track to the village of Long Lake, which had prospered with the arrival of the railroad. It now had two bars (one with a restaurant), a whorehouse, an expanded general store, and a doctor.

The men who were laying and spiking rails received a Christmas present from the Company: they were put on leave without pay. Aaron Howard was among them. "Do they expect us to hibernate like bears over the winter and poke our heads out when the snow melts?" he asked. "If we stay up here we'll freeze or starve to death. If we leave, we'll spend whatever we've saved just getting away."

Their plight gave Tommy an idea, which he talked over with the other jacks. On Wednesday December 24th, Tommy went to the office, which was no longer a boxcar but a small portable shack that could be loaded on to a flatbed car and moved as the terminus advanced. Only the thin boss was there. His fat associate had left on the supply train for a brief holiday the previous Monday and would return on December 26th. The supply train would head south again on Monday the 29th, carrying the thin boss who had New Year's off.

"Well, it's our young union man. We should have laid you off too."

"I guess I'm too valuable," Tommy said.

The boss let that pass. "Surely you didn't come back here just to wish me 'Merry Christmas.' What do you want?"

"About the men you fired."

"They're not really fired," the boss interrupted, "just put on leave until we can lay track again."

"Maybe they're on leave, if you want to call it that, but there won't be anything left of them in the spring."

"Look, Carter. Your sixty cents a day is almost bankrupting the Company. What do you want us to do? Pay them while they're not working?"

"We wouldn't go that far."

Again the boss interrupted, "'We'?"

"Yeah. I've talked it over with the other jacks. What we propose will hardly cost the Company anything, and it will get you a lot of good will." The boss looked at him quizzically. Tommy continued, "We want you to offer a free ride on the supply train on its next trip south. Since you bring a passenger car up here only on special occasions, the men can stay in boxcars. The only cost to the Company is to feed these men until the train leaves next Monday."

"You win this, it'll make you real popular. I'm not sure I like that."

"If you don't accept, the jacks'll walk off the job again. I'm sure the engineer and other trainmen will be as cooperative as they were last time."

The boss knew he was cornered. "I'll talk it over with my partner when he returns on Friday."

"What happens to the men in the meantime?"

"In the meantime," he paused, looking intently at Tommy who returned his glance resolutely, "In the meantime, they can stay in the bunkhouse and have their meals."

"Thank you." Tommy turned to go.

"Just a minute." Tommy walked back in. There's not much

snow yet. I want them to keep laying track until they go."

"The ground's frozen already," Tommy replied. "If it rains the water will freeze and we'll have dangerous conditions. The terminus is on an incline. Working up or downhill is hard enough when it's warmer. If there's an accident, it'll be on your hands."

"Take it or leave it," the boss said. Without another word, Tommy walked out. The men decided to take it.

After his ten-hour shift on Friday, Tommy walked to the office and confronted both the thin and fat bosses. They had talked over the men's demand and decided, without telegraphing the Company, that the men could go south in boxcars when the train left on Monday.

That Monday, the remaining workers stopped work in mid-morning to march down to the train to see their unemployed colleagues off. The bosses looked on in amazement. They had never seen this kind of solidarity before. The men on the train started to sing, "We shall be, we shall now be moved…" The train whistle blotted out their improvisation of the following lines.

———————

The first blizzard of the New Year came on Tuesday, January 13th. The next day a jack was badly injured by a falling tree. Tommy went with one of the other jacks to see the bosses. "This man is likely to die unless he gets medical attention in Long Lake. Why aren't you keeping the tracks cleared?"

The fat boss replied, "The supply train is not scheduled to return until Friday. We'll clear it then."

"This man's arm was crushed. We're not asking for a train for every injury."

When Tommy got back to the bunkhouse, the man was delirious with fever. The men talked about what to do.

Tommy went to see the backup engineer and firemen who stayed at the trailhead, living in a shanty close to the small locomotive and few freight cars that were used for local hauls. They agreed to fire it up the next morning, switch it to the main track and take the injured man to Long Lake. The engine was fitted with a snow catcher that would let it get through unless the drifts were high.

On Thursday morning, Tommy and a few others wrapped the man in blankets left by the departed tracklayers and carried him to an empty boxcar. Tommy and one other man climbed into the car to accompany the injured man. When the bosses heard the train whistle, they ran out of their shack to the locomotive. The fat man asked the engineer. "What do you think you're doing?"

"Trying to save an injured man's life. What are you doing?" The bosses conferred and walked back to their office.

It took less than an hour for the train to reach Long Lake. Tommy and the other man carried the patient to the doctor's office. The doctor examined him. "The arm is badly infected. The only way to save this man's life is to amputate." Tommy winced. To lose an arm or a leg meant the end of a jack's career. He nodded. "Who gets the bill?" the doctor asked.

"The Company, of course," Tommy replied.

"I'll operate this afternoon. I think he should stay in town for a few days."

The patient died the next day.

Tommy celebrated his eighteenth birthday on March 21, 1880 by having a beer in Long Lake with Peter. They walked back along the tracks singing happily. The snow was gone and the bosses had started to hire additional men for laying track. Only a handful of those who were laid off at Christmas returned. Aaron Howard was not among them. Men who had never laid rails before, as well as a few Chinese who had worked on Thomas Durant's Union Pacific railroad, were given jobs. Tommy made sure they were all paid sixty cents a day for ten hours' work.

At the end of April, the surveyors reported that the land along the planned route was flat until about three miles south of Axton where it dropped into a dry ravine, creating an unexpected obstacle. The northern side of the ravine was steep but then continued to climb gradually until close to Axton Landing. Either the track would have to detour around the ravine or a trestle would have to be built. The bosses discussed the problem with the foremen. If they bypassed the ravine they would add at least four miles to the track and would probably not reach Axton Landing in 1880. Building a trestle was dangerous and would also add time, though not as much. Danny Miller suggested that a small crew establish a camp near the ravine and begin to clear the ravine for the trestle so that when the track arrived on the southern side of the ravine, the massive posts, girders, and bents that would be needed for its foundation could be placed without further delay. That might require hiring a few more jacks to keep progress steady on extending the track, still less expensive than detouring around the ravine. Miller volunteered to take a crew of five to start the preparation. The fat boss said, "Why don't you take Tommy Carter? Get him out of our hair for awhile."

Miller was hesitant. "He comes from a family of trouble makers. His father helped send my cousin Frank to prison."

"For what?" one of the other foremen asked.

"For killing a man. But my cousin was only following orders from his boss. He should have been the one to go to jail."

"Is your cousin still in jail?"

"The judge gave him eight years. He's been out for the last five, but he's not well."

If the other foremen had opinions about what Miller told them, they kept it to themselves. The bosses prevailed, and Tommy plus four other jacks and Danny Miller were sent up to the ravine, two miles beyond the current terminus.

With timber they cut along the edge of one escarpment, the men constructed a crude log cabin for their lodging. They took turns returning to the terminus for supplies and food. Their water came from the Raquette.

After building the cabin, their first task was to clear the trees at the top of the escarpments where the track would be laid. Then they excavated the base of the escarpments to widen the ravine bed for laying posts to support the trestle. They completed this work by mid-May. By then, the rail bed was within fifty yards of the south bank of the ravine. More men joined in the construction of the trestle. The heavy squared timbers that would be used for the posts, beams, and bents were brought up on flatbed cars from the mill at Long Lake. The men carried the posts the rest of the distance to the south escarpment and slid them down the ravine where crews sank them deep into the bed of the ravine. To further anchor the posts, the men loosened rocks and boulders from the escarpments, letting them roll down to the bed where they were wedged firmly against the posts, making a jagged carpet of gray, black, and white chunks.

Now began the difficult task of building the trestle skyward. First, the men bolted horizontal beams between the posts, making edge-to-edge rectangular frames. Then they constructed bents or towers, the first layer of which was bolted to each rectangle. Successive bents were added on top of the previous layer until the trestle foundation was level with the top of the ravine. The work was dangerous; men had to climb up each bent and bolt it to the lower one. As the trestle got higher, the danger of a fall on to the rocky bed became greater. If a man slipped from the top tower, he had about a one-hundred-and-fifty-foot plunge to the rocky bed. The workers asked the two bosses to provide ropes for the men to tie themselves to the nearest horizontal beam, breaking their fall if they slipped. Reluctantly, the bosses agreed. Two men did slip but the ropes around their waists broke their fall.

The trestle was finished in July. Then the cross ties had to be laid and the rails anchored to the crossties. Its stability was tested in August when the locomotive pushed one car on to the trestle and stopped. Some of the timbers creaked as the joints set, but there was no movement. The locomotive pushed a second and a third, and finally a fourth car so they stretched the length of the trestle. The trestle held!

Miller and his men, including Tommy, were proud of the trestle and the speed with which they had built it without serious injury. The only sour note was the growing friction between Miller and Tommy. Miller resented Tommy's suggestions, many of which the men adopted because they made good sense. In successive weeks, as the train crossed over the trestle repeatedly, some minor damage occurred. A few ties loosened creating the possibility of derailment. While they were being repaired, the railhead advanced slowly toward Axton Landing.

Tommy was talking to Peter O'Rourke early one afternoon in September when Danny Miller interrupted. "Tommy, I need you to check the ties on the trestle. The train's heading north in fifteen minutes." He turned to O'Rourke. "I could use a spare hand, if you want to come along."

Tommy interrupted. "You don't have to go if you don't want, Peter. Miller is not your foreman."

"That's all right, Tommy. I want to see this beautiful trestle you keep bragging about." The engine was going to pull, not push, the train. The three men boarded the caboose when the train whistle tooted a few minutes later.

As they approached the trestle, Miller leaned over the rear of the caboose to look for loose ties. He found some midway across. Slowly, the train moved north across the trestle, finally coming to a stop on the north side. Miller ordered Peter and Tommy to walk back along the trestle and repair the damage. Tommy told Miller he could do it himself, a great relief to Peter who feared heights. Taking his tools, Tommy got off the train, walked out to the middle of the trestle, and began the job. Peter watched him from the rear of the caboose, unaware that someone had called Miller forward. He was back at Peter's side by the time Tommy completed the job in half an hour and started to walk back, carefully stepping from tie to tie. Tommy had gone about a third of the distance when the train whistle signaled that the locomotive was going to move farther up the tracks. He cursed that the train would not wait for him, but he was afraid he might trip over a tie and lose his footing if he ran for it.

Concentrating on walking from one tie to the next, he did not look up, until he heard the engine start to chug. He was surprised to see the locomotive pulling all but the caboose up the slope beyond the north side of the ravine. At first, he thought nothing of it, but as the space between the caboose and the rest of the train got larger, he realized not only that the first cars were getting farther away, but that the caboose was rolling slowly backwards down the incline, toward the trestle. Somehow , it had become uncoupled. Tommy did not immediately comprehend the danger, assuming that the caboose would come to a stop before it reached him. But as he watched, the car gathered speed, and suddenly he realized his peril.

His first thought was to try to outrun the caboose to the south side of the trestle, but he doubted he could run quickly enough without tripping on a tie. Then he thought of lying flat on the rail bed, hoping the car would clear his body. Rapidly, he judged there was not sufficient space between the rail bed and the bottom of the caboose. It was now only ten yards away, speeding toward him. Out of options, he dropped his tools and jumped off the trestle, hoping he could catch on to one of the bents or at least have it break his fall.

Standing on the rear of the caboose, Miller and Peter were powerless to stop it as it bore down on Tommy. Peter screamed, "Tommy, watch out!"

The caboose coasted to a stop on the flatter south side of the trestle. The two men got off and walked as quickly as they could back along the trestle. Peter had a new fear that superseded his acrophobia. They reached the place where Tommy had jumped and shouted his name. There was no response. Peter stood precariously on the edge of the trestle and peered over the side. He saw a shape sprawled on the ground near one of the posts. "Tommy," he yelled again. Still no response. He came back to the middle where Miller stood, his face pale. "We've got to get down there." Miller nodded but said nothing. They walked back to the north end of the trestle. "Look, dead or alive," said Peter, "we've got to get him out of there." Their roles reversed as Peter took charge. "Mr. Miller, walk up the track and let the men know. There should be a stretcher on the train. Get it back here as fast as you can. By then I should have reached the bottom and I can tell you whether Tommy's alive." Again Miller nodded and headed up the rail bed as Peter cautiously started to move down the escarpment.

Because it was so steep, he mostly sat and slid his way down, getting holds on roots and rocks so he would not go too fast. Once at the bottom, he picked his way along the rocky floor of the ravine. When he reached the midpoint, he walked amidst the posts to the side where he had seen Tommy. He found Tommy, sprawled and motionless. His legs lay on the rock bed but his head and chest were on the dirt where the rocks met bare earth. Gently, Peter rolled Tommy over on to his back. His face was covered with dirt. When Peter cleared off the dirt, he found Tommy's nose battered out of shape and his cheeks and forehead badly bruised. Blood clotted his cheeks. Peter put his hand over Tommy's heart. It was beating, slowly, and he was breathing.

Peter did not know how long he waited for Miller's return, but the sun had moved to the west, and Peter and Tommy were now on the edge of advancing shadow. Finally, he heard his name being called. "He's alive," Peter shouted back. Two men carrying a stretcher, accompanied by Miller, started down the escarpment, leaving three others on top. By the time they reached Peter, the entire ravine was in shadow. The only way of getting Tommy out was to place him in the stretcher and carry him up one of the escarpments, making sure he did not slide off. Miller, who had recovered his authority, shouted up to the other men. "Run up to the train and tell the engineer to bring the train back over the trestle. Have the engineer blow the whistle every few minutes so we know where the train is."

"We've got to get him to the doctor in Long Lake," Peter said. It was dusk before they got Tommy to the top of the trestle. The train was waiting for them. Gently, Peter and the other men lifted Tommy on to one of the boxcars.

When the train arrived in Long Lake, a worker ran ahead to notify the doctor. Peter and another man carried Tommy on the stretcher to his office, where Peter told the doctor what had happened. With one hand, the doctor lifted Tommy's eyelids and shined a small kerosene lamp at the eye. He told Peter, who had accompanied Tommy into the examining room, that his pupils reacted a little to the light, which was a good sign, although the pupils were large, which was not so good. Tommy also gagged when the doctor put a stick down his throat—another good sign, the doctor said. The doctor gently undid and pulled off Tommy's boots and trousers and banged on Tommy's knees with his little hammer, getting no response. When he banged in front and behind his elbow, Tommy's arm jerked. When the doctor stuck Tommy's feet with a needle nothing happened. When he pricked his hand, Tommy withdrew it. The doctor instructed his assistant to clean Tommy up and wrap him securely in blankets to keep him warm. "We'll keep him here until there's a change— one way or the other."

Outside the examining room, the doctor told Peter and Miller that Tommy would never walk again; his spinal cord must have been severed. Whether he lived would depend on how severely his head was damaged. Having it land on the dirt rather than the rocks could have saved his life. His nose was also broken.

Peter wanted to stay with Tommy, but he knew he could do nothing more for him. Feeling he had a duty to notify Cyrus and Mary, although he did not relish it, he told Miller that he knew Tommy's family in Saranac Lake and wanted to tell them. Miller nodded his approval.

The train remained in Long Lake overnight. The next morning, with Tommy unchanged, Peter boarded the train, which picked up other workers, and continued to the rail- head. There he set out toward Axton Landing, which was only two miles away. He reached the landing, waded across the river, and headed for Corey's. He found William sunning himself in a rocker on the front porch.

"Why Peter O'Rourke Junior, what brings you here?" With the sun shining over Peter's back into his face, Corey failed to notice Peter's anguish. "Don't tell me the railroad is here already?"

"No," Peter replied in a shaky voice, "but it's close." He didn't give William a chance to comment. "Mr. Corey, something terrible has happened to Tommy." Now William peered more closely at Peter and gripped the arms of the rocker, ready to get up.

"Is he dead?"

"Not when I left, but he might be now or soon."

With difficulty he lifted himself out of the chair. "What happened? Where is he?"

Peter quickly described how he and the foreman had watched helplessly from the caboose as it bore down on Tommy, forcing him to jump off the trestle. He told William that Tommy was barely alive and was now with the doctor in Long Lake.

"My god!" William exclaimed. "We've got to let Cyrus and Mary know. Maybe Dr. Weinberg in Tupper Lake, too. Peter, help me hitch the horses to the wagon and we'll go to the village."

They arrived at the Carter house just as Lisa and Mary were returning from school. When Mary saw Peter and how he looked, she knew something terrible had happened. Involuntarily she brought one hand to her throat and clutched Lisa's with the other.

"Tommy's been badly injured. He's in Long Lake. When I left he was still unconscious."

Mary collapsed into Lisa's arms. Peter helped sit her down in front of the house. Tears streamed down Mary's cheeks and she pounded her fists into the earth. "Damn you men," she shrieked. "Why must you put yourselves in harm's way?" She sobbed while Lisa tried to console her, crying as she did so. Finally, Mary calmed down. "How bad is it? Does the doctor know what's wrong?"

"The doctor said if he lived, he would never walk again."

"Oh! My Tommy," she started to sob and again hugged her daughter. Still sobbing, she hugged Peter. "Peter, thank you for bringing the news. I'd rather hear it from you than from a stranger." Next she hugged William. Lisa and Peter hugged, very tightly.

"Where's Cyrus?" William asked.

"He's up in Malone campaigning. He should be back tonight." She paused. "I don't want to wait for him, I want to go to Tommy now." Everyone understood.

Although Peter had used the railroad, he doubted that the train was still at the terminus or that Mary and Lisa would be welcome to travel on it to Long Lake. The alternative was to drive back past the inn to Tupper Lake and then south on the road to Long Lake. If they started immediately they might make it by dark. They climbed back into the wagon. "Don't you think you should leave a message for Cyrus?" William asked.

"I'll stay and wait for papa. He and I can come down together," Lisa said climbing down from the wagon.

William asked Peter to drive. Before he climbed up, he and Lisa hugged again. When they reached the inn, William said he would not go further. "Go on without me. Just give Tommy a hug for me."

They stopped at the Weinbergs' house in Tupper Lake, where Peter told Henry what had happened and what he remembered about the doctor's findings. "I know the doctor in Long Lake; he's competent," Henry said. Freda, in the meantime, had insisted that Mary and Peter have some nourishment. They quickly ate a few small cakes. Mary was eager to continue. Freda gave them a basket of apples. Henry said, "I don't think there's any point in my going. I'm sure you'll let me know how Tommy does."

They arrived in Long Lake after dark. The doctor had good news. Tommy had opened his eyes briefly but didn't seem to know where he was. He had not moved his arms, although the doctor told Mary he was capable of doing so.

Mary gasped when she saw Tommy's face, battered and bruised. She stroked his forehead and hair. Tommy opened his eyes. He recognized his mother and, as she bent over to kiss him, he raised his arms and put them around her. She tried to stop crying but couldn't for several minutes.

Cyrus and Lisa arrived the next day. Cyrus feared Mary would blame him for letting Tommy work for the railroad; in fact, he blamed himself. If Mary was angry with him, she did not show it. Instead, she hugged him. "Thank god you're here," she whispered in his ear, not letting go. Cyrus wanted to thank Peter for bringing the news but he had returned to work early that morning.

Mary insisted on staying in Long Lake, sleeping on a cot in Tommy's room in the doctor's house, and learning to nurse her son. He slept a lot, signaling his wakefulness by opening his eyes and raising an arm. He never spoke but nodded or shook his head in response to his mother's questions. Often, Mary's thought drifted to John. *Was he all right?* She knew he was as militant as Tommy when it came to workers, *Was he all right? Why haven't I heard from him?* While Tommy napped during the day she penned a brief note to John at the only address she could think of.

Long Lake, NY
September 30, 1880

John Carter
c/o General Delivery
Chicago, Illinois

My Darling Son,

No, we have not moved. I am sitting at your brother's bedside in the doctor's house here in Long Lake. Tommy was badly injured in a railroad accident last Monday. He is paralyzed below his waist and the doctor says he will never walk again. Worst still, he has not been able to speak since he recovered consciousness. We will take him home to Saranac Lake in a few days, when we are sure he is out of danger of dying.

I hope you get this, John. Please write, tell us where you are, and please, be careful and stay well,

Your loving mother,
Mary Carter

9

Adapting

TOMMY was soon able to take sips of fluid, but he could barely raise himself and had to be propped up. The most serious problem so far as the Carters were concerned was that Tommy was unable to talk. His frustration showed in his face. There was no change over the next week when the Carters brought him home in William's buckboard, fitted out with side rails and padding.

A week later, Cyrus hitched William's horse, and one of his own, to the wagon and rode west to the inn. Holding the reins loosely, Cyrus thought about making this same trip twenty years earlier when a tearful Mary realized she was pregnant with Jean's child but didn't let on to him. That he should marry Mary had not yet occurred to him. His thoughts flitted between the past—what harms he had done—and the future—what harms he might yet do. Would he and his family be better off if he quit his campaign for the New York State Assembly?

When he arrived, William was dozing in a rocker on the front porch. Quietly, Cyrus unhitched Corey's horse and set her to graze. His own horse pulled the buckboard to the shed in back of the inn where Cyrus's old boat leaned innocuously against the side of the shed, its hull lusterless even in the morning light. Cyrus kicked the boat, half expecting, half hoping it would fall apart. It didn't budge. He unhitched his horse from the wagon, opened the shed door, and pulled the wagon in. Emerging back into the bright sun a minute later, Cyrus shut the shed door, walked to the side of the shed, and stood in front of the boat. He grabbed the top gunwale, pulled, and then let go. The boat hit the ground with a thump, still intact, right side up, revealing its gaunt ribs and occasional cracks. "This boat's been nothing but trouble," Cyrus muttered. His original sin had been stealing it at Eighth Lake. Then he had insisted that Jean join his crew to break the logjam. Then he had let Peter O'Rourke Senior take the Reverend Loguen for a row. Then, a little over a year ago, he had used it to start Tommy on his journey to work for the railroad. Each time death or near death followed. He kicked it maliciously. It didn't budge. Maybe it was time to get rid of it.

———•———

The smack of the boat hitting the ground roused William. He saw his horse grazing, picked up his cane, and went to look for Cyrus. He found him staring at the boat. "Guess you returned the wagon?"

Cyrus raised his head. "I put it in the shed. Thanks for letting us use it."

"How's the lad doing?"

"As well as can be expected. He needs constant attention."

"Is he talking at all?"

"No. He understands perfectly and writes his answers on a pad that's always near him. He can use his arms just fine, but that's about it."

"Are you gonna hire someone to care for him?"

"Right now Mary wouldn't trust anyone else."

"She's gonna quit teaching?" Cyrus nodded and gave the boat another kick. Still, it didn't budge.

William hesitated before his next question. "Can you manage if Mary gives up teaching?"

"It'll be tough. My law practice can't be counted on. The Town Council pays a pittance," he intoned gloomily, again kicking the boat.

"If you get elected to the State Assembly that should bring in more."

"Not much. Anyway, I have to run and get elected first. And if I win, I'll be two days away from here when the legislature is in session. If Tommy should—" his voice trailed off. He kicked the boat again, so hard that his toes jammed against the front of his boot, causing him to wince and William to smile fleetingly. The boat remained impervious.

"You trying to destroy that vessel?" William asked.

"It's a worthless thing. Brought nothing but bad luck."

"Come on, Cyrus. You can't blame the boat."

Cyrus sighed and turned from the boat to look at the older man. "You're right, William. I only have myself to blame."

"I wasn't suggesting that. Tommy's a grown man. He settled on his course. That doctor, Jared Mason, put those union ideas in his head. That's what got him in trouble."

"You're not suggesting that Tommy's organizing had anything to do with the accident?"

"The Adirondack Railroad Company's a lot better off

with Tommy out of the way. He and the other leaders got the workers equal pay and a ten-hour day. It doesn't want that to spread."

Cyrus had been so immersed in worrying about Tommy's future that the thought that Tommy might have been intentionally run down had not entered his head. "We'd have a hard time proving the Company was involved."

"I'm sure you're right. I do recall Peter telling me that the foreman was on the caboose when it bore down on Tommy."

For an instant, Cyrus did not grasp the significance of William's remark. Then the lava bubbling below the crust erupted as Cyrus fused the event and its possible cause. His mind raced back to Thanksgiving. Hadn't Tommy mentioned a foreman named Miller? If he were related to Frank, he'd have reason to begrudge the Carters because of Cyrus' role in convicting Frank Miller, giving him reason to become an accomplice in a Company plot to get rid of Tommy. "He didn't happen to mention the foreman's name?"

"Not that I recall," William replied.

Cyrus's eagerness to find out if the foreman on the caboose was related to Frank Miller changed his mood. He grabbed the gunwales and lifted the hull, leaning the boat against the shed. Dusting his hands on his trousers, Cyrus smiled at William. "Well, we might just have a case against the Company."

William nodded, but thought, *when hell freezes over. The Company will say the foreman acted on his own.* Cyrus was walking to his horse, the old man hobbling alongside, when the wail of a train whistle startled him. "That sounds awfully close," Cyrus said.

"Damn right. I reckon the tracks are laid to Axton Landing. When the wind's from the south I can hear the jacks clearing the bed on the far bank of the Raquette. My refusal to sell didn't make much difference."

"Damn railroad!" Cyrus said angrily as he placed one foot in the stirrup and swung his other leg over the saddle. "We'll soon know, William, whether we've got a case."

———•———

Cyrus was home by midday. Mary had turned Tommy and was straightening his bedclothes. They brightened when Cyrus strode in. "I just returned from Uncle William's. Thanked him for the use of his horse and wagon—we couldn't have got you back here without them, Tommy—and then we started to talk about your accident."

"Don't you think it's best not talked about?" Mary interrupted. She was so thankful to have Tommy alive with his mental capacity intact that she didn't want to revisit the tragedy or engage in "what ifs?" Deep down she was relieved that he could never again be subject to the dangers to which lumberjacks and construction workers were exposed.

Cyrus looked at her blankly, not considering the pain of raising the subject. He turned to Tommy, who did not seem perturbed. "What was the name of the foreman who was on the caboose with Peter when the accident happened?"

Mary looked angrily at Cyrus and turned to leave. Cyrus gently took hold of her wrist. He whispered, "Be patient with me, you'll understand in a minute." Forgetting Tommy was mute, Cyrus expected him to blurt out the answer. Instead, Tommy reached for his pencil and pad, scribbled the answer and turned the pad so Cyrus could read it.

"Danny Miller," Cyrus read out loud. "Was he the one with red hair who I said might be related to Frank Miller?" Tommy nodded. Cyrus let go of Mary's wrist as she sat at the foot of Tommy's bed, curious where Cyrus the lawyer was heading. "Do you think Danny Miller might have uncoupled the caboose?"

Tommy looked at Cyrus, thought for a moment, and then wrote under Danny's name: *He's not smart enough, but if he was, we could never prove he did it.* He passed it to Cyrus but before Cyrus could reply, Tommy took the pad back and added, *"Besides, I think the RR is the bigger enemy, even if Miller was involved. Getting safety legislation after you're elected to the State Assembly is the most important thing.* Tommy had already insisted that his father not drop out of the race on his account.

On his way back from Corey's, Cyrus had decided that he would quit the race and devote his time to finding out just how the caboose had become uncoupled—and who, if anyone, had been involved. But Tommy's thoughts were headed in a different direction. Cyrus was less confident than his son that he could get the Assembly to pass the safety legislation Tommy wanted. He had another reason to withdraw: he could help Mary care for Tommy. After a long silence, during which he ran his fingers through his still-thick graying hair, he got up and went to his study.

A half hour later he asked Mary to accompany him to Tommy's room where he placed a single sheet of paper on Tommy's bed. Mary moved to the head of the bed to read it with her son.

My good friends,

As many of you know, my Son, Thomas Carter, was seriously injured when a runaway railroad car forced him to jump from the trestle that he had helped build. He will never walk, and may never talk, again.

It pains me that other workers have suffered even worse fates at the hands of the railroad companies. If working conditions remain as they are, countless others will be killed and maimed. I had hoped that my election to the New York State Assembly would enable me to seek legislation to require decent working conditions and compensation for workers injured on the job. For now, however, my duty is to Tommy, and to my wife, Mary, who has quit her teaching job to care for him, depriving the young people of Saranac Lake of her scholarship and wisdom. They both need my help. Consequently, this day I am canceling all appearances and withdrawing from the contest for State Assemblyman from Franklin County. Thank you all for your help. Perhaps I will be able to run in 1882.

Mary pulled Cyrus toward her and hugged him. Tommy wrote an emphatic "*NO!*" on his pad.

Despite his withdrawal, Cyrus's name remained on the ballot that November. He received over a hundred votes, not enough to beat the Republican incumbent. Tommy made him promise that he would run in 1882, although Cyrus shuddered when he thought about the most likely scenario that would let him.

Without the campaign, Cyrus helped Mary. The doctor in Long Lake had told her how important it was to turn Tommy and keep him clean, and he had shown her how to do it. Mary in turn taught Cyrus how to conduct these chores. Cyrus figured out how to change the sheets with Tommy still in the bed. He got so proficient that Mary agreed to return to teaching. The School Board had not yet hired a replacement for her, giving the students an extended holiday. Lisa, now fifteen, helped care for Tommy, too, but her parents, and Tommy, were intent that she finish school.

As winter approached and the shadows crept into his room earlier each day, Tommy became gloomy. *Can't you get me out of this bed?* he wrote on his pad. Cyrus, the only one who could lift Tommy without help, would carry him to a comfortable chair, and then do his own work. If Tommy got restless he'd ring the bell they fitted him with. If only Mary was about she kissed his forehead apologetically. "I'm sorry, Darling. I can't lift you myself. Papa should be back soon."

With the little spare money they had, Cyrus and Mary ordered a wheelchair to expand Tommy's freedom. While they waited for its arrival, Cyrus built a ramp over part of the front steps. One of the local saw mills had offered the wood as a gift. Conscious of the need to remain independent of the lumber industry, Cyrus insisted on paying. By the time the wheelchair arrived, snow was on the ground and did not melt until April. But the wheelchair made it possible for Tommy to move around the house, once his father got him in it.

By December, the Carters' supply of firewood was running low. Instead of buying, as he had done for many years, Cyrus decided to chop his own. He rummaged in his tool shed for his axe. There were some rust spots on the blade but the handle, smooth from years of twisting in his hands, still fit securely. He brought the axe back to the house together with a whetstone that had been lying on his workbench. That night and all of the next day a blizzard added three more feet of snow to the foot already on the ground. Cyrus got Tommy into his wheelchair and the two sat in front of the fire, as Cyrus sharpened his axe.

"Haven't used this for quite a while," Cyrus said. With the axe on his lap, he rubbed a drop of spittle into the whetstone, laid it almost flat against the blade, and began to sharpen with small circular movements.

Tommy put his book down, watched his father for a few moments, and then wrote on his pad. *Tell me what jacking was like.*

"You've done some." Cyrus kept sharpening. "You mean in the old days?"

Tommy smiled and nodded.

Cyrus thought for a while. "Well, first of all, the woods were different. We weren't felling the hardwoods, except when they got in the way. The forests were thick with maple and birch of a pretty good size, but still they were dwarfed by the white pines." He stopped for a moment, closing his eyes, visualizing the virgin timber. "You've never seen a mature white pine, Tommy, so big around that three men with their arms outstretched couldn't surround its trunk. It'll take a thousand years to grow them that big again."

Tommy wrote on his pad, *The lumber companies would never wait that long!*

Cyrus chuckled, "You're right, Son. They are a greedy bunch. Don't much care about the land—they just move on to the next forest—and the jacks move with them if they want to keep their jobs."

———•———

The family developed a new routine for the winter. While it was still dark, Mary cleaned and dressed Tommy, then Cyrus got him into his wheelchair, and Tommy guided himself into the kitchen where Cyrus had already stoked the wood stove. Mary and Lisa ate hurriedly and left for school. Over a leisurely breakfast and coffee, Cyrus related an episode of his logging saga. Tommy took prodigious notes. Leaving Tommy alone after breakfast, Cyrus went out to scavenge the near woods for fallen limbs that were not yet rotted and standing dead trees that were not too big for him to drag home. These he chopped and trimmed, leaving smaller branches in a pile, which he would retrieve later for kindling. He skidded the limbs and trunks across the snow to their house, limping slightly as he had since his leg had been broken. In the yard, he bucked them into two-foot lengths. Long dormant muscles resisted, but slowly Cyrus regained his old form, happily thinking, *this time I am jacking for myself.*

In January, without telling Mary or Tommy, Cyrus walked over to the law office he shared with Lawrence Venable to type a letter to the Adirondack Railroad under the letterhead, "Venable and Carter, Attorneys-at-Law." He described the circumstances of Tommy's accident as he had heard it from Peter O'Rourke, Jr.—Tommy still had no recollection—and requested that the company investigate the accident or, if it already had, inform him of the results. He did not say that he was representing Tommy because he doubted that Tommy would approve of his intervening. He walked to the village post office and mailed the letter.

During the days when Cyrus was out, Tommy read his notes and rewrote them coherently. By spring, he had enough to fill a book. In the evening, around the hearth in the living room, with Mary and sometimes Lisa present, Tommy presented a list of questions that took off from that morning's conversation with his father. Many of them asked for factual clarification, others for Cyrus's opinion. *If he didn't need the money, why did Jed Mason come to work in the Adirondacks? Could a brake be put on the destruction of the forests that would still leave jobs for lumberjacks? How difficult would it be to pass legislation to improve the well being of the workingman? What did Cyrus think about unions? Does violence inflicted on workers by their employers justify violence in return?* One of the many books Tommy had read that winter was *Civil Disobedience* in which Thoreau argued for citizens to take direct action when it disapproved what their government was doing. The action Thoreau took, refusing to pay taxes, was a peaceful one. But if the State, or companies, resort to violence, what then? Was violence ever acceptable? *If Durant's cops had fired into the workers in front of the locomotive, injuring or killing some, should the workers have retaliated?*

This last question evoked an almost violent response from Mary. "The workers should have known they were endangering their lives and should have found another way to express their grievances."

"I'm inclined to agree with your mother, Tommy," Cyrus added. "The workers must be patient. In time, the legal system will set things right in a democracy."

I and many of my fellow workers are not prepared to wait that long, Tommy wrote in reply, adding, *Women have waited one hundred years and still are deprived of the vote.*

———•———

In March, Lawrence Venable brought the Adirondack Railroad's reply to Carter at home. Cyrus invited Lawrence to sit in front of the fire as he read the letter aloud. The company thanked Attorney Carter for his inquiry and indicated that it had thoroughly investigated the "accident." The coupling between the caboose and the car in front of it, the letter stated, was in perfect operating order and the two men on the caboose were unable to say how the caboose could have become uncoupled. The letter concluded, "As there is no evidence of either faulty equipment or negligence, the company takes no responsibility for the unfortunate event. The possibility remains that Thomas Carter himself uncoupled the caboose."

Carter stood in disbelief about the final sentence. He crumpled the letter in his fist and threw it into the fire where its edges curled before erupting into flame. "Can you imagine Tommy uncoupling the caboose? I tell you, Lawrence, these companies are spelling their own doom by such stupidity."

"They think they can get away with it," Lawrence replied. "Only legal action will stop them. And I'm not sure you have enough evidence to make a case."

"I'm afraid you're right. No, the legal action that will work means changing the law, holding companies responsible for injuries on the job. I should be in Albany fighting for it."

Cyrus never mentioned his correspondence with the Adirondack Railroad to Tommy, Mary, or Lisa.

———•———

By April, Cyrus had brought his saga up to Tommy's last job. He reminded his son how he and Mary had rowed him up the Raquette to shortcut his trip to the railhead. Cyrus was surprised when Tommy wrote: *What happened to the boat?*

Cyrus chuckled, "It's lying up against Uncle William's shed in back of the inn." In unfolding his saga to Tommy, Cyrus had been generous to the boat. He gave it credit for bringing him (and Jean) to Mary, for helping restore Jed Mason's health, and for pleasant summer afternoons rowing with Mary and their young children on Upper Saranac Lake. He glanced into the fire, reminiscing. "I was getting to like Jean as we rowed up the Raquette to look for jobs until he blurted out, 'Da oars doan match.' That annoyed me, but I soon realized he was making an innocent observation." Smiling, Cyrus looked at Tommy. "I never did get a matching pair of oars. The originals are still in Uncle William's shed." He reflected for a moment. "You know, Son, I don't see why we can't take you out in the boat next summer. You might even be able to row!"

PART III

10

The Lobbyist

CONSTRUCTION of the State Capitol in Albany had begun in 1867. When Cyrus saw it in January 1883, it was only complete to the third floor with scaffolding rising above the fourth floor. He had never seen such an enormous building with so much granite and marble, its Romanesque columns dwarfing him as he walked through to the portal. With the building still incomplete, the Assembly moved into its chamber on the third floor in 1879; the Senate occupied its chamber two years later.

For his swearing-in as the Assemblyman from Franklin County, Cyrus Carter wore the only suit he had ever owned—the same one he had worn for his wedding twenty-three years earlier. Then, the muscles in his arms had bulged through the sleeves. Now that he only chopped enough to fuel his own house in Saranac Lake, the sleeves did not fit snugly. Lawyering did not keep him as trim as twelve hours a day of jacking, and Mary had to let out the waist of his trousers for the occasion. She also trimmed his beard and hair before he left Saranac Lake.

No friends or relatives accompanied Cyrus to Albany; Mary stayed home to care for Tommy, still paraplegic and mute. With the loving care of both his parents and his sister, Tommy's condition had stabilized and he had urged his father to stand for election in 1882 so he could fight to protect workers. The School Board, now under the Chairmanship of Lawrence Venable, had given Mary a leave of absence when Cyrus was elected, replacing her with Alan Philips, one of Mary's first students in the one-room school at Corey's and the young man Reverend Jones had chided for being bare-chested in Mary's classroom. Alan had taken up furniture making but until his business caught on he had time to teach.

With no friends or relations in Albany to congratulate him, Cyrus did not linger at the reception for new Assemblymen. He had almost reached the large doors that led out to the portico when a tall, well-dressed young man approached him, extending his hand. "Congratulations, Assemblyman Carter."

In the course of becoming a politician, Cyrus had learned to remember faces. He was sure he had never seen this man before. His tailored clothes were a cut above what the best-dressed men in Franklin County wore and his neatly combed hair and smooth, clean-shaven face did not reflect the hardships that living in the Adirondacks entailed. Yet, he had a pleasant open demeanor that Carter immediately liked. Smiling, Carter shook his hand. "Thank you, thank you very much." If his face showed puzzlement it was quickly erased.

"We haven't met before. I'm Lloyd Massing of the Lumberman's Association. We represent the logging companies in the Adirondacks."

Looking intently at Cyrus, Massing picked up the frown that momentarily crossed his face. "I know the Association endorsed your opponent," Massing said with a smile. "But I had nothing to do with it. From the newspaper accounts I could tell you had a better grasp of the issues and a platform that recognized the importance of logging to the well-being of the people of Franklin County."

They were at the large double doors that led out to the portico and the cold, crisp, January air. If through Mr. Massing the Lumberman's Association was extending an olive branch, Cyrus would not turn it aside, at least not at this stage. Although he did not equate the well-being of the people of Franklin County with the well-being of the lumber companies, or the railroads with which they were closely allied, he again said, "Thank you, thank you very much."

Massing continued forthrightly. "I know there are differences between your agenda and ours but there are also areas of overlap." Cyrus remained silent. "Perhaps you'll permit me to take you to lunch next week so we can explore our common ground."

Concerned about where this was heading, Cyrus replied, "That's very kind of you, Mr. Massing. I'd be he pleased to join you for lunch, but if you don't mind, I'll pay my own bill."

Massing laughed. "I don't mind, and I'm sure the Association won't mind saving a little money. How about next Wednesday?"

"That will be fine," Cyrus said. Massing again extended his hand. Cyrus walked through the columns, down the steps, and headed toward his boarding house as Massing turned to re-enter the capitol.

———•———

"Why don't you take the seat on the banquette?" Lloyd Massing suggested as the maitre d' pulled the table out. Cyrus slid in, quickly realizing that the leather-cushioned seat was uncomfortably low. Seated opposite, on a chair with lacquered arms whose red cushion was higher than the banquette's, Massing loomed over him. Cyrus did not complain. Although Massing had given him the more comfortable seat, Cyrus mused that the younger man would have been better off had he given Cyrus the chair. Even sitting ramrod straight, as he was accustomed to do, Cyrus was four inches shorter than Massing.

"Have you eaten here before?" Massing asked.

"No. It's beyond my means."

"Then why won't you let the Association pick up the bill for your lunch?"

Cyrus looked around. He recognized a few other Assemblymen at scattered tables around the spacious, ornate room. They seemed to enjoy being wined and dined by men like Massing who sat opposite them. "Mr. Massing, I'll listen to what you have to say, but I won't be beholden to you."

"Have it your way, but the lumber companies can afford this lunch a lot more than you."

A Negro waiter in a starched white apron approached, a linen napkin draped over his sleeve. "Good afternoon, gentlemen. Can I get you something to drink?"

"I'll have a whiskey neat. How about you, Cyrus?"

Already regretting that his obstinacy would cost him dearly, Cyrus declined.

"Not a teetotaler are you?" He didn't give Cyrus a chance to reply. "I've taken the liberty of ordering for us."

Cyrus winced inwardly, wondering how extravagant Massing had been.

When his drink arrived, Massing raised his glass to Cyrus.

"First of all Cyrus, I want to congratulate you for getting appointed to the Agriculture Committee. That's where the bills on woods and forests are introduced."

Of course I know that, Cyrus said to himself. After an uncomfortable pause Massing coughed into his fist and continued. "I understand you are acquainted with my father-in-law." The waiter arrived with their first course. Massing started his compote and Cyrus followed.

"Is that so?"

"Ben Anderson. Alice, my wife, told me you worked for her father about twenty-five years ago."

Cyrus was startled but maintained his composure. "How did she know?"

"She heard it from you, directly."

"Really? I don't recall meeting her."

"You didn't. When she was eleven her father took her to a murder trial in Saranac Lake."

"Frank Miller's trial."

"Your testimony and your wife's testimony made an impression on her. When I told her I was having lunch with you today, she asked if you were the Cyrus Carter from Saranac Lake."

"Give your wife my best wishes. Do you come from Westport, too?"

"No, I met Alice in Glens Falls, where my family owns the biggest sawmill. She worked as my father's secretary for a while. I met her after I graduated from Yale. She's a very smart woman."

"I have no doubt," Cyrus answered tactfully. "Do you have any children?"

"Just two, a boy of seven, Donald, and a girl of five, Jane. I know you have three." Massing raised his glass to Cyrus. "Here's to our children," he toasted.

Cyrus picked up his water glass in response. "You certainly know a lot about me, Mr. Massing."

"It's part of my job. Besides, you're widely known in the north woods. How else would you have been elected Assemblyman?"

"I hope it was because of what I campaigned on, not who knew me or who I knew." The waiter cleared the empty compotes and returned with dinner plates followed by a steaming silver platter. Massing nodded to the waiter to serve Cyrus first. "What will it be, Sir? Roast beef, venison, or duck? We have a black currant sauce that is excellent with the venison and an orange sauce for the duck."

Cyrus wondered whether they were all the same price. He concluded that if any were less it would be the roast beef. "I'll take the beef, please." The waiter expertly maneuvered a thick slice on to Cyrus's plate and offered him gravy. "Yes, please." He didn't think he'd be charged extra for it. Without asking, the waiter served Cyrus small roasted potatoes and a vegetable medley. He turned to Massing. "And you, Mr. Massing?"

"I'll have a bit of all three, George." The waiter served him.

"Is his name really George?" Cyrus asked after the waiter left the table.

"In this town, Cyrus, all Negroes are George."

The men ate silently for a few minutes. The clinking of silverware, subdued voices, and an occasional laugh reverberated around the room.

Cyrus was the first to speak. "Have you spent much time in the Adirondacks, Mr. Massing?"

"Please call me Lloyd."

"Have you spent much time in the Adirondacks, Lloyd?"

"As a matter of fact, I haven't visited the north woods. We got married in Westport and we honeymooned in Europe at my father's expense. I haven't done much vacationing since then."

"I prefer to call them the Adirondacks. 'North woods' is too vague. Some of my constituents have defined boundaries for the Adirondacks and in deference to them I prefer the term. Westport is not in the boundary. A pity you haven't ventured farther west." He paused to wipe a spot of gravy off his lips. "I suspect you invited me to lunch to talk about the Adirondacks. You'd have a better picture if you saw what you were talking about."

"You're right on both counts. Maybe after the session is over, I can get up there." Massing looked directly at Cyrus.

Cyrus saw genuine interest in Massing's look. Despite what he expected to be an unfriendly conversation, he liked Massing. Not many men in his position would boast of his wife being smart, even mention it, or would be open to seeing the damage the companies he represented had inflicted. Massing played the lobbyist role extremely well.

———◆———

It was no wonder. While at Yale, Massing had become interested in acting, to the neglect of his studies, starring in several local productions. His circle of friends in New Haven (most of them outside the University) included struggling thespians that often lambasted the parvenus who accumulated great gobs of money during and after the Civil War, like Lloyd's father. Lloyd kept silent about his lineage. Although dependent on his father's largesse, he became resentful of his family's wealth.

Lloyd just managed to graduate. His father would hear nothing of a career in the theater, threatening to cut off his son's allowance and inheritance if he pursued it. Massing thought seriously of saying to hell with his father until he met Alice Anderson when he visited his father's office. She was a petite, slim, beautiful brunette. He invited her to lunch, where he learned she could talk knowledgably about the lumber business. Alice was also interested in the theater, able to discourse on Shakespeare, but she could not afford to attend local theater. Lloyd remedied this and they were soon holding hands and having after-theater dinner together. Lloyd did not want to count on his inheritance to support a wife, but other than acting he was ill prepared to earn a living. His father arranged for him to get a job as the Lumberman's Association representative in Albany. By now he and Alice knew they were in love and she encouraged him to take it despite his reluctance to get involved in such mundane work. Shortly after he started as a lobbyist, he and Alice were married. Alice's father, Ben, was thrilled when she wrote that she was going to marry a Massing. She had not seen her father for years and neither Alice nor Lloyd thought it necessary to seek his permission. Lloyd's father did not approve—the Andersons were at least two rungs below the Massings on the social ladder—but he gave his consent. If he hadn't, Lloyd told Alice, they would have eloped.

Although Lloyd was very good at his job, he did not much like it. He hid his unhappiness well.

———•———

"I can arrange a camping trip for you in the Adirondacks," Cyrus replied.

"I hear you're an expert guide. I'll see if Alice and the children are interested."

The waiter returned with a bottle of red wine. "Some wine, Sir?" he asked Lloyd. Massing nodded and the waiter upturned his stem glass and poured. "For you, Sir?" he asked Cyrus.

"No thank you. I'll just have water." The waiter removed his wine glass and the two men ate silently for a few moments. Then Lloyd, adopting Cyrus's terminology, got to the point. "The Adirondacks are very important to us, Cyrus."

"'Us' meaning the lumber companies?"

"Not only the lumber companies but men like you. Had it not been for the lumber companies I daresay you wouldn't have found a job when you were younger. Now many more people live up there than when you jacked. They can't all be guides or Assemblymen. They'll have a hard time finding jobs unless we expand operations."

"Well, uhh, Lloyd, I'm not sure I was better off. Didn't put much money in my pocket, got a broken leg, and lost my best friend, both trying to break a logjam."

Massing knew what a logjam meant. "With the railroads we don't need to rely on log floats any more. That makes jacking a lot safer."

"Tommy, my son, was badly injured building the Adirondack Railroad. He's never going to walk again." Cyrus
swallowed down the lump in his throat with some water.

"I didn't mean to upset you. I know that's why you withdrew from the race in 1880. I'm sorry." Massing sipped his
wine. He realized he had made a mistake mentioning the
railroad. He was silent for a few moments. "Look, I'm not
representing the railroads—"

"Come on, Lloyd, the lumber companies benefit from
the railroads."

Massing was beginning to feel uncomfortable, and he
knew it was more than the alcohol and the heavy meal. For
the most part, the Assemblymen he invited to lunch were
complacent, seldom raising an argument, and never offering
to pay for themselves. He needed Cyrus's vote to kill a bill
prohibiting the sale of state lands; if Assemblymen from the
counties with timber were united in their opposition, the
bill stood little chance of passing. He decided to be blunt.
"Cyrus, I'm not going to beat around the bush. You know
that those downstate City do-gooders have introduced legislation to stop the selling of state lands. Last year, Governor
Cornell called for 'protection' of the state's forests. Protecting them is not going to protect the lumberjacks."

"It's not good for the lumber companies either," Cyrus
interjected.

"Regardless, if my companies can't purchase state lands,
it will mean fewer jobs."

Cyrus had stayed away from the logging issue in his campaign the previous fall. Massing was not sure where Cyrus

stood. "How do you feel about the selling of state land?" he asked. By now, both men had finished the main course. The waiter arrived to clear their plates and offer them dessert. Massing ordered an apple pie à la mode.

Judiciously, Cyrus decided against dessert. After a brief pause he responded to Massing's question. "That's not an easy question, Mr. Massing—uhh, Lloyd. The lumber companies are the biggest employers in Franklin and the surrounding counties."

"Yes, and a lot of your votes came from their workers. They sure would have a hard time finding jobs if the supply of trees dwindled."

"There's another side of the coin though, Lloyd." The waiter had refilled Cyrus's water and he took a sip. "You know, when I jacked, Smead and the other companies only took out the softwoods, the conifers. Now that the railroads have cut their reliance on floating logs to the mills, they're taking out the hardwoods as well. And with the demand for pulp, they're cutting small trees as well as big ones." Cyrus noticed that Massing had a vacant expression. "You know all this, Lloyd?"

"No, go ahead. It's very interesting."

"That means cutting almost every tree in the forest, Lloyd. And as your equipment gets better, you're gonna be able to remove the trees faster and faster, probably employing fewer jacks. And when you remove the trees, the animals will have no shelter. You pollute the streams with pulp chemicals, you destroy the fish. No trees, no animals, no fish. Are tourists going to come to the Adirondacks then? People downstate worry that their water supply, and the waterways themselves, will dry up when the trees are chopped and the land no longer holds the water."

"Cyrus, that's plain silly. There's no evidence of a water shortage. And what's more important: jobs for humans, or homes for animals and fish? Besides, Cyrus, we can plant new trees when we take out old ones. And if we continue to be able to purchase State lands with virgin stands of timber, we'll have an enormous supply. By the time we lumber those, we'll have new growth to harvest on the forests we're working now."

"Unfortunately, Lloyd, trees don't grow back as fast as you cut them. Besides, I haven't heard of any lumber company planting a single tree. Just the opposite! Once the companies strip the woods, the land becomes worthless to them; they move on, and they default on their taxes. That further reduces the county's ability to help its people."

Massing tried one last time to pin Cyrus down. "Cyrus, you haven't answered my question about the bill on the sale of state lands."

"Frankly, Lloyd, I don't know where I stand. It sure would be nice if we could keep the trees and have the jobs. Maybe we can't have it both ways." He took another drink of water and looked Massing in the eye. "Lloyd, you've got to see the Adirondacks where they haven't been spoiled to appreciate what logging them bare does."

"I'm ready to take you up on your offer to visit. Maybe this summer."

The waiter returned and laid a silver tray with the check next to each man's place. Cyrus blanched when he picked up his. It was almost all the money he had in Albany. Lloyd asked the waiter to bring a cigar. When it arrived he sheared off the tip and lit up, making sure the billows of smoke did not blow in Cyrus's direction.

"You sure you won't reconsider and let me pay for your lunch?"

"It's not necessary." Cyrus pulled out his wallet. He counted out ten one-dollar bills, leaving him with only two.

Massing laid a $20 bill on his silver tray. "We usually add on a tip, about 10%." Cyrus added on another dollar bill. He was ready to get up and concentrate on how he was going to replace the money, but Massing showed no sign of leaving. With every puff of his cigar the tip glowed red.

"I'll have to think about the bill some more and see how it comes out of the Agriculture Committee—if it does. I'll tell you one thing though, Lloyd. I'd be more likely to vote against it if I knew your Association did more to help workers. Most of your companies are still paying piece rate, which can be dangerous. But the jobbers and their foremen don't give a damn about safety because they know there are always men looking for jobs."

"I don't think that's fair, Cyrus. We've developed a code for workers to follow that aims to cut down accidents."

"Sure, you tell the workers to be careful, but the companies aren't big on protective equipment or adopting safe practices like paying a flat rate."

"You know we are, Cyrus. Healthy, contented workers make better workers, don't you think?"

Cyrus nodded. "Well, let's put that to the test. How about a fifty-hour work week? How about compensation for death or injuries due to work? How about a minimum wage of $10 a week?" Cyrus could not resist adding, "That would be the same as the price of my lunch and less than the price of yours. How about the right to join a union?"

"Well, I don't know about that last one, but the others sound reasonable to me. Let me bring those ideas back to the Association. They might be interested if they had your vote."

Cyrus said nothing and Massing got up. As Cyrus followed, he said, "I'll be in touch with you about visiting the Adirondacks. Your children would enjoy it, I'm sure."

"That would be splendid," Lloyd replied.

11

The Price of Integrity

CYRUS did not return to the Assembly after his lunch with Lloyd Massing. He went to his boarding house, folded his arms on the small desk, and laid his head on them. After a time, he drew out a piece of paper and took the pen from his pocket.

Albany, New York
February 1, 1883

Dearest Mary,

Do you remember when Jed Mason lectured us about danger to the integrity of elected officials? Well, maintaining my integrity has cost me a great deal. Lloyd Massing, representing the Lumberman's Association, invited me to lunch. I agreed but insisted on paying for my own meal. Of course, he picked a real fancy restaurant. Now I am out $10. I'll have to skimp on meals for a while and find a job when I am not legislating to get enough money to return home.

How are you managing with Tommy?

Your loving husband

Cyrus Carter

Cyrus didn't have supper that night and skipped lunch the next few weeks. He arranged with the couple who ran his boarding house to sweep out the floors, empty the trash, and do other light tasks for two dollars a week. At that rate he would have just enough for transportation back to Saranac Lake at the end of the session.

———•———

Cyrus was not the only one to write his wife following the lunch. Lloyd's letter, however, was typed rather than handwritten thanks to the typewriter in his association's office.

Albany, New York
February 1, 1883

My Dearest Alice,

Your memory is accurate. Assemblyman Cyrus Carter, with whom I had lunch today, is the Carter who testified in that murder trial in 1866. He sends his best wishes.

Carter is stubborn as a mule. I—or rather the Association—offered to pay for his lunch but he refused. I'm sure the lunch cost him a good part of his meager salary. Nor could I persuade him that the lumber companies' primary interest is providing jobs for workers. To placate him, I said I would try to get the Association to support a minimum wage for workers and compensation for injuries if he would vote against protecting the state lands,

However, I'd jeopardize my own standing if I brought ideas like that to the Board.

Alice, Dear, this lobbyist role is hard to play when I come up against a man of Cyrus Carter's integrity, though I can play it well enough as long as most of the legislators are not like Carter. But where is my integrity?

Carter has invited you, me, and the children to visit the Adirondacks, probably this summer after the session ends. I am eager to see this beautiful land that you rave about. The trip may unravel me even further. Here in Albany, I will continue to do what I'm paid for.

I expect to be home either next weekend or the following one. I cannot wait to see you, Donald, and Jane.

With all the love in the world,

Your husband
Lloyd Massing

Alice knew how conflicted her husband was about his job. She immediately wrote back:

Glens Falls, New York
February 7, 1883

Darling Lloyd,

I would like nothing more than to visit the Adirondacks with you and the children this summer! Please convey my sentiment to Mr. Carter and make arrangements with him for our visit.

Lloyd, Dear, when I took the children to your parents last weekend, your father said that the Association was extremely pleased with your work. (Of course, I did not tell him that you were not so pleased.) That means your reputation as a lobbyist is growing and that you might expect job offers (or even seek other jobs) from organizations that you might like better. You are also earning more and more. In a few years, that will give us more freedom.

The children are well and eager for your next visit. You have instilled a bit of the theater in them. They have been working on a surprise performance, which will première upon your return. Neither they nor I can wait.

Your loving wife,
Alice

———◆———

Over the next few weeks, Cyrus noticed Massing talking to the Assemblymen from the counties near his. Most of them were veterans of the Assembly and seemed to prefer the civilized atmosphere of Albany to their home districts. Some of the wealthy ones had houses in Albany where they lived with their families during the legislative season. Others preferred to leave their families behind. One of them, Stanley Zack from Clinton County, came up to Cyrus's desk at the end of one session, threw his arm around Cyrus as he started to leave, and said, "How about a beer, Cyrus? Help us get better acquainted. I'll buy the first round."

Reluctantly, Cyrus agreed. They went to a saloon near the Capitol.

Zack paid at the bar and they retreated with their mugs to a small table. After exchanging pleasantries, Stanley asked, "Has Lloyd Massing spoken to you yet?"

"Yeah, a couple of weeks ago."

"Whaddya think?"

"About what?"

"About the bill to forbid the sale of State lands."

Having not eaten since breakfast, and having not had any alcohol for many years, Cyrus's beer made him woozy. He had to concentrate hard on what Zack was saying.

"The Agriculture Committee is going to debate it tomorrow," Cyrus said.

"I know." Something clicked despite the wooziness. Was it a coincidence that Zack had approached him on this particular day?

"How are you gonna vote?" Zack asked.

Cyrus struggled to clear his brain. "How would you vote?"

Now it was Zack who was wary. He didn't want Cyrus to think that he was trying to pressure him. "It's a tough call. The lumberjacks I've heard from don't like the idea."

"Lumberjacks or the lumber companies?" Cyrus doubted that lumberjacks would write to their Assemblyman.

"Actually, it's the jobbers who I've heard from. But they

represent the workers."

Cyrus refrained from reaching for the handle of his mug. His mind was clearing. He thought of Ben Anderson.

"I guess you've never jacked, Stanley."

"How do you know that?"

"The jobbers are middlemen. They get paid by the companies to hire the jacks who do the work."

"So they need the jobs as much as the jacks."

"True. But they also want to keep as much money as they can for themselves, and squeeze as much work out of the jacks as they can." He paused, reached for the mug, and then decided against it. "But I guess you're right. Most of the workers would see limiting the supply of land for logging as cutting down their work."

"Well, the Lumberman's Association is against it. You know, Cyrus, if you get the association angry, your career here could be over in one term."

Cyrus grabbed the mug and drained it. Zack had finished his a few minutes earlier. Cyrus got up and steadied himself momentarily by placing his hands on the back of his chair. "That might be okay with me. I'm sorry, Stanley, one round is enough for me. I'll buy next time."

They shook hands and Cyrus headed back to his boarding house. The cold evening air felt good on his face.

Zack wondered whether the beer had been worth it.

———•———

When he got back to his boarding house, Cyrus found an envelope addressed to him propped on the breakfront in the sitting room. Quickly, he opened it and unfolded the letter. It was wrapped around a $5 bill. He went up to his room, lit the small kerosene lamp, and sat on the bed. The room had no chairs.

Saranac Lake

February 23, 1883

Cyrus,

I'm proud you didn't let this Mr. Massing pay for your lunch but disappointed that you agreed to dine with him. If you continue with this half-hearted "integrity" in Albany you might do more good at home.

The enclosed $5 comes from the money jar we keep for Tommy. Tommy is waiting to hear what you are doing to protect workers and the woods.

On Saturday, Lisa stayed with Tommy while I attended a meeting of the American Woman Suffrage Association whose leaders think we will get the right to vote by campaigning state by state. You should be talking to the suffragists in Albany instead of Mr. Massing and urging your colleagues to vote for women's suffrage.

The Weinbergs visited yesterday. They said that Jed is getting worse, and that he and Eleanor are likely to come up here soon.

Your wife,
Mary

Cyrus's head ached from just the one beer and Mary's letter didn't help. The five dollars she sent made him feel even worse. He hadn't asked for the money, which was needed for Tommy's well being more than for his.

The next morning he checked out of the boarding house. At the Capitol he collected the first part of his salary and left for Saranac Lake without going to the hearing room where the Agricultural Committee was scheduled to discuss the bill prohibiting the sale of state lands. He took the Delaware-and-Hudson train from Albany to Ausable Forks, the last stop. From there he took the cheapest seat on top of the stage back to Saranac Lake. Windblown and chilled, he walked briskly to his house on Helen Street in the darkness, avoiding the snow that had been piled up on the side of the street. Mary and Lisa were sitting around the kitchen table. Lisa got up as soon as he entered and ran to hug him. Mary got up more slowly and concentrated on clearing the table of dinner dishes. After a few moments Cyrus relinquished his grip and Lisa helped her mother clean up.

Matter of factly Mary asked, "Have you eaten?"

"Not for some time."

"Let me see what I can get." She busied herself in the pantry and came back with a plate of beans. "We finished all the smoked meat you left so the pickings have been slim."

Cyrus reached for his wallet and took out the five-dollar bill. He placed it in the jar for Tommy. He looked at Mary to make sure she noticed. "Do you think Tommy's asleep?"

"He dozes on and off at this hour. He needs to be turned or he'll get bedsores again." Mary reached the door to his room just before Cyrus. They went in together. Tommy lay propped on several pillows. "Hi, Darling," Mary cooed. "Look who's come home."

Cyrus came up to the bed and took Tommy's hand. Tommy grabbed it tightly.

"I'm gonna turn you a bit, honey, and then I'll change your pajamas." Tommy was taller and heavier than Mary. Mary had not shaved him since the previous day and he had brown-blonde stubble on his face. He put his arms around his mother as she bent and put her arms under his. She began to straighten up with her heavy load. Cyrus went to the other side of the bed and helped. "How do you manage without me?" he asked Mary.

"Lisa's strong enough to help. We've managed," she said curtly.

After Tommy was turned and cleaned, he reached for his pad. *Did you get the Assembly to vote for an hourly wage and compensation for injuries?* he wrote.

"Let's talk about it tomorrow, Tommy," Cyrus replied. Tommy nodded agreement.

By the time Cyrus returned to the kitchen, Lisa had gone to her room. Mary returned from the well, adding water to the pot simmering on the stove. Finally, after throwing another log into the stove, she sat facing Cyrus. "I didn't want to say much until Lisa left," she started. Cyrus nodded. She continued, her voice slightly hostile. "Whatever possessed you to eat lunch with that Massing fellow? You know you're going to vote to protect the woods." She paused. "I hope you told him that."

Cyrus finished chewing, got up, and with a glass scooped some water from the pot on the stove, returning to his seat to take a long swallow.

"I told him that if the State continued to sell land to the

lumber companies it would destroy the Adirondacks."

"You told him you'd vote against the sale, didn't you?"

"When we talked, the bill was still being drafted. I told him I wanted to look at it before I made any commitment." Mary got up in disgust; she grabbed Cyrus's empty plate and put it in the bucket for dirty dishes.

She turned back to him. "What's happened since then?"

"The bill was sent to Agriculture. The Committee started to debate it today."

"What? You left before the debate?" Mary asked in disbelief.

Cyrus put his head between his arms on the table. After a few moments he raised himself. "Your letter upset me a lot, Mary. I thought I could do more good here than in Albany."

Mary walked back to her chair. "Oh Cyrus, I didn't mean instantly. I thought I mentioned contacting the women suffragists in Albany so they could help you prepare a motion to give us the vote. Our movement is growing, even among men. There are other issues besides protecting the land."

That gave Cyrus an opening, although he did not mention the horse trade he had proposed to Lloyd. "Yes. I told Lloyd I hoped his association would support bills I was going to introduce to improve conditions for jacks—the bills Tommy was asking about."

Mentioning Tommy mollified Mary. "What did your friend Mr. Massing say?"

"He thought they were reasonable."

"He might think so, but surely the lumber companies aren't going to support laws telling them what to do."

"You might be right. But I think Massing will bring

them to his association. He isn't all bad."

"What's good about him?"

"He admits he's never been to the Adirondacks."

"What's good about that?" She thought for a moment, trying to read Cyrus's' mind. "You mean he's willing to come up here to see what damage logging has done?"

"That's right. I offered to take him and his family hiking for a few days after the session is over this summer."

Mary was taken aback. "Well, don't expect me to be nice to them."

"Oh, I forgot to mention that he's married to Ben Anderson's daughter."

"Was she the one he brought to Frank Miller's trial?"

"Yes. She apparently remembered our testimony."

"That's nice, but I'm surprised you think you can influence his views. He's got to do his association's bidding. Besides, you haven't even drafted those labor bills and the sale of state lands is going to come up this session."

Cyrus got up. "I'm glad I came home, Mary. I can't talk things through with anyone else."

———

Cyrus returned to Albany a week after he left. Once again, he arranged to do menial chores in his boarding house to earn back what the luncheon with Lloyd Massing had cost him plus his trip back to Saranac Lake. He was not too surprised to find a note Massing had left the day before. In it, Massing asked for another meeting when the Assembly recessed for lunch on Cyrus's first day back.

While Cyrus had been home, the Agriculture Committee had favorably reported the "forever wild" bill, prohibiting the sale of State lands in the Adirondack counties, to the Assembly floor. The bill had gotten its name from the clause proclaiming these lands to be forever wild. The bill was on the calendar to be debated by the Assembly in two days.

As Cyrus left the chamber on his first day, he saw Massing approaching him. His first reaction was to pretend he did not see him and walk away. But they had already made eye contact. Rather than meet Massing halfway, Cyrus stayed put and waited while Massing came up to him.

"I was surprised you weren't at the Agriculture Committee when it debated the 'forever wild' bill," Massing started.

"I had to return to Saranac Lake last week."

"Nothing serious, I hope."

"Giving my wife some relief in caring for our son." Cyrus did not say he went to consult with his wife. "Tommy's too heavy for his mother to turn him by herself. I don't know how she manages."

Massing took a small step backwards. "I'm sorry," was all he said. He started to say, "I hope he's better," but realized there was little likelihood of that. He had to make a quick decision about whether to proceed with lobbying Cyrus or withdraw.

After the Committee had passed the bill, Massing had traveled up to Glens Falls to meet with the Board of the Lumberman's Association. They had pressed him on the need to round up every last vote to defeat the bill, no matter what it took. Cyrus was his toughest nut; only verbal persuasion would work. "I know it's difficult for you, Cyrus, but now that you're back, are you going to let those rich City bosses tell you that more jobs can't be provided to the people of your county?"

Cyrus started to walk toward the exit, Massing close at his heels. "I'm sorry, Lloyd. I still haven't decided what to do. If your lumber companies showed signs of protecting the lumberjacks, it might help. Good day, Sir." Cyrus quickened his pace, leaving Massing, who quickly buttonholed another Assemblyman.

That night, Cyrus decided what he would do. He had not yet spoken on the floor of the Assembly, and the notion of speaking before that august body, with its polished orators, filled him with dread. Yet he had not run for office or been elected to be a passive participant. He stayed up late drafting his speech on the backs of envelopes with a pencil that grew shorter in a matter of hours as he whittled it down to keep the point sharp.

The bill was called to the floor the following morning. The sponsor from the Committee on Agriculture was the first to speak, followed by Stanley Zack from Clinton County. Zack opposed the bill saying it would leave his and the surrounding counties of the Adirondacks bereft of jobs. The Speaker recognized a few other Assemblymen who made brief remarks both pro and con. Cyrus listened attentively. His palms grew sweaty and he could feel his heart beating. When no other Assemblyman requested to speak, he raised his hand and was recognized by the Speaker. He approached the platform and stepped to the podium. With trembling hands he arranged the sheaths of envelope backs before him.

"Mr. Speaker, I have the honor to represent Franklin County, in the heart of the Adirondacks."

He looked up and departed from his written remarks to acknowledge Assemblyman Zack.

"As my esteemed colleague from neighboring Clinton County, Assemblyman Zack, has noted, the citizens of the Adirondacks depend on the forests for their livelihood. I myself was once a lumberjack. Many local farmers spend their winters chopping trees and bucking logs for the lumber companies. A good part of their produce goes to feed the lumberjacks. The lumber mills and, lately, the pulp mills, would not be there were it not for the forests. Homes are built with Adirondack lumber. The tanning industry, a large one in the Adirondacks, depends on hemlock bark. Most of the railroads that have come in the last ten years would not be there were it not for their role in getting logs to the mills."

Cyrus's hands stopped shaking as he became absorbed in his message. In the gallery, Massing listened with increased interest. Maybe he had won Cyrus's vote.

"Lumber is not the only resource the forest offers. Every year the number of tourists visiting the Adirondacks grows. Cutting down trees robs the land of its game, its fish, its pristine beauty, the features that attract travelers from downstate and beyond, even from foreign countries. They require food, accommodations, and guides. But the travelers are transients; they do not stay the year round and cannot sustain the local population.

"The lumber companies tell the citizens of Franklin County—and the other counties of the Adirondacks—that they are our saviors, that we cannot survive without them. But look what they do. When they finish logging the land they own, they move on, as they have done from Herkimer County, no longer paying taxes on the land they have pillaged, and leaving communities with lower revenues than when the companies started. If the companies buy state lands, the process will be repeated again and again. Mr. Speaker, we may be postponing the loss of livelihood for the people of Franklin County by giving the lumber companies access to State lands, but sooner or later we, or our children, or our children's children, will be devastated, along with the forests. Now these unborn have not elected me and my primary duty should be to those who have. I should, the lumber companies tell me, be grateful to them and oppose this bill. But, Mr. Speaker, I hesitate to do so for two reasons.

"First, the lumber companies are not interested in the health and welfare of their workers; they treat them only as a means to an end—the end of getting the most profit from their labor. Lumberjacks work from before dawn to after sunset, sometimes more than twelve hours a day. In many places they are still paid on the basis of the number of trees they cut; this saps their energy and increases the likelihood of accidents. When jacks are paid by the hour or day and not by the piece, as is beginning to happen over the vigorous, sometimes violent, opposition of their employers, the rate of accidents goes down without any appreciable decrease in the number of trees cut.

"Despite the long hours at hard labor, most lumberjacks receive only two meals a day, not always of the highest quality. They sleep in crowded, vermin-ridden quarters, with poor sanitary conditions. In one camp I worked in, several workers were brought down with typhus. The next year, in another, cholera killed two workers and three others got very sick. Sadly, the situation has not changed much over the twenty-five years since this happened.

"The second reason has to do with the condition of the forests themselves. Now that railroads are replacing river floats as the means to get logs to the mills, the forests are being stripped bare. Hardwoods, which don't float, are now falling under the axe, along with the softwoods, which do. The companies make sure that saleable logs get transported, but they leave the lopped branches to become tinder on the ground. Lightning strikes sometimes ignite fires, which spread rapidly through the dead wood and often reach live stands of trees, quickly demolishing them. I'm told by loggers who work with the railroads that sparks from wood-burning locomotives can also ignite dry tinder, starting fires and destroying forests.

"The lumber companies think only of today and not tomorrow. They want us to think the same way. For every forest destroyed by cutting or fire, new seedlings can be planted. The current owners won't be around to see them grow to harvestable timber, but future generations of owners will. Cut trees can be replaced with seedlings and a rate of cutting managed to sustain the forests at all times, but the companies will have none of that.

"Mr. Speaker, I might be induced to support the sale of State lands with their valuable stands of virgin forest, but not without safeguards to the lumberjacks and to the forests. I am talking about hourly wages replacing piecework, about a ten or even an eight-hour day, and about compensating workers injured or killed on the job, or their families. When I jacked, a co-worker died after a foreman's backswing accidentally struck his head. My best friend was killed trying to break a logjam, and just three years ago, my son—who cleared trees for the Adirondack Railroad—was paralyzed from the waist down and lost his speech when he had to jump off a trestle to avoid being crushed by a runaway railroad car. In none of these cases did the worker or his surviving relatives receive a penny.

"I am talking about good forest management: about replacing every cut tree with a seedling, about leaving some trees standing, and about building towers to spot forest fires and establish water reserves to douse them. These measures will not reduce jobs. They might even create new ones.

They will preserve the forests so not only will the
workers of today benefit, but the workers of tomorrow as well. I am also talking about good human
management. Mr. Speaker, I intend to vote for the
bill before us. Thank you very much."

Cyrus walked back to his seat in the Assembly to only a
quiet ruffling of papers. The Speaker recognized Assemblyman Zack who rose from his desk. "Mr. Speaker, I call the
question."

The Speaker looked around the floor. No hands were
raised. "Without objection, we will proceed to vote on the
proposal offered by the honorable Assemblyman from New
York County to forbid the sale of state lands. All in favor sig-
nify by saying 'Aye.'" The loudness of the "ayes" that echoed
through the chamber surprised Cyrus. "All opposed?" Most
of the "nays" came from Assemblymen representing the
Adirondack and Catskill counties. Among the Assemblymen
from those regions, only Cyrus and the Assemblyman from
Herkimer County, where the forests had already been heavily lumbered, had voted "aye." (Cyrus wondered whether
the speech had persuaded him.) The populous cities and the
downstate and west state farmers had carried the vote. "The
bill passes," intoned the Speaker, pounding his gavel. At his
seat, Cyrus took out his handkerchief and mopped his brow.

12

Poaching

A S was his custom when little work was waiting to be done and the weather was not too cold, William sat in the rocker on the front porch of the inn, smoking his after-breakfast pipe contentedly, the early summer sun warming his wrinkled face and the breeze ruffling his soft white hair. He could make out the purple and yellow pansies and the white and striped petunias Lisa had planted along the edge of the clearing a few days ago. He knew Lisa did not come out to the inn just to keep William company. If he was not mistaken a wedding would soon take place.

After Tommy's calamity, Peter O'Rourke Jr. had continued to work for the Adirondack Railroad as its tracks were laid all the way to Tupper Lake. When the last stretch was completed in 1882, he got the job as stationmaster at Axton Landing, making sure the tracks were clear and in good repair. The job required Peter to live at the station with a skeleton crew. On Thursday and Sunday, when fewer trains ran, he was able to get away midday to meet Lisa at Corey's Inn, weather and Lisa's schedule permitting.

When Lisa galloped up and hitched her horse, William was fast asleep in his rocker. She tiptoed up the inn steps and into the large room. At the moment, there were no guests, and William had given his helpers off until the next day, Friday, when he expected several to arrive. She rummaged in the kitchen, preparing lunch for Peter, William, and herself. When she finished, she went to the porch again, carelessly letting the screen door slam behind her. William opened his eyes. "Thought someone was shooting at me," he smiled, feeling himself all over to make sure he was intact.

"I'm sorry for the noise, Uncle. How are you?"

"Other than being rudely awakened, couldn't be better, child. Perfect weather and now you've come to keep me company, at least until that whippersnapper friend of yours arrives."

Lisa laughed and looked down the trail on which Peter would arrive. "I'm not a child anymore, Uncle."

William ignored the remark. "Have you fixed us a nice lunch, Lisa?"

"I had to make do with what you have. Looks like the remains of a roasted turkey. I fixed it on the bread you baked last week and I'm on my way to get some greens from the garden to moisten it up. Your ice is running low, Uncle; I hope you've scheduled another shipment soon."

"The iceman comes on Monday. I reckon we'll manage until then. It would be nice if your father would pick up his rifle and shoot down a couple of geese. I hear 'em yakking overhead."

"He just got back from Albany yesterday. Give him a few days."

"How'd things go in Albany?"

"Papa made his first speech, opposing the sale of state lands to the lumber companies."

"Must've convinced everybody."

"He doesn't think he did, but the bill protecting the state

lands won! Papa thinks his vote may have cost him reelection. The lumber companies are sure to go after him. He invited the lobbyist for the lumber companies to come up here with his family for a few days. The man's never been to the Adirondacks. Papa says he should see what damage the lumber companies have done."

"Lobbyist? Those are the fellas that try to persuade the legislators, right?" Lisa nodded. "Sounds like Cyrus is trying to lobby the lobbyist. If he thinks the green of the woods is any match for the green of lumbermen's money, Cyrus is a bigger fool than I thought."

"Uncle! You shouldn't speak about Papa that way."

Lisa's repeated glances down the trail were finally rewarded as Peter appeared on the cutoff trail from the Indian Carry. "Excuse me, Uncle, I see Peter coming." Before he could even grunt she flew off the porch and ran down the trail. The two lovers greeted each other with a passionate kiss and tight hug. Hand-in-hand they approached the inn. Peter was old enough to sport a black beard that he kept well trimmed. He was taller and sturdier than his father, Peter Sr., who he had already surpassed in years. Lisa, who resembled a young beautiful Mary, was proud and pleased to have kept friends with Peter as he matured from a small, scrawny boy into a handsome man who now had some authority over others. The boys at Saranac Lake who eyed her knew that she could not be pried from Peter.

"Your uncle's not going to be happy with what I have to tell him."

Lisa turned as they walked, to fasten her eyes on Peter's. The gesture was enough to express her concern.

"You know your uncle's southern boundary is the river

after it bends to the west." Lisa nodded. "Well, coming back last Thursday, I saw some of Smead's men marking trees on the north bank, Corey's stand of virgin timber. They told me they were following orders. When I returned today, several of Corey's trees had been cut. Smead—or at least the jobber—is poaching."

"Maybe we shouldn't tell Uncle. It will upset him. He's an old man—he can hardly see or walk."

"We've got to tell him. The boundary is clear."

They were almost at the steps to the inn. "Yes, you're right, but let's have lunch before you say anything." They glanced up at William who sat slumped in the rocker, his unlit pipe in hand. They took the opportunity for another kiss and hug.

William opened one eye. "You two are acting as if you're already hitched. How much longer am I going to wait for my lunch?" he asked with mock irritability.

"Uncle, you shouldn't pretend to be asleep and spy on us."

"Pretend? I was fast asleep but your sparking was loud enough to wake Rip van Winkle." William bent down to pick up his cane. With one hand on the cane and the other on the arm of the rocker he slowly pulled himself up and headed for the door to the inn. Lisa and Peter went to the garden to pick some lettuce, and then entered the inn through the kitchen door.

The dining room was cool and dark despite the midday heat, and they ate on one of the dining tables. As he did every time they met, William asked Peter, "How's the railroad doing, young man?"

"Nothing new, Mr. Corey, but Smead's poaching." Lisa kicked Peter under the table, but it was too late.

"What do you mean?"

"They're felling trees on your stand along the northern bank of the Raquette."

"I thought maybe my hearing was getting better lately. Seemed the clang of axes was louder. I'll be damned."

"How about asking Lisa's father what he thinks?" Peter suggested. "He should be able to put a stop to it."

William turned to Lisa. "Lisa Dear, will you bring your father up to date and ask for his opinion on the matter? You can be his messenger, but I wouldn't mind a visit from the Honorable Cyrus Carter and his charming wife."

Peter got up reluctantly, having to return to work. Lisa rose with him. "Of course, Uncle. I'll tell him as soon as I see him. I'm sure he and mother will come and visit and discuss the matter further." She walked outside with Peter and started toward the Carry trail with him and continued partway down the Carry until they reached the junction with the Axton trail where they embraced and parted. Returning to the inn, Lisa cleared and washed the dishes, fondly gave William a gentle good-bye kiss, mounted her horse, and returned to the village.

<hr/>

The following Sunday Cyrus, Mary, and Lisa drove out to Corey's in the family wagon. Peter had arrived first and when the Carters pulled up, he suggested to Lisa that they go down to the foot of the Carry for a swim. The weather had been unremittingly dry and hot. Lisa had brought swimming attire, thinking a swim would be nice, and they scampered off as if they were children half their age.

Cyrus pulled out four dressed ducks from the buckboard and brought them into the kitchen where William was puttering around. "What a surprise," William said. "I didn't expect my prayer for your visit to be answered so quickly." He eyed the ducks and Cyrus promptly handed them over. "I prefer geese but ducks do make better eating. You'll stay for dinner I hope?" He handed the ducks to one of his helpers, who had returned since Lisa's last visit. "And maybe supper."

"As long as it's not too late. We don't want to leave Tommy home alone for too long," Mary replied.

"How's the lad doing?" William asked.

"Amazingly well," Mary replied. "He's strengthened his arms and shoulders and wheels himself around almost effortlessly. We asked him to come today but he signaled that he'd rather stay home, read and write, and move around the house in his wheelchair. It bothers him that he needs other people's help for simple tasks, like getting into the wagon. He's written letters to John and the Masons and seems more cheerful. I still hope he'll speak one of these days."

"Only problem," Cyrus complained, "is the wheelchair is almost as wide as the door frames and if Tommy's not careful he skins his knuckles. I might have to widen the door jambs."

William spoke to his helper about preparing the dinner, took his cane, and led Cyrus and Mary out to the porch where he sat down in his rocker. Mary and Cyrus pulled up chairs with slanted, slatted bottoms and backs that were already being called "Adirondack" throughout the country.

"Lisa told us about the poaching," Cyrus said. "After dinner, I'll walk over to Axton Landing and see for myself. If the jobber is there, I'll discuss it with him. If not, I'll ride over to Smead headquarters early in the week. Smead might not even know about it. In either case, we'll put a stop to it or they'll have to answer to the Courts."

"Thanks, Cyrus. I'd like to know how many trees they took down. You think we can get something back for them?"

"I'll see what I can do."

Lisa and Peter came racing up the Carry trail, Peter chasing Lisa but obviously letting her win. They reached the steps and stopped to catch their breath. Their heads were still wet.

"If you don't mind," William uttered to them, "why don't you go in and lend a hand to get the meal ready. We've set a table for our guests on the porch, and we can eat here, too." The two youngsters went inside, Mary accompanying them. William chuckled to Cyrus. "Seems about twenty-five years ago I remarked to you that it looked like Jean and Mary were serious. Sure looks as if Peter and Lisa are serious."

The comment startled Cyrus. He hadn't thought of Jean with Mary for a long time, but he well remembered Corey's remark. "I only hope that Peter lives much longer than Jean," Cyrus replied.

After dinner, Cyrus accompanied Peter up the trail to Axton. Before they left, Peter openly kissed Lisa on the lips. William let out a long whistle, causing Lisa to step back and blush. "When are you two going to get hitched?" William asked bluntly.

"I've got to build up my savings," Peter answered, seemingly prepared for the question. "Lisa's going to start teaching in the fall. That should help. Maybe next year." His voice rose with this last sentence; he looked at Mary and Cyrus as he talked, as if expecting approbation. "I haven't officially asked you for her hand, and until I do, I can't propose."

"But we've talked about it," Lisa said.

On the trail, Cyrus said to Peter, "You don't need my permission to marry Lisa. Mary and I would tell Lisa if we thought she was making a mistake, but we haven't and we won't. You two have been very responsible, and we know you'll make the move when you're able and ready." Cyrus was surprised that his youngest child would be the first to marry. "How's your mother, Peter? We haven't seen much of her lately."

"She's doing all right since my grandfather died. He left her a little money, and I give her part of what I earn. That's adding to the delay, too."

They turned southwest before reaching Axton, coming on to Corey's land on the north bank of the river. Cyrus commented that the river was below its usual level for July; Peter added that he had noticed it falling over the past few weeks. "They are already talking of drought downstate. If it doesn't rain soon, we'll have the danger of forest fire," Cyrus said. The forest in front of them thinned out, and soon they came to an open area marked by tree stumps whose light tan-yellow surfaces indicated they had been recently cut. Lopped branches, pine needles, and leaves already turning crisp brown were strewn over the ground, trampling small shrubs struggling to rise. Across the Raquette, they saw logs piled not far from the railroad track, which ran parallel to the river. Presumably, Corey's logs had been floated across. Beyond the other bank, on Smead's land, the forest was decimated. Only the dead toppings of the evergreen softwoods remained, along with a few scrawny maple, beech and birch. They continued walking west along the north bank for another quarter of a mile where the cutting on both sides of the river ended and forest closed in, with a thick canopy of leafy branches arching across the river. Retracing their steps to the Axton trail, they entered the lumber camp. Peter walked over to the office of the lumber camp and knocked. No one answered.

"Just as well," said Cyrus. "I'll go see Smead's people tomorrow or the next day."

———•———

After Peter and Cyrus had gone off investigating, William sent his paying guests on a short hike up Little Panther Mountain. Then, Mary invited her uncle on a walk to the Carry. "You can hold my arm in the rough spots where your cane won't help and we can turn around anytime."

"I would love it," answered William. Mary helped him down the steps and they headed toward the Carry trail, not talking for a while. The air was still in the afternoon heat. Despite the shade of the spruce and birch arching overhead, it was not long before they both were sweating. Bent with age, William held Mary's arm with his right hand and used the cane with his left. Mary was still a handsome woman, standing tall and straight, her hair a luxuriant brown with a few streaks of grey and a few furrows on her forehead, but her face was otherwise unblemished. They walked in silence until William finally spoke. "Mary, Dear, I think I would have died a long time ago had you not been around and had your family here."

Mary did not reply immediately. She helped William over a few rocks and exposed roots. "I have no regrets, Uncle. But you're sounding old and nostalgic. We still have a lot to look forward to."

"Lisa's wedding for one I suppose. You'll become a grandmother and I would become a great grand uncle." He thought a few more minutes. "I reckon the inn will prosper, but I am worried about the woods shrinking."

"I know. Cyrus showed me the speech he gave in Albany opposing the sale of state lands. He wrote it on the backs of envelopes. It was brilliant! Of course, I'm biased, but Eleanor Mason wrote me that it was mentioned in the New York City papers."

"A powerful speech will be no match for the lumber companies. They'll be out to get Cyrus now."

"People downstate are blaming the drought on the logging that's already been done."

"It's too bad people have to suffer in order to make change, but I guess that's the way it is." William let out a small "ouch" as his ankle twisted off a small rock and he momentarily lost his balance, leaning heavily on Mary. He was not as heavy as he had once been, and Mary was able to keep him from falling. She worried that when no one was about he skipped meals. They stood still for a moment, William clinging to Mary. "I'm okay," he said after a moment, "but maybe we should start back."

They reversed direction and walked quietly, William holding Mary's arm tightly. "What do you hear from John?" he asked after a while.

"We've had two letters since I wrote him about Tommy's accident. So far as I know he's still in Chicago working for the McCormick Harvester Works. He's joined the Knights of Labor and is advocating for the eight-hour day—"

William cut her short. "Eight-hour day. What's the world coming to? I used to work almost double that without anybody telling me. What are workers supposed to do the rest of the time—drink, go whoring?"

Mary blushed. "Uncle, it's not the same. You could pick when you wanted to work and what you wanted to do. Workers like John have no choice. If they want to survive they have to take what they're offered. And it's not only men. To feed their families, women have to work, too. John writes that seamstresses work up to sixteen hours a day and take home only a dollar and a half a week! It's criminal. They barely see their children; sometimes the children have to work, too."

William did not answer right away. "What's he aiming to do about it?"

"The workers have formed unions. When they get angry enough they'll strike and eventually get their demands met. You remember Tommy organized the jacks working for the Adirondack Railroad Company and got a standard wage and a ten-hour day. Peter Junior tells me that still is the rule."

"You know, Mary, I've always wondered how that railway car became uncoupled. I know it's no comfort to you, but maybe it wasn't an accident."

They stopped walking and faced each other. "Yes, Uncle. That's occurred to me, and Cyrus, too," she said with a catch in her voice and tears welling in her eyes. No more words came out. Simultaneously, they hugged each other until Mary regained her composure. "Cyrus and I have talked about it but concluded it would be too difficult to prove. Tommy agrees. We'll never know."

Cyrus and Peter and Mary and William returned to the inn within an hour of each other. The guests who William had sent off to climb Little Panther returned a little later, complaining of the black flies and not much of a view. "Well, you could try Ampersand Mountain tomorrow, but you'd need to get an early start," said William. He turned to Cyrus. "What do you think, Cyrus?"

"There's a good trail now, steep in some places, but I've taken many a party up it without mishap and with considerable delight at the magnificent view. Thanks to Verplanck Colvin burning it for his survey, the top has become bare. You can see many lakes and mountains. Mile-for-mile it's one of the best climbs in the Adirondacks."

They had supper on the porch, William lighting smudge pots whose smoke kept the mosquitoes at bay. When they finished and the Carters prepared to depart, Cyrus said to William, "By the way, a gentleman I met in Albany is bringing his family up to the Adirondacks next week. I want to show them around a bit."

"You mean the lobbyist for the lumber companies?"

"How did you know?"

"I told him, Papa," Lisa blurted out, sensing William's embarrassment if he had to reveal his source.

Mary chimed in. "I told Cyrus he would be a fool to think that he could change Mr. Massing's mind."

"Massing's the name of the lobbyist?" William asked.

"Yes," Mary replied, and he's married to Ben Anderson's daughter."

William looked puzzled for a moment until the name struck a chord. "You mean the jobber at Axton Landing when Jean was—" He realized what he was about to say and thought the better of it.

"Yes, the very same," said Cyrus. "I know it seems ridiculous, but I can't let a man who has never seen the Adirondacks take the word of the lumber companies that they're not doing harm. Anyway, William, I'm going to meet them on Saturday at Ausable Forks, camp near Keene Heights, and hike up Noonmark with them early on Sunday, unless they're churchgoers. I want to show Massing the result of the cutting and the fire damage. If the weather holds, we'll return to Saranac Lake on Sunday evening. If we get bogged down, we'll camp at the Cascade Lakes Sunday night and get home on Monday. If we get home on Sunday, I'll bring them over here on Monday for a few days, until they return to Glens Falls Thursday or Friday. If not, they'll come on Tuesday. I don't know whether Mr. Massing or the Lumberman's Association will pay their lodging with you, but I don't expect you to give them any special consideration."

"I won't. You can also show them how Smead has poached on my property."

"I intend to do that."

———•———

When Lisa, Mary, and Cyrus returned home at dusk, they found Tommy lying on the ground a few feet from the house. He was on his back but grinned at them sheepishly. Alongside him was the wheelchair, which had toppled over. Mary looked him over quickly, finding nothing wrong. Tommy put his arms around her as she pulled him to a sitting position. Cyrus righted the wheelchair and the two of them seated Tommy in it. He insisted on rolling himself up the ramp into the house. He grabbed a pad and a new Ticonderoga pencil, which he had sharpened, and scrawled a note: *I guess I am still reckless. Went too fast over an exposed root. Sorry for the trouble.* He showed it to Mary and Cyrus, who both laughed and hugged him again.

13

The Massings' Visit

CYRUS was at the Ausable Forks station when the midday train arrived from Glens Falls. Lloyd Massing descended the steps from the passenger car and then helped his wife, a small woman wearing a beige-colored hoop skirt, a white blouse, and a wide-brimmed pink hat covered by a gauzy scarf tied under her chin. Next, Lloyd helped his two children, also dressed as if they were going to church or a wedding. While Lloyd headed to the baggage car to retrieve their luggage, Alice and the children turned in the opposite direction toward Cyrus, who, at the same time, walked toward them. She offered her hand. "Alice Massing, Mr. Carter. Thank you so much for the invitation. We are looking forward to our visit. The children have never been in the mountains, and I only came through once before. It's also new to Lloyd."

"Pleased to meet you, Mrs. Massing." He bent slightly to shake hands with her two children as she introduced them: "Donald, Jane, this is Mr. Carter." Donald thrust his hand out boldly and gave Cyrus a good squeeze for a seven-year old. Shyly, Jane extended one hand while the other clutched a doll.

With the help of the porter, Lloyd came up with their luggage—a hatbox, several suitcases, and two long woolen sheaths, which Cyrus guessed contained Massing's fishing rod and rifle bought for the occasion. Cyrus was astounded. He remembered telling Massing to bring comfortable clothes for roughing it. Lloyd shook Cyrus's hand. "Cyrus, so good of you to meet us. We are ready to begin our voyage." Cyrus grasped Massing's arm above the elbow, pulling him out of earshot of his family. In low tones, he said, "Lloyd, you have brought too much uh…uh…stuff. I won't be able to fit it all in the buckboard along with the four of you. I know the stationmaster, and I suggest we leave most of the luggage here. I hope you've each brought some rugged clothes, which you can change into in a private room here."

"Won't we need a change of clothes? What about dinners? Won't we dress for them?"

Cyrus laughed. "We are not going to the Governor's Ball or to Mr. Durant's great camp, Pine Knot. For the first few days, we'll eat and sleep in the same clothes. A swim now and then will keep you from smelling ripe."

Looking doubtful, Lloyd returned to confer with his wife, while Cyrus remained a distance apart. Much to his surprise—he thought it would be the other way round—he heard Mrs. Massing say, "I told you we were bringing too much."

Cyrus helped the Massings take their luggage into the small station house where Alice rummaged through the suitcases to pull out the "rugged clothes"—denim overalls and work shirts—for the children and her. She led the children into the adjoining room while Massing got his clothes out and then closed the valises. In the meantime, Cyrus arranged with the stationmaster to store the luggage until their return.

A simpler Alice Massing emerged with her children. Shorn of the finery, Alice Massing was small and slim. She had fine features and bright eyes. Her face was unblemished. To Cyrus, Alice bore no resemblance to her father, Ben Anderson.

Although they were now dressed more suitably, Cyrus recognized immediately that their clothes were being inaugurated that day. A few minutes later, Massing emerged similarly attired. They walked over to the buckboard, where Cyrus assigned seats, Donald between Cyrus and Lloyd in front, and Alice and Jane on the second seat. They loaded the essential baggage, including Massing's rod and rifle, in back where Cyrus had laid in basic supplies and his own sparse gear. As she mounted, Jane politely asked Cyrus, "Mr. Carter, do you think there's room for Betsy?"

Cyrus looked at the doll. "I think we can squeeze her in."

Holding the reins, Cyrus summarized their itinerary, including a visit to the Ausable Lakes, then a Sunday hike up nearby Noonmark. "The mountain's a bit out of the way, but it has a splendid view and teaches us a few lessons." They had no objection. "I'm sure climbing a mountain will be more instructive to the children than squirming around in the pew at church," Alice said.

They covered the twenty-five miles to Beede's Hotel at Keene Heights in three hours. The Massings were astounded to see the three-story structure emerge in the woods as they rounded the trail approaching it. "Are we sleeping here tonight?" Donald asked.

"No, we'll ask Mr. Beede if we can go farther toward the Lakes," Cyrus replied. "We'll water and feed the horses, set up camp, and do a little fishing."

"Are we going to sleep in tents?" Donald asked.

"It will be too warm in tents. I suggest we sleep under the stars." Cyrus pointed up to the puffs of clouds. "If the clouds haven't gathered this late in the day, it's not likely to rain. If I'm wrong, I can build a lean-to very quickly." Obtaining Beede's permission, Cyrus led his party two miles farther, at which point the road narrowed to a trail too narrow for the wagon. "We'll unload here." He gave each of them, including Jane, something to carry to a small, flat clearing a few yards away where they heard the rush of the Ausable River.

The children dropped their loads and ran toward the river. "Be careful," Lloyd yelled after them. Cyrus took the horses to the river for a good long drink and then tethered them to nearby trees and gave them their oats.

After arranging camp to his liking, Cyrus got his and Lloyd's fishing rods from the wagon. He led Alice and Lloyd to the river, where they gathered the children and walked a half-mile to the junction of the river and Rainbow Brook. "If I'm not mistaken the fishing should be good here." At Cyrus's suggestion, Alice and the children stepped across the river on stones to follow the brook a short distance to Rainbow Falls.

Removing his battered felt hat, Cyrus undid a hook from the hat band, attached it to one end of the fishing line that was wound around the crown of his hat and tied the other end to his pole, a sapling whittled its entire length and worn especially smooth at the root end by frequent handling. He dug for a worm and tied it onto the hook. Carefully unwinding the line from around the hat, which he placed back on his head, he dropped his line into the water below a promising eddy. Lloyd, in the meantime, had assembled his rod and, from the large collection on his jacket, was deciding on a fly. By the time he was ready to cast, Cyrus had caught two ten-inch trout. Lloyd stepped out on a partially wet slab of concrete wedged in the river where the brook entered. He whipped his rod back and forth a few times and then let the line go. The fly caught on a low overhanging hemlock branch. "I'm sorry, Cyrus, I don't have the knack yet."

Cyrus climbed on a boulder and reached up to free the fly. "Fly fishing is not easy; just keep trying."

Lloyd gave up flexing his rod back and forth. He imitated what Cyrus was doing, gently tossing his line into a promising pool. After ten tries he got a bite. In his excitement he started to slip off the slab. To keep from falling he let go of his rod. Cyrus tried to catch it, but the fish had swallowed the hook and darted off at great speed, trailing the rod behind him. "That's one dead trout won't come to anyone's table, but someone might fish out a nice rod someday."

Empty-handed, Lloyd stood up and brushed his hands on the seat of his pants. "Where'd that slab come from, anyway?"

As Cyrus continued to fish, he pointed upstream. "From the dam at the outlet of the lower lake. We'll see it later. Your lumber industry got the State to build the dam so logs could be stored on the lake. In the spring, the rising water would float the logs over the dam to a mill on the Ausable River. The first dam washed out while it was still under construction, but a second one held for a couple of years, until some freak fall rains caused an avalanche of mud and rocks down Rainbow Brook."

"You mean the brook Alice and the children are climbing?" Lloyd asked with alarm.

"The very same—but don't worry, Lloyd, there isn't going to be an avalanche today. Anyway, the rubble blocked the river, and water backed up to the dam, bursting it and sending fragments, like the one you're standing on, downstream. The worst part was that when the dam broke suddenly, water flooded the whole valley. Bridges were washed out and six people were killed, not to mention livestock. All to help get logs to the mill." While he was talking, Cyrus gutted the fish he had caught. He thought he heard Lloyd mutter, "damn lumber companies," but he wasn't sure. Before he finished they heard Alice and the children talking and laughing as they approached the confluence of the brook and the river. They emerged soaking wet. "Did you take a slip, too?" Cyrus asked.

"No," Alice answered. "Why? Did someone slip here?"

"I did," Lloyd answered, "and lost my rod, too." Alice came up and threw her arms around him. "Oh dear, I'm so sorry. You just bought it. Now we'll have to rely on Mr. Carter for our catch."

"Please call me Cyrus."

Alice eyed the fish that Cyrus had strung up, five in all. She turned to her husband. "How many did you catch, Darling?"

Before he could answer, Cyrus pointed to the biggest one. "This one's his, Mrs. Massing."

"My goodness!" She hugged her husband. "Cyrus, if I'm going to call you by your first name then you have to call me Alice." They started back up to their camp.

"Daddy," said Donald as they walked up the trail, twisting his head back to speak to his father who followed him closely, "we saw this enormous waterfall. There wasn't much water coming down, but it was really high."

"How did you get wet, Son?"

Donald faced forward to check his footing, and then continued. "The water was low enough for us to walk out on the rocks and stick our heads under the falls. Our clothes got splashed, but mommy said they'd dry soon." Lloyd shot a glance back at Alice who was holding Jane's hand as the girl chattered away.

Cyrus built a fire. The children and Alice stood close by to dry. He went to the wagon and took out a loaf of bread, some other victuals, lard, and a frying pan. With his hunting knife, he cut some summer squash and potatoes into small cubes and fried them for a couple of minutes then added the trout, turning them once after about three minutes. He gave a bucket to Donald and asked him to fill it with water from the river.

"Is it clean enough to drink?" Lloyd asked.

"I'm sure it is. The water's flowing rapidly—lots of bubbles," Cyrus explained.

After supper, Cyrus cut hemlock boughs for mattresses and then invited the Massings to walk to the Lower Lake. "There's still two hours of daylight and tonight's a full moon, so it'll be up early. If we walk briskly we can make it in twenty minutes." Cyrus doused the fire with the rest of the water Donald had drawn.

They started off at a quick pace, but after five minutes, Jane began to lag and Lloyd put her on his shoulders. "Just be careful of low branches," Cyrus cautioned.

The sun was still above the horizon as they reached the narrow, mirror-smooth lake. Alice let out a gasp of delight. "I've never seen anything so beautiful." Close by on the left, as if carved in the cliffs by a master sculptor, was an Indian head in profile—standing sentinel over the lake—his craggy face reflected upside down in the water. Beyond, two peaks, the recently named Colvin and the other nameless, jutted upwards. Straight ahead the lake ended in a stand of evergreens. Cyrus followed Alice's glance. "This is Lower Ausable Lake. A short distance beyond is the Upper Lake." Alice turned to her right, took in the jagged peaks of Sawteeth Mountain above the lake and followed them to the most awesome view: the bare rock face of Gothic Mountain. Glinting in the setting sun, it towered over the verdant mountainside. "I can hardly breathe. It's so overwhelming." Lloyd came up with Jane and set her down. "It is rather nice," he commented as he took in the same panoramic view.

Alice spied a guideboat pulled up on the shore a few yards from where they stood. "Wouldn't it be wonderful to go out on the lake and catch a better view of the mountains?"

"As a matter of fact," Cyrus replied, "I have Beede's permission to use the boat as long as we're back by dark."

Alice took Jane's hand and started toward the boat. Jane pulled back. "I don't want to go, Mommy. I'm tired."

"I'll take her back, Darling," Lloyd said. "I'm tired myself. What about you, Donald?"

The boy had been skimming flat stones on to the lake, disturbing its placid surface as the waves rippled out from each impact. "Do you want to stay or go?" Alice asked him as Cyrus set the oars in the locks and readied the boat.

"If I go back now, can we build a fire, Dad?" Donald asked.

"It is getting chilly. I suppose we can if you gather wood," his father replied.

"Then I'll go back with you and Jane."

Cyrus told them, "If you build a fire, cut some green sticks, and carve them to a point at one end, I've got a treat for you when your mom and I get back."

Lloyd put Jane on his shoulders and took Donald by the hand. "Are you sure you want to go without us, Dear?" he asked his wife, whom Cyrus was helping to get settled on the stern seat.

"Yes I do. I'm in good hands. You heard, we've got to be home before dark."

Cyrus was amused that she already called their camp "home." He pushed off and took his seat, facing Alice. They rowed without speaking until they were about a third of the way across the lake. Lloyd and the children had disappeared into the woods.

"I see what you mean, Mr. Carter—"

"Cyrus," he corrected.

"—About the beauty of this place. Lloyd didn't really believe you when you told him he had to see it to understand it."

"Do you think he's beginning to understand?"

"I don't know. He's been awfully quiet. Losing his fishing rod—he was so looking forward to using it—upset him. And he does worry about the children. I do too of course, but I know them better than he does. They are not likely to do anything that will get them in trouble."

"Like ducking their head under the falls?"

"That was my idea!" They both laughed. "So far as beginning to understand, ask Lloyd at the end of the trip."

Cyrus pointed to the hills on the north shore. "That's what the Adirondacks were like before the lumbering started. Through the spruce you can pick out the white pines on the hillside; they're the trees with a girth of about twenty feet. You'll see a contrast in a few minutes. Tomorrow, we'll climb to some lovely vistas but you'll see more damage that lumbering has done."

"I hope the climbing won't be too strenuous. Jane is getting too big to sit on Lloyd's shoulders. If he aches, he might curse the mountains more than embrace them."

"I can carry her without any trouble." Alice's face, framed by her auburn hair, glowed as it reflected the setting sun. Seeing her enchantment, Cyrus turned around to look southwest. A few clouds were bathed in orange, others were red. At the horizon the blue sky turned turquoise. They reached the west shore in silence. Cyrus got up and took Alice's hands to help her out of the boat. He noticed how soft they were compared to Mary's. He pulled the boat farther up the beach while Alice looked back to see more of Gothics and beyond it the shoulders of Armstrong mountain and the Wolfjaws.

"It's just a short walk to the Upper Lake. You can't have come this far without seeing it."

"Let's go," she said, following Cyrus briskly up the trail alongside the brook that ran between the two lakes. The Upper Lake was more desolate. The hills rising out of its shores were barren, mostly stumps and low lying shrubs and saplings. Farther back, however, Haystack Mountain rose gloriously out of the gathering dusk. Pointing to it, Cyrus said, "That's the third highest peak in these parts."

Alice turned her glance from the peak to the bare, brown hills in the foreground. "Lumbering?" Cyrus nodded. "Will the trees grow back?"

"It's been twenty years or more since this hillside was cut. A few white birches have sprung up. You can't see them in this light but there are lots of blueberry bushes just coming into bloom. In another ten or twenty years, the spruce, cedar, hemlock, and fir will dominate; the white birch will decay and the berry bushes won't have enough light. The process will take longer if there's fire. There are plenty of dead limbs and branches that lightning could ignite like a tinderbox if this drought continues."

Alice shivered. Cyrus couldn't tell whether his narrative affected her or whether it was the cooler evening air. He took off his top shirt and placed it around her shoulders. "Thank you," she said. "I guess we'd better head back."

On the Lower Lake, Alice faced east and watched the moon rise. "I can see why you love these woods." She paused, letting her hands trail in the warm water. "And yet you've helped destroy them."

Surprised by her frontal attack, Cyrus did not answer for almost a minute. When he started, Alice immediately regretted she had been so brutal. "I knew your father, Alice, and I daresay you've never been poor and your husband's family is even better off than yours." He pulled hard on his left oar to head the boat to the landing. "When I was eight my drunken father destroyed our home and himself. At sixteen, I decided

I could best help my mother and younger brothers and sisters by getting a job. As soon as I earned enough to buy an axe, I got a job jacking—the best job around, which isn't saying much. For awhile, I sent money home, but I never saw my mother again." The moon, now above the water, made Alice's face pale. "When I started jacking, I didn't see the forest for the trees, as the saying goes. The difference you make isn't noticeable when you're chopping ten trees a day. You can look at the mountainsides, like we just did, and not even see the stumps. But then after five, ten years and swarms of lumberjacks, the hills are naked," he paused in mid-sentence, "and the jobs are gone, and so is the beauty." From the shore, a blue heron took off and flew across the lake. "What puzzles me is how the greed of the lumber magnates and mill owners blinds them to the beauty. No! That's not quite right. Those magnates have their own hunting and fishing preserves that won't be cut. But they could care less whether ordinary people can partake of the beauty."

"I'm sure Lloyd sees the beauty. But he's trapped."

"Trapped?"

"Lloyd's not altogether happy working for the Lumberman's Association. When he graduated from Yale he wanted to act—he's really good at it—but his father would have none of it. He got Lloyd the job with the Lumberman's Association. I hope Lloyd will strike out on his own when we have saved some money, but—"

"But you have your doubts?"

"He doesn't like taking risks. You can see that from the way he treats Donald and Jane. If he had gone into the theater despite his father he would have had to settle for a lot less than he was used to; he wasn't ready to take the plunge."

Cyrus beached the boat. He gave his hand to Alice—again aware of how soft hers was—but she tripped as she stepped over the gunwale and fell into Cyrus's arms on the beach. Neither looked at the other and they separated quickly. A pair of loons called to each other across the water.

They walked up the path along the river. Alice remarked, "I remember you as a man who spoke your mind at Frank Miller's trial. I've changed much more than you."

"How old were you then—ten, eleven?"

"Eleven. The trial changed me." He looked at her inquiringly but said nothing. "For one thing, I no longer thought my father walked on water. For another, I became much more interested in the world around me. I've been involved in the suffrage movement—"

"Mary is too. She'll be pleased to hear that."

"I know your wife's been involved. She's often spoken of in Glens Falls."

Just ahead they saw the glow of Lloyd's campfire. Cyrus was sorry to see his interlude with Alice end.

"We couldn't keep Jane awake for the surprise," Donald told Cyrus. We did cut green sticks though."

Alice looked at her daughter sleeping peacefully on boughs Cyrus had cut to fashion a bed. "She looks so comfortable, Cyrus. I don't think I'll wake her for the treat." Cyrus walked over to the buckboard and brought back a small box and a pile of blankets. He covered the girl without waking her.

"Is the surprise in the box?" Donald asked. Cyrus nodded and handed Don the box. He lifted the cover off. "What are they?"

Alice peered in. "Marshmallows!" she exclaimed.

"One of my clients purchased them in a French confectioner's shop in Quebec," Cyrus told them. "He told me they're very good gently roasted over an open fire. Let's try it." He picked out a white cube and threaded it on to one of the green sticks that Lloyd had carved to a point. Then he added two more. Cyrus held the stick so the marshmallows were just above the flame. He rotated the stick slowly, watching as the cubes turned brown on each side. When they started to sag he pulled them out of the fire and waved the stick gently to speed cooling. He held the marshmallows in front of Donald, who started to reach for one. "Not with you hands, Donald. Open your mouth and bite off the marshmallow at the point."

Donald followed Cyrus's directions and rolled the marshmallow around in his mouth.

"Wow! I never tasted anything as good as this before."

Cyrus let the next one slide down to the pointed end and offered it to Alice who took it the same way. He gave Lloyd the last one. Then they each prepared the tasty treat on their own sticks and tried to repeat what Cyrus had done. Donald's caught fire and were a charred mess by the time Cyrus extinguished the flame. The boy did better on his second try.

While the Massings continued to roast their marshmallows, Cyrus got up, took one of the blankets, and moved about ten yards away from the fire to find a place where he could spread out. Returning, he announced, "I'm turning in. You might want to save some of the marshmallows for tomorrow in case we have to camp out again." He cleared some brush away from one side of the fire. "Why don't you folks sleep here, around the fire? You'll be warmer." He inspected the fireplace and concluded there was no danger of fire spreading. "Just let it die by itself. The weather shouldn't get much colder."

Alice spread two blankets, one on top of the other, near the fire, while Lloyd returned the remaining marshmallows to the wagon. When he returned he asked Alice, "Do you think we should take our shoes off?"

"Of course, Dear, and maybe our pants, too." She hesitated. "It might get colder, I'll leave my blouse on." They undressed partially and crawled under the blanket side-by-side, lying on their backs. Neither spoke for a while. Slowly the fire died, casting them into black night; only if Alice looked directly into the ashes could she see a glowing coal. As their eyes became accustomed to the darkness they saw more jewels in the sky above the clearing than they had ever seen before. Under the blanket, Alice took Lloyd's hand. "Oh, Lloyd, this is fairyland." They spoke softly, not wanting to wake the kids or have Cyrus overhear them.

"I don't see much destruction. I think Cyrus is exaggerating," Lloyd said.

"You should have come out on the lake with us. It's desolate where the mountainside's been logged. I think Cyrus will show us more destruction."

"I'm not sure I want to see it, Alice." He was silent for a moment. "I thought this would make a nice vacation for you and the kids—"

"It does," she interrupted, squeezing his hand. She rolled

on top of him and kissed him. She was surprised that he did not become aroused, and after a few moments she rolled off. "Would you rather be back in our bed in Glens Falls?"

"Probably, but that's not what I started to say." They were both quiet for a few moments.

"So far, I don't find this outdoor life agreeable or something I'm good at—"

"You caught the biggest fish and built a wonderful fire," she interrupted again. "Donald loved it."

Ignoring her he continued, "Although I find the lakes and mountains beautiful, I fear that Cyrus will convince me that the lumber companies are doing harm. And I am their agent. I am not prepared to argue with him."

Alice took his hand again. "Then just look and listen, Darling." Again she kissed him. This time he was more responsive.

⸻

They broke camp after a hardy breakfast—eggs, trout, and biscuits—and climbed on to the buckboard. Back at Beede's, Cyrus confirmed with one of the local guides the location of the Noonmark trailhead. The horses led them through a meadow over which massive Giant of the Valley loomed. Cyrus pointed to a much lower crag and said, "That's our morning's destination, Noonmark." They left the wagon at the edge of the meadow and started toward the peak. After a few minutes, Jane said she was tired and Cyrus put her on his shoulders. Lloyd opened his mouth to say, "I can carry her," but his back was sore and his feet ached inside his stiff boots. He closed his mouth without a word.

Alice had little difficulty. "You're not the first woman to climb in the Adirondacks," Cyrus told her, "but there haven't been many." As they climbed, Alice noticed that the forest floor was saturated by sunlight, although the trees were plentiful. She glanced up and saw that most of the trees were shorn of branches. She asked Cyrus, "Are these trees blighted?"

He turned back to her, Jane still on his shoulders. "Not unless you call lumbering a blight. These woods fell victim to what we call a crown fire after the softwoods had been lumbered." He pointed to old partially rotted stumps interspersed with the trees that still reached skyward. "When the wind is right, a fire fed by dead stumps and wood on the ground is pulled upwards along tree trunks, then spreads along the treetops. The heat creates tremendous updrafts so the flames don't descend but race along the canopy killing the trees from the top."

"What started the fire?" Donald asked.

"Lightning most likely. Maybe a careless camper who didn't douse his fire."

Frequently during the climb, Alice, the children, and Cyrus had to wait for Lloyd to catch up. At one point, Cyrus kidded him, "You need more exercise, Lloyd."

Huffing, he replied, "You're probably right, Cyrus, but I don't have the time."

Toward the summit the trees were stunted by wind and cold. Cyrus put Jane down and held her hand as they clambered up the bare rocks to the top. He pointed to the blackened earth.

"What a view!" Donald exclaimed. Far below, Keene Valley, with homes and farms, rolled in front of them. Across the valley, Giant looked down at them, but didn't seem quite as high as before. Turning to the west, the great range of the Adirondacks came into view. They all were silent for a few minutes.

Close below Noonmark's summit, surrounded by the dull gray of dead forest, a dense grove of intensely green spruce stood out. Cyrus saw Alice looking at it. "The fire spared those trees; a shift in the wind often decides the path of a fire. Noonmark may be luckier than most mountains. The seeds from those trees will speed up growth down the mountainside. If we went down the north side, we'd see the spruce saplings."

On the way down, Alice asked, "Do the lumber companies ever plant seedlings to replace what they've cut?"

"Nope," Cyrus replied. Silelntly, Lloyd echoed Cyrus's monosyllable.

14
Corey's Last Stand

THEY were off the mountain by noon, heading to Chapel Pond where they replenished their water supply and had a lunch of sandwiches Cyrus had packed. "We've got to ride north through the valley in order to skirt the mountains. Then we'll turn west and climb through the pass between Cascade and the Pitchoffs. We might camp near there, depending on the time."

Alice spoke. "When he took me to the trial in Saranac Lake, my father drove us past the Cascade Lakes. They were almost as beautiful as the Ausables."

"But not as secluded," Cyrus noted.

Without rain, the dirt road was packed hard and they covered ground quickly, reaching the Cascade Lakes, almost at the head of the pass, in a couple of hours. Cyrus watered the horses and decided they would go on to Saranac Lake. Before they climbed on to the buckboard, Cyrus asked Donald to change places with his mother; the two children sat in back. He wanted to prepare Lloyd and Alice for seeing Tommy, so, in turn, they could prepare Donald and Jane. After a few miles traveled in silence, he began. "I'd like to tell you about my son, Tommy, before we get to my home."

"He's the one who had the accident, isn't he?" Lloyd asked. Cyrus nodded.

"What accident?" Alice asked.

Cyrus proceeded to tell them how Tommy became paraplegic and mute, concluding, "So don't be surprised when he doesn't say 'hello.'"

"Is his thinking okay?" Alice asked.

Cyrus turned from his driving to look at Alice. She was pale. "He's always been a smart lad and still is. We have to keep him supplied with Ticonderoga pencils for his writing." He turned to Lloyd. "That's one good use of Adirondack lumber." They rode on silently. The children talked and giggled in the back seat. Cyrus skirted the little village of Lake Placid by taking the Military Road. When they passed Raybrook, Cyrus added, "I don't know if you want to tell the children. I'm sure they'll ask."

They arrived at the Carter home about six in the evening. The sun still dappled the house. As they pulled up, Mary was watering flowers in front. She stood as they arrived, not smiling.

"Hello, Dear," Cyrus said to her, still holding the reins. "The roads are in good condition, so we decided to come all the way today."

"That's nice," she said coldly. Alice was sitting on the side nearest Mary. Perfunctorily, Mary offered her hand as Alice jumped down. To Mary's surprise, Alice took both her hands and looked in her eyes, "Mary Carter! I've wanted to meet you for a long time."

Mary replied, skeptically, "Really?"

"Yes, I'll explain in a minute. Let me help the children down first."

Cyrus jumped down after Alice and hugged Mary. He whispered in her ear, "I think you'll be surprised." He let go of her and went to collect the Massings' luggage. Lloyd,

Alice, and the children stood in a little knot in back of the wagon. Cyrus carried the suitcases into the house. Mary followed him. "Did you tell them about Tommy?"

"Yes, I told Lloyd and Alice. I don't know whether they're telling the children."

"What will I be surprised about? You know, Cyrus, I don't like surprises. Most of them are bad."

"I don't think this one will be. It'll be best if Alice talks to you herself. Right now we'd better tend to dinner."

With the sun still up, the air was warm. Cyrus pointed the Massings toward Moody Pond, suggesting they might like to cool and clean off with a swim. They returned, wet hair plastered down, looking content.

Dinner and the evening that followed passed uneventfully. Whatever Donald and Jane had been told, they seemed to enjoy Tommy's company. He had learned several string tricks, which he first demonstrated with Jane. Then, he showed Donald how to tie a cat's cradle and a few others, which the boy played with his sister, although she couldn't learn to tie them. At dinner, Lloyd did not say much, but Alice, Mary, and Cyrus carried on a lively conversation.

By the time they finished eating, night had fallen. "It looks like another mild, clear night," Cyrus said. I hope you don't mind sleeping outside again. Tomorrow night you'll have deluxe accommodations at Corey's Inn."

"Who's Corey?" Jane asked. "And where does he live?"

"William Corey is my uncle, Jane," Mary answered. "He lives about ten miles away. You'll meet him tomorrow. You'll like him."

As they got into bed that night, Mary said to Cyrus, "You were right. Alice did surprise me. She's a suffragist all right.

The way she wears her hair—short—is becoming popular among them. Apparently, I have a reputation—at least as far as Glens Falls—for being a militant member of the movement." She threw her arm around Cyrus and kissed him. "Maybe now that you've got the 'forever wild' bill passed you'll work on getting the vote for women in New York."

Still embracing Mary, Cyrus replied softly. "First of all, *I* didn't get the bill passed. Second of all, the Adirondacks aren't 'forever wild' yet. The lumber companies can buy up private land and poach on state as well as private land. Look what's happening to William. Third of all…" His voice trailed off as he realized from her breathing that Mary was asleep.

———•———

Corey's helpers prepared two cabins for the Massings, whose arrival William doubted would be before Tuesday. Other guests departed on Sunday and Corey gave his help Monday off. William said to himself, *Cyrus'll never make it back to Saranac Lake Sunday unless he can keep his mouth shut. And I don't think he aims to do that.* Since Cyrus had become an Assemblyman he had, in William's opinion, become more vocal.

As was their custom, Lisa and Peter met at Corey's late Sunday morning and had lunch with him. They parted in the early afternoon, Peter returning to Axton and Lisa to Saranac Lake, leaving William alone.

———•———

On Monday morning the locomotive chugged up to the Axton station from Long Lake, pulling three flat bed cars. Smead's jobber joined stationmaster Peter as he discussed the day's work with the engineer and fireman. A crew of jacks would accompany the train, which would stop periodically at the piles of logs spaced at half-mile intervals along the track. The jacks would lever the logs onto the flat beds for delivery to the mill at Tupper Lake. When the crew was assembled, Peter warned them to be on the lookout for sparks from the locomotive that might ignite small fires. They carried shovels to damp down the earth and dig ditches to isolate any fire that might be ignited.

Mary decided to accompany Cyrus and the Massings to Corey's on Monday morning. She and Alice sandwiched Cyrus in the front seat as he held the reins while Massing sat in back with the children. Shortly before they reached Corey's, Cyrus turned to Alice, and then to Lloyd in back, and said, "I want to show you Bartlett's before we reach Corey's. We won't be long." As he finished, the wail of a train whistle pierced the rattle of the wagon's wheels on the road. "That'll be the Adirondack Railroad pulling into the Axton station." Cyrus turned off the main road on to the path to Bartlett's. They passed the trail to the cemetery on their left and then the small bridge from which Bartlett's Inn was visible. Cyrus stopped and hitched the horses. He went ahead to the inn to let the Bartletts know what he wanted to do. Shaking his head as he came out, he said to Mary, "Virgil's not well. I don't think he'll see another summer." Then he turned to Lloyd and Alice. "Let's walk up the knoll." Lloyd trudged along besides Cyrus. Mary put her arm through Alice's and they followed the men up the hill.

"This is the hill Cyrus and I were married on," Mary

told Alice. They reached the top. The Saranac River surged beneath them, plunging under the wooden bridge, emerging with less vigor as it expanded into a broad stream lined with rushes and water lilies. Alice's eyes followed the river's winding path toward Round Lake. Its surface was still, the air sultry. She looked out over the river to Ampersand Mountain. "That mountain must have remarkable views."

"It does," Mary replied. "I've climbed it many times. At first, there were trees all the way to the top. Now the top is bare and the views are better."

"Did logging go up to the top?"

"No. Verplanck Colvin who has surveyed the Adirondacks burned the top bare so he could make sightings from the summit." She paused for a moment as she looked around. "Maybe you can climb it tomorrow or the next day. I don't know what Cyrus has planned for you."

They descended the knoll. Cyrus led them past the buckboard, over the small bridge, and up the trail to the cemetery that stood on a smaller hill overlooking the river. He opened the small gate in the picket fence, which demarcated the cemetery, and led them in. "The oldest graves in this cemetery aren't thirty years old." He pointed toward two stones in the center of the cemetery. "The Bartletts lost two children soon after they arrived, and Virgil built the cemetery for them. He's let other folks in this neighborhood bury their kin here, including his workers." He led them over to a cluster of four stones on one side of the cemetery. Sensing that the adults were going to have a prolonged conversation, which held little interest for them, Donald and Jane wandered off. They started a game of hide and seek with Jane the first to hide behind a tombstone on the other side of the cemetery.

Although already fading, the names and dates were readable. Alice and Lloyd walked around the cluster of small headstones. "These men all died in 1858," Alice said.

Lloyd calculated their ages. "Twenty, twenty-four, twenty-five, twenty-six."

"So young. Was there an epidemic?" Alice asked.

"Two of them died of cholera."

"Cholera?" Lloyd asked.

"All four of these lads worked for the Smead Lumber Company that winter," Cyrus continued. "So did I. We'll visit the camp this afternoon; it's adjacent to Corey's property. Smead cut back on the food for the jacks, probably making the men more vulnerable to contaminated drinking water. After another jack and I diverted the water supply, there were no more cases of cholera."

Mary, who had fallen behind as they crossed the bridge, came up holding a bouquet of wild flowers she had just picked. She knelt and laid them at the bottom of the stone marking Jean's grave a short distance away.

"What about this one?" Lloyd pointed to the stone of Michael O'Rourke, the twenty-year old.

Cyrus replied, "He was killed by an axe blow, although Frank Miller denied it."

"Frank Miller?" Alice inquired. "The murderer?"

"The same one," Cyrus replied. "Michael had gone to speak with Frank, his foreman, when Frank swung his axe without looking around. The back of his axe hit Michael in the side of his head." Cyrus felt the side of his own head, just above his ear. "He died the next day."

"Oh, how terrible," Alice said. "Did he have a family?

How did they manage after he died?"

"He had two brothers, who were also jacks. The jobber advanced the money for Michael's tombstone, but he took it out of Michael's brother Sean's pay." Cyrus realized he was speaking of Alice's father but made no mention of it. Pointing to Sean's grave, he said, "Sean was the one who Frank Miller shot."

Cyrus led them over to a fifth grave where they stood silently in back of Mary.

Cyrus said softly, "Jean Entremont, from Quebec, was only eighteen when he was killed trying to break a logjam. Mary had improved his English and he was speaking it almost as well as we do."

Mary stood up. "Jean and I were going to be married. Cyrus tried to rescue him. After Jean drowned, a log smashed into Cyrus's leg. You've noticed that he still walks with a limp."

They were all silent.

Then they summoned the children and started down the knoll together. In the distance, they saw a breeze coming from the south ruffle the surface of Round Lake.

"Would you kids like to go for a row later?" Cyrus asked. They clapped hands delightedly. Telling about the logjam had reminded Cyrus about the guideboat.

———•———

William heard the steam engine's whistle as it pulled away from Axton Landing. As he busied himself in the kitchen, he felt the breeze. It blew the curtains into the room through the open windows on the rear of the building. Leaving his cane hooked over the kitchen table, he hobbled from the kitchen into the windowless pantry to collect food for his lunch. When he came out, he smelled smoke. Feeling along the edge of the kitchen table, he accidentally knocked the cane to the floor. He got down on his hands and knees but could not find it. He was surprised how quickly the room filled with smoke. *Must be a fire down near the tracks*, he thought. Crawling, he groped his way toward the main room of the inn.

———•———

As they headed south back to the main road, Cyrus saw a plume of smoke rising from the forest about a mile ahead of them. "Looks like a fire near Axton. If it's close to the river the men should contain it." As they continued, clouds of smoke spread to the west and the acrid smell of burning trees reached them.

"Oh my god! Mary shouted. "It looks like it's near Corey's." Cyrus flicked the reins, getting the horses to move faster. They turned right on the main road as smoke seeped out of the woods to the south, obliterating the sun.

———•———

After the train left the station, Peter raked the ground between the tracks and the station house. He was about to go inside when he noticed smoke rising from the west, less than a mile distant. He ran into the house yelling "Fire!" Then he ran to the jobber's office, again yelling "Fire!" The jobber came out, saw the smoke, and blew a whistle to summon men from the nearby woods. Peter and one of his men returned to the tracks and pushed a small handcar from a siding on to the track. By this time, half a dozen men carrying shovels and axes reached the handcar and climbed on with Peter and the jobber. Two of the jacks pumped the large lever, getting the car to move up the tracks about as fast as the men could run.

The fire started after the crew had loaded a pile of logs on to one of the flatcars less than a mile west of the station. As the engine pulled out, a heavy shower of sparks emerged from its stack, landing on tinder between the tracks and the Raquette River. Within minutes, fire reared up. When the train stopped at the next pile, the crew glanced back to see a red glow through the sparse trees with smoke rising above. They ran to the engine. Hearing their cries, the engineer backed the train eastward, getting close enough to the flames for the crew to feel the heat. The fireman attached a long hose to the boiler to spray water on the fire, but needing to retain enough water to make steam, and realizing the fire was out of control, the engineer ordered the hose disconnected. The train crew dug a ditch just beyond the perimeter of the fire to try to contain it.

The handcar arrived at the eastern side of the blaze as it reached the bank of the Raquette. As fast as they could, the men chopped the few standing trees and dug a ditch perpendicular to the tracks extending to the Raquette. Peter jumped off the handcar and raced toward the river. The fire, which had been burning less than an hour, generated so much heat that the gentle breeze that had blown it north took on gale force, fanning the flames higher. When Peter reached the river he was horrified. He watched the fire climb up the trunks of the few standing trees, ignite the canopy that arched across the River and spread to the crown of trees on the north bank. The fire was on a direct course to Corey's. Peter waded into the river. In midstream, he was soaked up to his neck, and he felt the river getting deeper. Holding his breath, he half swam, half walked under water until he regained a footing on the river bottom. He struggled up the bank about twenty feet east of the fire. Dripping wet, but warm from the heat radiated by the fire, he was standing on Corey's property where the poachers had thinned out the woods. He ran north reaching the road from Saranac Lake and then turned left, running toward Corey's. As he ran, Cyrus's wagon caught up to him. Certain that Cyrus had seen the fire, Peter motioned for him to keep going; he only had a few hundred yards to reach the inn.

Cyrus reached the front of the inn at the same time that flames leaped on to the roof at the back. Cyrus and Lloyd jumped off. Cyrus instructed Mary to return to Bartlett's and raise the alarm. She hesitated for a minute, her face grief stricken. "Cyrus, save Uncle. I'm sure he's inside." She took the reins, turned the wagon around and with Alice beside her and the children in back they rode back toward Bartlett's. They did not get far before a group of riders approached them, carrying shovels, picks, and axes; Bartlett's workers had already seen the fire. "We'll try to save the inn," they shouted at Mary as she reined in the horses. No longer needing to call for help, she turned back toward Corey's.

While Cyrus had been giving his brief instruction to Mary, Lloyd had run up the steps to the inn. Cyrus was a step behind him. "Lloyd, what do you think you're doing?"

"I'm going in to save Corey."

He put his hand on the door. Smoke was seeping out from its bottom.

"Don't be foolish. You don't know the layout of the inn.

You won't be able to see anything in there." Lloyd opened the door anyway and started to enter.

Cyrus grabbed him by the back of his collar, dragged him out, and punched him in the jaw sending him sprawling on the porch. He did not move right away. Cyrus went in and immediately dropped down to crawl. "William!" he shouted. He thought he heard a groan from near the kitchen. Putting his face as close to the floor as he could, Cyrus held his breath. He managed not to cough as he crawled towards the kitchen door where his path was blocked by William's body. Cyrus grabbed the old man's arm and dragged him toward the door of the inn. Halfway there he could hold his breath no longer and let it out as slowly as possible, finally gasping the smoke-filled air. He stood up, still dragging William by the arm. Through the smoke the dim light from the open door showed him where to head. On the porch, Lloyd had gotten to his feet. He knelt as Cyrus handed William to him. Cyrus stood for a moment then stumbled down the steps coughing and trying to get enough air to keep from suffocating. He glanced back at the inn. Smoke was pouring from the front windows. Through them he could see a red glow. A tremendous crash told Cyrus the back of the roof had collapsed into the kitchen.

Lloyd carried William down the steps and laid him on the ground beyond the hitching post, almost at the side of the road. The old man was ashen gray and showed no signs of life. By then, Peter, Bartlett's men, and Mary with Alice and the children had all converged on the clearing in front of the Inn. Flames leaped from the roof. Inside the main room of the Inn, they could see flames leaping up the walls. In another minute, the entire roof collapsed. Within half an hour the house was a hot, smoldering mound of ashes, except for the stone fire-places. The clearing in front of the inn had stopped the fire. Bartlett's men dug a ditch on either side, parallel to the road that prevented the fire from spreading across.

Mary ran to Corey, kneeling beside him. She threw her arms around him and yelled into his ear, "Uncle, Uncle." He did not respond. She looked at his unseeing eyes and, sobbing, gently closed his lids. Watching William grow old, she had in recent years thought about his death, imagining it would be peaceful. To go down with his inn—his life's work and joy—crumbling and smoldering around him was too cruel.

Cyrus, still coughing and clutching his throat, gently lifted Mary and put his arms around her. He walked her back to the wagon. Lloyd was standing alongside it, rubbing his bruised jaw.

"I'm sorry to have hit you, Lloyd," Cyrus wheezed. " I know you wanted to save the old man, but you would have died in that inferno before you found him." Cyrus put his hands on Lloyd's shoulders.

On Wednesday, after the Massings were gone, William Corey was buried in the cemetery on the knoll at Bartlett's.

15

The Lobbyist Returns Home

CYRUS arranged for the Massings to take the stage-coach from Saranac Lake to Ausable Forks early Tuesday morning. They retrieved their stored luggage, boarded the southbound train, and were back at their home in Glens Falls that afternoon. As Lloyd was not expected back to work until the following Monday, he took the rest of the week off, much to Alice's dismay. Each day, he sat around their living room, staring into space, ignoring the morning sunlight pouring cheerfully through the windows. He continued to sit as the sun traversed the sky, leaving the room in shadow by mid-afternoon. On Wednesday, he poured himself a drink before dinner. By Friday, when he started drinking after lunch, Alice realized she could do nothing to rouse him from his torpor, and she took the children out. When they returned, Lloyd was dozing in his favorite chair.

"Where the hell were you?" he asked in an uncharacteristic, menacing tone.

"I took the children to play in the park. Then we visited some of their friends." Lloyd got up and poured more whiskey in his glass.

"Lloyd, what's troubling you?" She knew the answer but thought it might help if they talked about it.

"You know damn well what's troubling me. My life is

worthless. I couldn't even save that old man. What was his name?"

"William Corey."

"Yeah, Corey." He took a swallow of his freshened drink.

"Darling, Cyrus really appreciated your help. What you did showed you had real courage."

"Courage? When I go back to the Lumberman's Association on Monday, am I going to show them I have courage? If I really had courage, I'd quit." Alice thought for a moment. She knew Lloyd was right. But if he quit, what kind of work would he get? Making a living by going into the theater, his first love, was out of the question. They would have to sell their house, stop entertaining, and find other ways to cut down expenses. Now it was Alice who was conflicted. "You don't have to quit. You can suggest changes that would be to the benefit of the lumber companies; actions to stop forest fires, for instance."

"Believe it or not, Alice, while I've been sitting here I've thought about that. The lumber companies can't afford to clean up the lopped branches, to build fire towers, or plant seedlings. With competition from other companies in the south and west, their prices are so close to the bone they can't invest in improvements."

"The government could insist on it. That way, every company would have to do it. No one would gain an advantage." Alice thought for a moment. "The fire problem seems mostly due to the railroads. You could lobby for the government to make them put spark collectors on their engines. That wouldn't cost the lumber companies anything."

"You think you're so smart?" Lloyd replied nastily. "The

last thing the lumber companies want is regulation. You may recall, my dear," he said sneeringly, "interference by the legislature is what started the whole trip. When I encouraged Cyrus to vote against prohibiting the sale of state lands, that's when he invited me to visit the Adirondacks. No! I can tell you my bosses won't hear of any government interference with the railroads or the woods."

On the following Monday, Lloyd was so badly hung over he could not go to work. Alice sent Donald down to the Association's Glens Falls office, just a few blocks away, to tell them his father was sick. When Donald returned, his father was asleep. He told his mother that the man in the office said he was sorry to hear his father was sick. "He asked me if I had seen the fire up there and whether I thought Papa would be at work tomorrow."

"What did you tell him?"

"I said I had seen the fire and the man die. I didn't know whether Papa would be well enough to work tomorrow."

"Good boy," Alice replied.

"He said one other thing, Mama." Alice looked at Donald inquiringly. "He said the fire committee was meeting tomorrow and he hoped Papa would be able to give them a report."

Alice was determined that Lloyd would go to work on Tuesday. She knew she was courting danger, but she gathered up the whiskey bottles, made sure they were tightly corked, and hid them in the bottom drawer of her dresser.

Lloyd woke about noon. Alice brought him some tea and toast. Grumblingly, he ate it. She ran her hand softly over his four-day beard as he chewed. "I sent Donald to tell the Lumberman's Association you were sick and wouldn't be at work today. They told Donald that the fire committee will be meeting tomorrow and wants an eyewitness report about the fire."

"I'm not surprised they've heard about it already. What can I tell them?"

"Tell them what happened."

Lloyd was silent. He got out of bed, washed, and shaved. Alice suggested he take Donald and Jane for a walk, which, after encouragement from the children, he did. They returned a few hours later. Usually they came back laughing. This time they were silent. The children went to their room where Alice soon could hear them chattering away. Lloyd went to the sideboard to fetch a drink. Not finding his liquor, he went immediately to the kitchen where Alice was preparing dinner. He grabbed her by the wrist and spun her around. Glowering into her face he asked, "What did you do with my whiskey?"

Alice tried to break out of his grip, but he held tight. "I hid it."

Lloyd raised his arm. "You hid it. Am I a child? Tell me where it is!"

"No," she replied, trying to hold back tears. "Lloyd you've got to—"

At that moment the children came out of their room. Lloyd dropped Alice's wrist, which she began to massage. He turned to the children. "Your mother and I are having a private conversation. Please go back to your room."

"What's it about, Mama?" Jane asked.

"It's between your father and me. Your father asked you to go back to your room."

"But we're hungry," said Donald.

"We'll be done in a minute, Dear," Alice replied. They returned to their room.

Alice took a step backward. Lloyd did not advance. "Darling," Alice said, "I did it for your own good. You've got to go to work tomorrow. If you start drinking now, you'll end up with another hangover."

Lloyd sat down, planted his elbows above his knees, and put his head in his hands. "I suppose you're right," he said mournfully. "Better get the children." There was not much conversation at the table until dessert, when Donald asked, "Are you going to work tomorrow, Papa?"

"It's none of your—" Lloyd started.

Alice quickly interjected, "If he's feeling better, I'm sure he'll go." The rest of the meal was eaten in silence.

Lloyd went to work Tuesday, coming home a little later than usual. Although he seemed sober, Alice smelled liquor on his breath as she went to kiss him.

"Since you hid my whiskey, I stopped at the tavern on the way home."

Alice ignored the remark. "How was work?"

"I gave them my 'eyewitness report,' as you put it."

"Did you include your attempt to rescue Mr. Corey?"

"No, they wouldn't have been interested. All they wanted to know was how we could prevent this from happening again. Their companies are taking terrible losses because of fires this summer. The drought is killing them."

"What did you tell them?"

"I said I didn't know."

"But you do—" Alice started and then decided there was no point in discussing it.

"Where's my whiskey?"

Reluctantly Alice returned the bottles.

Lloyd missed several days of work over the next few weeks. The Association gave him a warning; then they put him on probation. His father's intervention prevented them from firing him on the spot.

———•———

The next day when Lloyd was out of the house, Alice wrote Mary Carter.

Glens Falls, New York
September 16, 1883

Dear Mary,

I apologize for my tardiness in writing to express our appreciation for your kindness during our trip. Once again, I offer my condolences on the loss of your uncle. I know how trying these months must be for you. Please also convey to Cyrus my appreciation for his arranging our trip and guiding us so expertly. I am sorry it ended in tragedy.

You may have noticed that during our visit, Lloyd had little to say. His feelings emerged after he saw firsthand the destruction caused by logging and the disasters it could unleash. That is what drove him to try to rescue your Uncle William.

Lloyd has been despondent since we returned from the Adirondacks. He began to drink heavily

and threatened me when I hid his whiskey.
He's missed so many days of work that the
Lumberman's Association put him on probation.
Were it not for his father's intervention, they
would have dismissed him by now. With his
parents' help, I hope and pray we can work it out.
I apologize for burdening you with this in your
moment of need. All our friends here are with the
Lumberman's Association. They would not be
sympathetic.

Your friend,
Alice Massing

Mary showed the letter to Cyrus. "Your little tour had quite an effect. Of course, you didn't plan Uncle's death."

"No. And I didn't expect that Lloyd's visit would have such a profound influence on his life. Now it's my turn to feel guilty."

Saranac Lake, New York
September 23, 1883

Dear Alice,

Your letter arrived Friday and this is the first chance I've had to write. The weather here is so beautiful, with the leaves beginning to turn, that Cyrus and I climbed Ampersand yesterday. He was planning to take your family up when you were here in July.

Thank you for your condolences. The initial trauma has passed and we are now waiting for the will to be probated. Uncle William left the property to me. I doubt we will rebuild the inn. We may sell the property and improve our house here in the village.

Cyrus and I were very distressed to hear about Lloyd. It was never Cyrus's intention to jeopardize Lloyd's job with the Lumberman's Association, only to have him appreciate the problems caused by logging and, perhaps, to influence the companies' policies. Both of us hope fervently that Lloyd can overcome his problems.

In any case, please count us both as friends and call on us anytime.

Affectionately,
Mary Carter

Lloyd's parents, Ann and George, were both in their sixties. They loved Donald and Jane as their only grandchildren and invited them over often, with or without their parents. On a weekday in early October, while the children were in school, Alice visited her mother-in-law. Lloyd and his father were at their respective jobs. Aware of his mood changes, Ann asked what was troubling her son, noting, "He refuses to talk about it with us."

"I'm not surprised," replied Alice. "He's having second thoughts about whether he should be lobbying for the Lumberman's Association. I don't think George would understand why and surely wouldn't sympathize."

"And George worked so hard to get him that job. What on earth is wrong with it?"

"On our trip to the Adirondacks, we witnessed some of the damage caused by logging. Not only damage to the woods, but damage to people. The forest fire we witnessed— and the death of our hostess' uncle—was the culmination."

Lloyd's mother seemed to be thinking ahead. "Certainly, he can't quit. He's not trained to do anything else." She thought of his acting, but dismissed it without a word. "I hope you haven't been encouraging him," she commented icily.

Alice ignored the admonition. "I think he could find another job if he wanted to. But he doesn't want to. He's drinking too much."

"Yes, I've noticed," Ann replied. "Is there anything George and I can do?"

"I don't know." Alice pulled a handkerchief out of her sleeve and dabbed her eyes. "I don't think you or George can argue him out of his concern about what's happening to the woods. I've suggested that the Lumberman's Association might look favorably on policies to reduce the risk of forest fires, but Lloyd doesn't think the Association would be interested in anything that needs regulation." Alice was silent for a while thinking over her mother-in-law's question. "I think maybe telling him that he's got to pull himself together for the children's sake might help."

"I could probably do that better than George. But I'll discuss it with him first."

When George returned from his office that day, Ann

told him about Alice's visit. He agreed—for the good of the children—that his wife needed to talk to Lloyd. "I'm not good at that sort of thing," George admitted. He then added, "You know Alice has some funny ideas sometimes—that suffrage thing. You don't think she's responsible?"

"I asked her that directly," Ann replied and thought for a moment. "Come to think of it, she never gave me an answer."

The following Saturday, Alice asked Lloyd to take the children over to his parents while she cleaned the house. They were gone several hours and shortly after their return Lloyd took Alice aside. "I see you've been talking to my parents," he said.

"Lloyd, they didn't need me to see that you've changed. But, yes, I tried to explain what was bothering you."

"Mother warned me that if I continue the way I've been going, I am going to hurt Donald and Jane. Do you think that's true?"

"I think there's been some hurt already. They're wary of you; they worry they'll say the wrong thing, and you'll explode. So they keep quiet, which is not their nature." Lloyd walked over to his bar and turned around. Alice was looking at the bottles. He hesitated and then walked back toward her. Alice continued, "And if you lose your job, we'll all suffer."

Lloyd did not miss any work the next week. He came home on Friday, his breath clean, and announced to Alice that the following week, the first in October, the Association was going to discuss the candidates they would support, or oppose, in the 1884 elections. "That includes Cyrus Carter, you know."

"What will you tell them?"

"Nothing unless they ask."

"They're more than likely to ask. It's no secret that he invited you to spend a week in the Adirondacks. In any event, don't you think you should be prepared?"

Lloyd sprawled on his favorite cushioned chair, his legs stretched in front of him. He looked at Alice and smiled. "Don't you think a drink would help me formulate my thoughts?"

She came over and straddled his legs, her skirt rising above her knees. She put her arms around his neck. "Try this instead," she said, kissing him firmly on the mouth.

Lloyd bent his knees, which brought her body closer to his, and put his arms around her. "That's much better than a drink."

Alice moved her mouth away from his. "Are you going to be for Cyrus or against him?"

"I guess I know where you stand. But what if I recommend that the Association endorse him and then he continues to vote against their interests? You know who'll pay for that."

Alice moved backward, climbing down from Lloyd's lap. "I suppose. But you know he's going to call for stricter measures against forest fires, and that's in the best interests of the lumber companies."

"I've told you how the companies feel about regulation." He thought for a minute. "You might be right though. They have so much to lose from forest fires, they just might agree."

The couple continued to discuss the endorsement on and off through the weekend. Donald and Jane were peripherally aware of the issue that preoccupied their parents. What most pleased them was their parents talking to each other again in loving tones. The children became more playful, too.

———•———

At its monthly meeting in October, the Board of the Lumberman's Association had its first discussion of candidates for the 1884 election, more than a year away. As their lobbyist, Lloyd was invited to sit in on the meeting and give his impressions of the current Assemblymen and Senators as they went county by county. When he arrived home afterwards Alice kissed him and immediately asked, "Well?"

He pretended he didn't know what she was talking about.

"You know darn well what I'm asking."

He broke into a big smile. "I told them Cyrus could be counted on to favor legislation to reduce the chance of forest fires. That didn't bother most of them; like you keep telling me, fires are their bane too. But like I thought, some were worried about a precedent for regulation. Several were angry about his vote preserving state lands in the last session." He took his jacket off and went to hang it up.

"So what do you think they're going to do?"

"For now, they've decided not to make an endorsement."

"I suppose that's a victory of sorts. What do you think?"

Lloyd approached Alice, put his arms around her waist and lifted her off the ground. "I don't think we could have done any better. I have to tell you, Alice, that the Board member from Smead said he would be very angry if Cyrus was reelected and then supported legislation to protect the forests. He asked me if I thought he would."

"What did you say?"

"I had to be honest, Alice. I said he might." A shadow crossed Alice's face. Lloyd looked at her. "What's keeping them neutral is Cyrus's popularity in Franklin County and the absence of another decent candidate. But that could change in the next year before the election."

16
Tommy's New Career

THE return address on the envelope was headed *The Nation*. Mary took it to Tommy while he was writing at the kitchen table. She laid it alongside him and went to the sink. He did not glance at it until he finished the paragraph. He picked it up and opened it, expecting the worst.

New York, New York

September 25, 1883

Dear Mr. Carter:

    Thank you very much for submitting your article. We have verified the information it contains. We admire your courage in penning this and plan to publish it in our next issue.

    As you probably know, we cannot pay for articles we do not solicit. We would, however, invite you to write on related labor topics as you wish. We will pay you $10 for each article we accept.

    Thank you once again.

    Sincerely,

E.L. Gotkin, Editor

Tommy smiled and moved his wheelchair back. Mary looked over her shoulder to see Tommy waving the letter. His mother grabbed it from him, read it, let out a yelp, and hugged him tightly. "We have a published author in our midst."

Cyrus read the piece when the proofs were mailed to Tommy. Tears came to his eyes as he read.

THE NATION
Saranac Lake, New York
August 6, 1883

Report from the Adirondacks
By Thomas Carter

My mother's uncle, William Corey, was buried last month in a tranquil cemetery overlooking the Saranac River as it flows sedately into Round Lake. The circumstances of his death were anything but tranquil. The cemetery also holds the remains of men who died as a result of the practices of the lumber companies that are trying to make the Adirondacks their own province with the help of the railroads.

Uncle William owned the only inn between the villages of Saranac and Tupper Lakes. He also owned first-growth forest that surrounded the inn on three sides. [Editor's note: "First-growth forest," also known as virgin forest, consists of land whose trees have never been cut.] The Raquette River bounds his land on the south; the land on the other shore belongs to the Smead Lumber Company. The tracks of the Adirondack Railroad run parallel to the Raquette River through a right of way on Smead's land. The Railroad wanted to buy a right of way from Uncle William, claiming the location would help bring downstate tourists to his inn. Uncle William refused; the noise and the despoliation of the woods were more than he could bear.

The railroad makes most of its money hauling logs for the lumber companies. That's what its train was doing on Monday morning, July 16. In the previous weeks, Smead had logged the woods on its side of the Raquette and some that belonged to Uncle William, which they floated across the river and stacked with Smead's logs. We call that poaching. The train stopped at the pile and Smead's crews loaded the logs on to flatbed cars for transport to the mill at Tupper Lake.

The lumber companies are not interested in the thin limbs and branches of the enormously thick trunks of these trees. They lop them off to die on the forest floor.

Dead wood is tinder waiting to be ignited. That is what happened. Sparks escaped from the wood-burning steam engine after it picked up its load. They ignited the wooden debris on the forest floor. The fire engulfed the remaining standing trees between the track and the river. It raced up trunks to the canopy, spreading in a matter of minutes across the river to Uncle William's property.

Uncle William was sixty-eight years old. His vision was failing. Rheumatism forced him to walk with a cane. Having no guests, he was alone in the inn when the fire started. My father, who arrived at the inn before the fire engulfed it, groped his way through the dense smoke to find William sprawled on the floor of the kitchen. We'll never know whether he was already gone or whether he died in the few minutes that it took my father to pull him out before flames engulfed the house. We do know that this good man who loved the woods and who entertained us with his wry humor was a victim of the careless policies of the lumber companies and the railroads. The lumber companies don't have to leave dead wood on the forest floor. The railroads could use arresters to prevent sparks from escaping, or use fuels, like kerosene, that burn clean.

In 1879, refusing to heed my mother's pleading that I go to college, I got a job clearing a railbed for the Adirondack Railroad. Learning from my father, I helped organize the local railroad workers to demand a standard wage for a ten-hour day instead of getting paid according to the number of logs we chopped. We stood across the tracks in front of the engine and refused to move until the company met our demand. One of the owners of the Railroad, William Durant, son of Thomas Durant who built the Union Pacific, had come up in his private railroad car to break the strike. He ordered the train to mow us down, but the engineer and his crew refused. Next, he ordered the Company's private militia, hidden in the car next to his own, to fire on us. They fired one round over our heads but refused to fire into our midst. Durant agreed to our demands.

I continued to work for the Adirondack Railroad until late the following summer. I and a few other workers built a trestle so the railroad could traverse a deep ravine. One day in September, after the trestle was completed, my foreman ordered me to walk out on the trestle to make some minor repairs. I don't know whether it was negligence or intentional, but the rear car of the train became uncoupled and when the engine started up, it coasted back on to the trestle, gathering momentum as it headed toward me.

I don't remember anything that happened until I awoke in a bed in a doctor's office in Long Lake late the next day. Apparently, I jumped off the trestle as the car approached, my head landing on relatively soft earth just outside the jagged rock bed of the trestle. The fall broke my back, paralyzing my legs. I also lost the ability to speak.

The events I have related are not unique. They can happen anywhere that unregulated logging and railroad building take place. They can be prevented by laws and by workers' unions. Neither will happen without protest from many people. My uncle did not expect to die the way he did. I hope his story, and mine, will help spark the protest.

Cyrus was silent for a moment when he finished. Then, with a rare grin, he rose and hugged Tommy, who was sitting in his wheelchair reading. "Tommy, if I could afford it, I'd hire you as my speech writer. You've got a natural gift." Now it was Tommy's turn to grin. Cyrus turned to Mary, who was beaming. "Of course, Thomas, your mother had something to do with this, considering you haven't been to college and she's responsible for most of your education, at least your formal education."

In November, Tommy received a letter from Chicago, banged out on a Remington typewriter.

Chicago, Illinois
November 4, 1883

Dear Brother Tommy,

What a surprise: To pick up The Nation in the Knights of Labor office and see your article. You have paid homage to Uncle William brilliantly! I wish you could come to Chicago and see how McCormick Junior is exploiting his workers, of which I am one. The story is much the same as in jacking: Horribly long hours, accidents that the Company blames on workers and refuses to do anything about, although its ruthless negligence is almost always the cause. We get a pittance for the work we perform. The workers and their allies are not content to take it. Some here talk of an-

swering violence with violence. I don't think
we should go that far until peaceful means,
including strikes, have been exhausted. The
police are in league with the companies, and
even if we protest peacefully, their response
is violent. Demand for an eight-hour working
day is growing and will be the focus of strikes
until we attain it.

I didn't realize that you were a union orga-
nizer until I read your piece and learned what
you had done while working on the railroad.
You can help us organize by continuing to
write. Your story gave my friends here a big
boost.

I think often of you, Cyrus, Lisa, and our
mother. The dirt, grime, and general destitu-
tion that are rank here are repulsive. I dream
of coming home to the beauty and clean air of
the Adirondacks. With my meager wages, I am
slowly accumulating savings. Someday, I hope
to use them to return to Saranac Lake.

Happy Thanksgiving to everyone there.
Not much to be thankful for around here.

Your brother,
John

In New York City, Eleanor Mason purchased *The Nation*
at a newsstand on her way home from work at the Bellevue
clinic for the indigent. She fixed a simple meal expecting

Jared at any minute. When she finished and he was still not home, she sat down to read the magazine and was startled to see Tommy's byline. The Masons had not communicated with the Carters since before the summer and so did not know of Corey's death. After finishing, she sat for several minutes in the fading light, wondering how the news would affect Jared. He was becoming increasingly frail, coughing and tiring easily. If only he would agree to return to the Adirondacks instead of working long hours, literally killing himself, he could be cured again. Finally, she got up, lit the kerosene lamp over their kitchen table, and finished setting the table. She started to write a letter of condolence to Mary. It was dark before she heard Jared dragging himself up the last flight of stairs to their one-room flat on the fourth floor. She left the letter unfinished and opened their door to meet him on the landing with *The Nation* in her hand. After a fast hug and kiss she held the magazine up and turned to the page with Tommy's article. "Look at this!" she said excitedly.

Jared took the magazine and walked to the kitchen table. Pale and still puffing, he laid the magazine on the table and leaned over it, his eyes adjusting after a few moments. Seeing the byline, he sat down and gave the article his undivided attention. His face suffused with anger when he came to the part about Corey, and he started to cough. Eleanor feared that he would continue to get angry, worsening his condition, but he finished the story with a smile. "I hope Tommy doesn't count me as a pernicious employer. I was his first boss. You remember?"

"I do. He and John formed a union to negotiate with you. You made him a union man!" Eleanor said proudly.

"What a crime, to have his opportunities cut by that 'accident.'" Jared said the last word sardonically.

"Yes, of course," she replied, "but he's got plenty of potential left."

Jared was still short of breath. Eleanor stood behind him, rubbing his shoulders. "Jared, you're working too hard—destroying yourself. Sometimes I think we would do well to go back to the Adirondacks and take over father's practice."

Jared seemed to ignore Eleanor's last comment. "I wasn't at work. I went to the Knights of Labor office. The Board called a meeting with women hat makers to discuss a strike. They're less inclined to accept their plight than a few years ago."

"Jared, do you have to serve on the Board? The extra exertion, going downtown, staying out late, it's killing you."

"Eleanor, the working people have to know they have allies, that they're not alone. We can't stand by them if we're off in the wilderness."

"Look what Tommy did, not only from the wilderness but from a wheelchair. If you're dead, Jared, you won't be of any help."

Jared sighed. Having been on death's door once he was not ready to face it again. "I guess I have to admit I'm not invincible."

Encouraged that Jared might think of returning to the Adirondacks, she broached a subject that she had suppressed for many months. "Besides, Dear, we once talked of having children. I'm thirty-three, already old for child bearing. I would like us to have a child—maybe even two—but I can't think of having one in this city. With our work, either of us might bring home contagious diseases. The air itself is filthy and we can't always be sure of the water. I was raised in Tupper Lake and I'm healthier for it."

"A child? Into this world?" (Eleanor was not surprised by this rejoinder.) "The air may be cleaner at Tupper Lake but the future is as grim there as it is here. Besides, the child might soon be deprived of a father. Could you continue to be a doctor and raise him?"

"My parents are still there and thank goodness they're both healthy, or so they claim. Up there, you'd have another recovery and then you could join me in practice or do your public health work in Franklin County. Except for Papa, I daresay few people up there have ever heard of public health. You might accomplish more than you do here, banging your head against the City bureaucracy."

Jared washed up and they sat down to eat the one-dish meal Eleanor had cooked. Breaking some bread, Jared mused. "It would be lovely, watching a little tyke grow. I could manage to carry him up Little Panther but he'd have to be big enough to climb Ampersand on his own."

"What if it was a girl?"

Jared put his hand over Eleanor's. "No difference. You know I treat men and women, boys and girls, equally."

For the first time in several weeks, they both smiled. Jared continued, "With both his—or her—parents doctors and one grandparent, too, the child probably wouldn't be able to take a step if he—or she—had a sniffle."

Gently, Eleanor slapped Jared's hand. "You know that's not true. Daddy made me do lots of walking and swimming to keep me strong." She stopped, reminiscing for a moment. "Remember, I'm a better swimmer than you."

The rest of the evening was spent making plans. They had saved enough money for the trip and could afford to rent, or even possibly buy, a house in Tupper Lake. Jared would enlarge the cabin on Huckleberry Cove so the family could spend the summers there. One practical question was whether to leave before winter or wait until spring. They both had worked up such enthusiasm that they decided not to delay.

Eleanor finished her letter to Mary. After extending their sympathy, Eleanor announced that she and Jared had decided to return to the Adirondacks. She would work with her father as a doctor. "Once he gets his health back, Jared would like to improve the health of the community. Perhaps Cyrus can tell him who to contact in Franklin County." Her last line was in parentheses: "(I hope Jared does not change his mind.)"

In bed that evening, Jared moved close to Eleanor and whispered, "Do you want to start the baby now or wait for the clean air?" She cuddled close to him and did not answer.